The King in the
Golden Mask

The King in the Golden Mask

and other writings
by
Marcel Schwob

Selected, translated and introduced
by
Iain White

Carcanet New Press Limited, Manchester

to
Ingrid

First published in 1982 by
CARCANET NEW PRESS LIMITED
330 Corn Exchange Buildings
Manchester M4 3BG

ISBN 0-85635-403-1

The publisher acknowledges the financial assistance of the
Arts Council of Great Britain.

Printed in England by Short Run Press Ltd., Exeter.

Contents

From *Vies imaginaires*

The Children's Crusade

Translator's introduction

To at least ninety per cent of British or American readers the question will be: 'Marcel Schwob? But who *was* Marcel Schwob?' The short answer is that Marcel Schwob was an outstandingly talented writer of the *fin-de-siècle* period and that, in the French-speaking world, he has a faithful – and numerous – band of readers whose existence has kept his writings in print for over eighty years. Nevertheless, in the English-speaking world he has remained all but unknown. This book is an attempt in some degree to remedy that deficiency.

But the question remains: 'Who *was* Marcel Schwob?' What I want to do here is to give some sort of an adumbration of the man, his milieu and his influence.

First a few contemporary reactions:

> You are the most marvellous, the most hallucinatory resurrector of the past: you are the magical evoker of antiquity, of that *Heliogabalesque* antiquity to which fly the imaginations of thinkers and the brushes of painters, of mysteriously perverse and macabre decadences and of the ends of old worlds.
>
> Edmond de Goncourt, writing to Schwob on the publication of *Le Roi au masque d'or*

> History, linguistics, poetry, prose, astrology, chemistry, criticism, English, German, Greek, Latin, Italian, Spanish, Hebrew – Schwob animates, sets in motion, orders, reconstitutes, associates all these branches of knowledge in his immense and precise imagination. He evokes adventuring sea-captains with the exactitude of Quicherat and the verve of Cervantes. He describes the customs and manners of prostitutes and pimps in the city rookeries as eloquently as he does those of sixteenth-century scholars or Spanish *conquistadores*. With all that goes a perfect taste; never a false move, never is anything over-stressed. His whole attitude is summed up in pity, pity which he applies without distinction to criminals and saints, to traitors and to heroes.
>
> Léon Daudet

To write this book *(Cœur double)* was required, over and above a visionary gift and the vastest erudition, a spirit wide open to life, simple and serene. Those who love Marcel Schwob have already recognised in him these traits. They would be better able than I am to divine the profound humanity there is in this scholar, in this observer, in this evoker and how, out of all this, a great writer could and should emerge – a sort of encyclopaedist of the nineteenth century, a more modern Diderot, less spontaneous perhaps, but at all events more of an artist and no less good and straightforward.

Henry Berenger

The peculiar genius of Monsieur Schwob lies in a species of tremendously complex simplicity; that is to say that, by the arrangement and the harmony of an infinity of telling and precise details, his stories present the sensation of a unique detail ... Like Paolo Uccello, whose geometrical genius he has analysed, he sends out his lines to the periphery and brings them back to the centre.

He is one of the most substantial of writers, one of the decimated race of those who always have on their lips some new words of good odour.

Rémy de Gourmont, *Le deuxième Livre des Masques*

Next a 'chronology' of his short life:

1867   Marcel Schwob born in Chaville-sur-Seine, on the outskirts of Paris, the descendant of a long line of rabbis and physicians on his father's side and, on his mother's side, descended from the Jewish Cayms who fought in the crusades with Saint Louis. His father, Isaac-Georges Schwob, had been Flaubert's schoolfellow at the Rouen Lycée; he had participated in a literary circle that included Théodore de Banville and Théophile Gautier and contributed to the *Corsaire-Satan* at the time when, in the 1840s, Baudelaire was making his début in its pages; in 1849 he collaborated with Jules Verne in writing a 'vaudeville' in two acts (called *Abdallah*), and he was a contributor to the *fourieriste* journal *La Démocratie pacifique*. Later he spent ten years in Egypt, working on the foreign-affairs staff of the Khedive. In 1876 he brought his family to Nantes where he purchased the newspaper *Le Phare de la Loire.*

We may fairly safely dismiss the claim that at three the young Marcel was as fluent in English and German as he was in French; but we can surely accept Paul Léautaud's statement[1] – the statement of a close friend – that at the age of eleven he (Schwob) acquired a copy of Baudelaire's translations of Poe, and that the translation sent him to the original. From this moment the major influence of Poe over Schwob may be dated.

1882 Sent to Paris where he lodged with his maternal uncle, Léon Cahun, keeper of the Bibliothèque Mazarine; the aim was that he should prepare for the entrance examinations of the *École normale supérieure.* His fellow students at the Lycée Louis-le-Grand included Paul Claudel and Léon Daudet. The breadth and 'indiscipline' of his reading – Greek philosophy and drama, Schopenhauer, Mark Twain and Sanskrit Grammar – led to his failing his examinations (1884).

1885 Enlists for his two-year *volontariat* in the 35th regiment of artillery.

1888 Again 'refusé au concours' at the École, but passes his 'licence ès lettres' at the Sorbonne, the first of fourteen new *licenciés* drawn from a field of a hundred. Writing a great deal: poems, stories, translations (of Whitman) etc.

1889 Publishes *Étude sur l'argot français* (written in collaboration with Georges Guieyesse).

In correspondence with R. L. Stevenson.

1890 *Le Jargon des Coquillards en 1455.*

1891 *Cœur double;* the book is dedicated to R. L. Stevenson.

Translates (with Auguste Bréal) W. Richter's study of *Les Jeux des Grecs et des Romains.*

Joins Catulle Mendès as editor of the literary supplement of *L'Écho de Paris;* his friends include Jules Renard, Barbusse, Courteline and Willy and Colette.

Schwob's acquaintance begins about this time with 'Louise' – *'ma petite Vise chérie'* – of whom practically

4

nothing is known except that she was an uneducated working girl, possibly also a prostitute, and certainly mortally ill. Schwob cared for her as best he could; she became the 'Monelle' of *Le Livre de Monelle* (1894).

1892 *Le Roi au masque d'or.*

1893 *Mimes* (prose poems 'imités d'Herondas').

Schwob's friendship with Alfred Jarry begins.
Death of 'Vise', 7 December.

Along with Pierre Louÿs, Schwob corrects the final draft of Wilde's *Salomé*.

1894 Schwob's translation of R. L. Stevenson's *The Dynamiter.*

Le Livre de Monelle: certainly Schwob's strangest work (considered by some to be his 'masterpiece' – others favour the *Vies imaginaires).* Mallarmé declared that the book 'fascinated' him; the critic Edouard Julia wrote: 'the best memory you could leave of your dearly loved mistress is your work, in which she will live on, whole and entire'; Maeterlinck wrote of '... the most perfect pages... the most simple and the most religiously profound it has been given to me to read... (a work that) by I know not what admirable magic seems to float ceaselessly between two doubtful eternities'; Pierre Champion, Schwob's biographer, called the book 'a gospel of pity and a manual of nihilism'. (To a large extent Schwob became 'identified' with this work: if, later, he replied brusquely when introduced as the author of *Le Livre de Monelle,* this was not something to be surprised at – he had done a good deal besides...) [2]

1895 Translation of Defoe's *Moll Flanders.*

Schwob's health breaks down. The first of a series of operations that are to leave him more and more an invalid.

Paul Valéry dedicates his first book, *L'Introduction à la méthode de Léonard de Vinci* to Schwob. (By a printer's error the dedication was in fact omitted in the first edition, to be restored only in the second edition, 1919, long after Schwob's death.)

1896 *La Croisade des enfants* ('... un petit livre miraculeux', Rémy de Gourmont).

Spicilège (a collection of critical essays).

Vies imaginaires

Alfred Jarry dedicates his *Ubu Roi* to Schwob.

1900 Marries Marguerite Moréno, a leading actress of the Comédie française (in London).

Visits Meredith (whose work he has been successfully promoting in France).

La Tragique histoire de Hamlet, Prince de Danemark, a prose version by Schwob and Eugène Morand, presented at the Théâtre Sarah Bernhardt. ('... her most ambitious performance', R. Shattuck; '... the most curious and most beautiful of Sarah's creations', Lysiane Bernhardt).

Friendship with Guillaume Apollinaire begins.

1901
1902 Scholarly work on Villon.

Travel: Jersey – and later Samoa – a Stevenson pilgrimage. Taken ill (pneumonia) and returned, penniless, to France.

His adaptation of F. M. Crawford's *Francesca da Rimini* presented at the Théâtre Sarah Bernhardt: dedication by Crawford to Sarah Bernhardt 'who by her creative magic has after five hundred years reincarnated the soul of Francesca *che piange e dice'*.

1903 *La Lampe de Psyché* (containing *Mimes; La Croisade des enfants; L'Étoile de bois; Le Livre de Monelle).*

'Loyson-Bridet' (i.e. Schwob), *Mœurs des Diurnales: Traité du journalisme* (a satire on journalism).

1904 Further travel – Portugal, Spain, Italy – and further decline in his health.

Lectures on Villon at the École des Hautes Études Sociales.
1905 Dies, Paris, 26 February.

Le Parnasse satyrique du quinzième siècle (anthology of 'pièces libres' edited by Schwob and seen through the press by Paul Léautaud).

Friendships and influences
Jarry

It was in the *Écho de Paris littéraire illustré* that Jarry's work first appeared in 1893. The poem 'La Régularité de la châsse' (as it is called in *Minutes de Sable mémorial*) was soon followed by 'Guignol' (also collected in *Minutes*), the first text of the Ubu cycle to see the light of public print – and the first appearance in print of the name of *'Pataphysique,* 'the science of imaginary solutions'. Three years later Jarry dedicated his *Ubu Roi* to Schwob. The copy Jarry presented to the dedicatee is inscribed: 'Just as this book is dedicated to him, this copy is offered to Marcel Schwob because his writings are among those I have admired the longest.'[3]

Schwob's name continued to recur in Jarry's writings. In 1899, in the *Almanach du Père Ubu illustré,* he is cited as 'Celui qui sait' – after the style of the titles handed out to others, including: 'Valette, celui qui Mercure; Allais (Alphonse), celui qui ira; Debussy, celui qui Pell (et as et Mélisande); Degas, celui qui bec; Becque, celui qui gaz; Toulouse-Lautrec, celui qui affiche'. Chapter XXI of the posthumous – and brilliant – *Gestes et opinions du Docteur Faustroll, 'pataphysicien,* was dedicated to Schwob and written for him; it contains a couple of oblique references to characters in the *Vies imaginaires:* 'l'Ile Cyril' takes its name from the Elizabethan dramatist Cyril Tourneur and, on the island, the intrepid Faustroll swigs gin with Captain Kidd. (Nor should it be forgotten that *La Croisade des enfants* is one of the twenty-seven 'livres pairs' in Faustroll's library.) Noel Arnaud[4] notes that far more than their common love of Rabelais and Shakespeare united Schwob and Jarry. For all their superficial dissimilarities of personality they shared many common attitudes. Arnaud quotes the definition of art given in the 'Introduction' to the *Vies,* one to which – he claims – the 'pataphysician could not but subscribe: 'Art is opposed to general ideas, describes only the individual, desires only the unique. It does not classify: it *de*classifies.'

Jarry was always a difficult man, and especially so in his later years when his diet became increasingly restricted to absinthe. His dress then was that of a racing cyclist – skin-tight sweater, bumfreezer jacket and ancient trousers tucked into his socks. But he was also a faithful friend. 'As a symbol of great respect at Marcel Schwob's funeral, he pulled them out, something he neglected to do at Mallarmé's funeral, for which he borrowed a pair of Madame Rachilde's bright yellow shoes.'[5]

Valéry

It would be hard to imagine a writer more different from Jarry than Paul Valéry: yet, at about the time in the early 1890s when Schwob and Jarry were close, Schwob was also on friendly terms with the young Valéry, newly arrived in Paris. It was to Schwob that Valéry dedicated his first book, the *Introduction à la méthode de Léonard de Vinci*, a characteristically subtle analysis of the mind of a genius which prefigured his lifelong interest in the workings of the creative intellect. Their relationship was, sadly, to be cooled by the Dreyfus affair (in which Valéry was swept along, not at all unwillingly, on the wave of chauvinism while Schwob was a staunch Dreyfusard); but Valéry remained faithful to his erstwhile friend's memory and to his talent. Writing many years later Valéry set down this recollection:

> ...I knew Marcel Schwob very well, and I recall with deep feeling our long twilight conversations in which this strangely intelligent and passionately clear-sighted man told me about his research, his intuitions, his discoveries in the pursuit of his quarry – which was the truth about the Villon case. He brought to this task the inductive imagination of an Edgar Poe and the sagacity, in matters of minute detail, of a philologist inured to analysing texts, as well as that peculiar interest in exceptional people, in lives that diverged widely from the norm, which led him to discover a number of books and establish many literary reputations.[6]

And, more than thirty years previously, when their political differences were about to come to a head, Valéry was writing in an almost identical vein:

> ...I recall long conversations with Marcel Schwob: nothing – except perhaps for the dialogue of our characters – could have been more diverting than my surprise when he drew some sort of a thread from a word or phrase by which to attach it, according to the most subtle probabilities that can be imagined, to something far far away, the devil knows where, in a certain niche of a certain epoch. Often I would be delighted by a sudden proof. The argot of all the brigands, as he sifted and conjured it up by the fireside, filled me with childlike pleasure, with literary enjoyment, with the extreme happiness conferred by a perfect analysis. And miraculous to say: I could press him with all the questions I pleased; he left none of them unanswered.[7]

Apollinaire

Another of Schwob's friends was Guillaume Apollinaire, and Roger Shattuck – among others – stresses Apollinaire's debt to Schwob. Apollinaire's paradoxical character as traditionalist and revolutionary, modernist and simple lyricist, owed much to 'the men he most admired in the preceding generation (who) had displayed equally paradoxical temperaments – Rémy de Gourmont, Marcel Schwob, Jarry. Apollinaire prolonged their erudition and their "decadence" and refreshed it with a new youthfulness and robustness.'[8]

It was in 1900 that the twenty-year-old poet made the acquaintance of Léon Cahun in the Bibliothèque Mazarine and, through him, that of his nephew, Marcel Schwob. Cahun was a man calculated to fascinate the newcomer to the capital. A scholar of the first rank, Hellenist, Latinist, Hebraist, historian and master of such obscure tongues as classical Turkish, Cahun was also a Cabalist and steeped in Jewish legend and folklore. Significantly – as it happens for both his nephew and for Apollinaire – he was also the author of historical novels with such redolent titles as *Hassan le Janissaire, Les Aventures du Capitaine Magon* and *La Tueuse.* According to Apollinaire's biographer Cecily Mackworth,[9] Cahun not only initiated Apollinaire into the Jewish folklore that was to appear and reappear in his work (notably in *L'Hérésiarque et cie),* but also introduced him to other writers and to the Bibliothèque Nationale, where he was later to catalogue the *'enfer';* and it was Schwob who provided Apollinaire with his contact with the literary circle of the Closerie des Lilas and Paul Fort, so crucial to his career, as well as arranging the introductions that led to his practice of what he called 'littérature alimentaire' – ghost-writing.

Schwob's influence on Apollinaire as a writer is clear in the stories that make up *L'Hérésiarque et cie.* Although the book appeared in 1910, the first of these 'gothic narratives' (as Shattuck calls them) were published in *La Revue Blanche* as early as 1902 – in other words soon after Apollinaire's meeting Schwob; and the learned, folkloristic themes of the stories very probably attest the influence of uncle and nephew. The Apollinaire scholar Pascal Pia[10] is quite specific. 'If the prose of *L'Enchanteur pourrissante,* his first work, betrays a certain awkwardness, that of the stories he sent to *La Revue Blanche* and which were collected in *L'Hérésiarque et cie* already reveal a greater facility. Whilst the text of *L'Enchanteur* often seems to hesitate between verse and prose, the prose of *L'Hérésiarque* is that of a prose-writer who is master of his style, as he is of his subject. The influence of Marcel Schwob seems to me not unconnected with this rapid progress in the art of writing... None of the 'bad habits' of symbolist writing, none of the absurd preciosities of *l'écriture artiste* mar the stories of *L'Hérésiarque.* If by chance a rare word insinuates itself this happens, as with Schwob, in the most natural of ways and in the very place where both sense and verisimilitude justify its use.' Pia does not limit Schwob's influence to matters of style. In the attention Apollinaire gives to odd individuals, to eccentrics, he again sees a residue of Apollinaire's reading of his friend's stories: indeed he visualises the possibility of composing *vies imaginaires* of Isaac Laquedem and the other heroes of *L'Hérésiarque.*

Borges

The question of Schwob's probable – to my mind certain – influence on Jorge Luis Borges is suitably labyrinthine in terms of the clues that are scattered about in his life and works – and positively *Borgesian* in its indirectness. There are, of course, the traits of personality the two share (and have in common with Stevenson, significantly a favourite of both). Both are enormously and curiously erudite men of the library, fascinated by the mechanics of storytelling, who are also fascinated by murderers, pirates, outcasts and heretics. There is also the influence, exercised in varying degrees and in different ways on both writers by Poe. Then there is the common anglophilia and interest in oriental cultures – not to mention the interest both have displayed in Schopenhauer.

To those who are minded to take hints, I believe the clues are pretty convincing, leaving aside the like cast of mind.

Chronologically the first – and admittedly tenuous – link between the two is through the person of Victoria Ocampo who, in 1931, was to found the journal *Sur,* to whose foundation Borges also contributed. It was his collaboration with *Sur* that properly launched Borges as a writer; so it may safely be said that Victoria Ocampo played a part in Borges' literary career. Now in the early years of the century it was customary for well-to-do Argentinian parents to send their children to French schools, and Victoria Ocampo had been no exception; in fact her first writings were in French. What *may well* be significant from our point of view is that she had lessons in French diction from

Marguerite Moréno – Schwob's wife.[11] It is hard to believe that
Ocampo did not at least *mention* Schwob to Borges.

Earlier, from Borges' point of view, is his encounter with Rafael
Cansinos-Asséns. (At this point remember that whatever else Borges
may do, he never wastes words or deals in irrelevancies.) In his
'Autobiographical Essay' – a crucial text – Borges underlines the
impact of this strange character. The period is about 1920. 'Next we
(the Borges family) went to Madrid, and there the great event to me
was my friendship with Rafael Cansinos-Asséns. I still like to think of
myself as his disciple. Cansinos was a wide reader. He translated De
Quincey's *Opium Eater,* the Meditations of Marcus Aurelius from the
Greek, novels by Barbusse and Schwob's *Vies imaginaires.*'[12] I should
be surprised if the mention is fortuitous.

This is not the only reference to Schwob in the 'Autobiographical
Essay' – and the work runs to only forty-one pages in the English
translation. Reaching the critical point in his life as a writer, Borges
makes himself fairly plain: 'The real beginning of my career as a story
writer starts with a series of sketches entitled *Historia universal de la
infamia* (A universal History of Infamy), which I contributed to the
columns of *Crítica* in 1933 and 1934. (. . .) In my *Universal History* I did
not want to repeat what Marcel Schwob had done in his *Imaginary
Lives.* He had invented biographies of real men about whom little or
nothing is recorded. I, instead, read up on the lives of known persons
and then deliberately varied and distorted them according to my own
whims (. . .) I did the same for Billy the Kid (. . .) and the veiled Prophet
of Khorassan (. . .).[13] I suppose now the secret value of those sketches –
apart from the sheer pleasure the writing gave me – lay in the fact that
they were narrative exercises. Since the general plots or circumstances
were given to me, I had only to embroider sets of vivid variations.'[14]

The importance of Schwob for Borges is not lost on Borges'
biographer, Rodriguez Monegál:

> One of the general sources Borges never mentioned in print prior to
> writing the 'Autobiographical Essay' is Marcel Schwob's *Imaginary
> Lives.* Although he did not use any of the French symbolist's
> stories, it is obvious to any reader of both writers that the model for
> the Borges stories could be found in Schwob's book, especially in
> the best story, MM. Burke and Hare, murderers.[15]

Rodriguez Monegál goes on to quote the American critic Suzanne Jill
Levine to the effect that Borges had remarked that the 'concept' of

Imaginary Lives was 'superior to the book itself' and that the last story, 'Burke and Hare' was 'the best, and the only one in which Schwob achieved his concept'. (And it is certainly the case that 'Burke and Hare' *is* a beautifully constructed piece, as well as being perhaps closest in 'concept' to the stories in the Borges collection...) The essence of the style of *The Universal History of Infamy,* according to Levine (quoted by Rodriguez Monegál), 'is precisely the selection of relevant details' – a good description of the style of *Imaginary Lives* too – and, the biographer goes on, 'Borges had already acknowledged the style without identifying the general source'. This acknowledgement was in the preface to the first edition of the *Historia universal,* where Borges stated that:

> The exercises in narrative prose that make up this book were written in 1933 and 1934. They stem, I believe, from my rereadings of Stevenson and Chesterton, and also from Sternberg's early films, and perhaps from a certain biography of Evaristo Carriego. They overly exploit certain tricks: random enumerations, sudden shifts of continuity, and the paring down of a man's whole life to two or three scenes (...) They are not, they do not try to be, psychological.[16]

At the time however, and in the place where the stories had first appeared (in the pages of the literary supplement of the Buenos Aires paper *Crítica),* Borges had obliquely 'acknowledged his interest in Schwob'. 'Apart from contributing at least twenty-nine original pieces to the magazine, Borges also selected and translated pieces by his favourite authors for *Crítica.* Chesterton, Kipling, Wells, and the German-Czech author Gustav Meyrink shared with Swift, Novalis and James Frazer the gaudy pages of the supplement.'[17] What is significant is that among the translated pieces was Schwob's 'Burke and Hare'.

Whether or not in 1944 Borges actually 'translated and wrote a preface' to the *Vies imaginaires,* as Hubert Juin firmly states,[18] I do not know. But in 1949 Borges contributed a 'prólogo' to a translation of *La Croisade des enfants:* in the couple of pages it occupies, this brief and telling paragraph occurs – which, I think, makes clear Borges' deep understanding of Schwob and the uncommon sympathy and likeness of mind that exists between them:

> In certain books of Ancient India it is written that the universe is no more nor less than a dream of the unmoving god that is individuate

in every human being; towards the end of the nineteenth century Marcel Schwob – creator, actor and spectator of this dream – set out to dream again that which for many centuries had been dreamed in African and Asian solitudes: the story of the children who longed to recover the Holy Sepulchre. He did not attempt – you may be sure of that – Flaubert's greedy accumulation of detail; he preferred to saturate himself in the ancient pages of Jacques de Vitry or of Ernoul and then give himself over to the practice of imagination and selection. Thus the pope was dreamed, thus the goliard, thus the three children, thus the cleric.[19]

Notes
1. Paul Léautaud, *Passe-temps* II, Paris 1944, p.23.
2. It was only after some thought that I decided not to include any extracts from *Monelle*. It seems to me the book is simply not excerptible; it must be taken as a whole – as a quite exceptionally subtle, shifting whole whose delicate blend of the vague and the precise, the *précieux* and the anarchic, defies the anthologist's scissors.
3. R. Shattuck, *The Banquet Years: the Origins of the Avant-garde in France, 1885 to World War I*, London 1969, p.193. And N.B. Marguerite Moréno: 'I remember the day Jarry came to read him his *Ubu Roi;* he (Schwob) laughed till the tears ran down his cheeks at that coarse schoolboy joke – but not at its author, whose fine turns of phrase delighted him.' (*La Statue de sel et le bonhomme de neige,* Paris 1928, p.133, quoted in B. Eruli, 'Schwob, Jarry ed altri ribelli', *Saggi e Ricerci di Letteratura Francese,* XV n.s., Rome 1976).
4. Noël Arnaud, *Alfred Jarry, d'Ubu Roi au Faustroll,* Paris 1974, p.410. *If* – and the question is more than an open one – Schwob actually *influenced* Jarry, *Messaline* (1901) is the most probable source for the temerarious scholar.
5. Shattuck, *The Banquet Years,* p.211.
6. In 1930, in an article on 'Villon and Verlaine': *Collected Works of Paul Valéry,* vol. IX, pp.239–40.
7. A review of Michel Bréal's *La Sémantique (Mercure de France,* Jan. 1898), in *Collected Works of Paul Valéry,* vol. XIII, p.257.
8. Shattuck, *The Banquet Years,* p.256.
9. *Guillaume Apollinaire and the Cubist Life,* London 1961, p.23.
10. *Apollinaire par lui même,* Paris 1965, pp.138–9.
11. Emir Rodriguez Monegál, *Jorge Luis Borges, a Literary Biography,* New York 1978, pp.17–18.
12. 'An Autobiographical Essay', in *The Aleph and Other Stories 1933–1969,* edited and translated by Norman Thomas di Giovanni in collaboration with the author, London 1973, p.138.
13. The reference to the Veiled Prophet of Khorassan looks like a fine example of Borgesian subtlety and indirectness: Hubert Juin remarks in his préface to Schwob's *Le Livre de Monelle/Spicilège/l'Étoile de bois/Il libro della mia memoria,* Paris (10/18), 1979, p.8: '...how, in fact, is one not to evoke – in an indirect fashion, to be sure – 'The King in the Golden Mask' when one reads the tale of Hakim of Merv in Borges' *Universal History of Infamy?'*

14. Borges, 'An Autobiographical Essay', *The Aleph,* p.151.
15. Rodriguez Monegál, *Jorge Luis Borges,* pp.256–7.
16. *A Natural History of Infamy,* Harmondsworth 1975, p.8.
17. Rodriguez Monegál, *Jorge Luis Borges,* p.252.
18. In the préface to *Le Livre de Monelle* (etc.), Paris 1979, p.8. Juin is an experienced critic and editor and vastly learned, but in this instance he is vague about his sources; and the standard Borges bibliography does not list the supposed translation. On the other hand the catalogue of the Library of Congress *does* list a translation of the *Vies,* not by Borges, as appearing in Buenos Aires in 1967 – is this a case for investigation by Borges' detective, Don Isidro Parodi?...
19. *Prólogos,* Buenos Aires 1975, p.141; reprinted from Marcel Schwob, *La cruzada de los niños,* Buenos Aires 1949. The entry in the catalogue of the Library of Congress records that the book has five illustrations by Nora Borges, the sister of Jorge Luis Borges.

Acknowledgements

Five of the pieces collected here – 'The King in the Golden Mask', 'Herostratos, incendiary', 'Cecco Angiolieri, malevolent poet', 'Paolo Uccello, painter' and part of the 'Introduction' to *Vies imaginaires* appeared in *Comparative Criticism* II, 1980; I am indebted to the editor, Dr Elinor Shaffer, and to the publisher, Cambridge University Press, for permission to reprint.

I should also like to thank Dr Sylvia Morton for her attentive and sensitive reading of my semi-final draft of the entire text. Her corrections and suggestions were apt, valuable and greatly appreciated.

from
CŒUR DOUBLE
1891

The Strigae

Vobis rem horribilem narrabo...
mihi pili inhorruerunt.
T. Petronius Arbiter, *Satiricon*

We were stretched out on our couches about the sumptuously laden
table. The silver lamps were burning low; the door had just closed
behind the juggler who had in the end wearied us with his trained pigs
and, because of the flaming hoops through which he had made his
grunting beasts leap, an odour of singed skin hung about the room.
Dessert was brought in: hot honey-cakes, and candied sea-urchins,
eggs wrapped in batter-rissoles, thrushes in sauce with a fine wheaten-
flour stuffing, raisins and walnuts. As the plates were being passed, a
Syrian slave sang a shrill mode. Our host played with the long tresses
of his catamite who lay at his side, and elegantly picked his teeth with a
gilded spatula: he was fuddled by numerous cups of mulled wine,
which he drank avidly and unmixed, and so it was in some confusion
that he commenced:

'Nothing is more saddening to me than the end of a meal. I am
obliged, my dear friends, to part from you: that inescapably recalls to
me the hour when I must leave you in all earnest. Ah! ah! What a trivial
thing man is then! Slave; sweat; serve on campaign in Gaul, in
Germany, in Syria, in Palestine; amass your fortune coin by coin; serve
good masters; work your way from the kitchen to the table, from the
table to a place of favour; wear your hair as long as this one here, in
whose hair I wipe my hands; have yourself manumitted; keep house in
your turn, and have clients as I have them; speculate in land and in
commercial consignments; bestir yourselves! Strive! From the
moment a freedman's cap touches your head, you will sense yourself
the slave of a more powerful mistress, from which no quantity of
sesterces will deliver you. Let us live while we have the health to!...
Boy, pour out some Falernum!

He had an articulated silver skeleton fetched in and laid it in various
postures upon the table; he sighed, wiped his eyes, and continued:

'Death is a terrible thing, the thought of which besets me especially
after I have eaten. The doctors I have seen can offer me no advice. I
suppose my digestion is bad. There are days when my belly bellows like

a bull. One should be warned by these discomforts. Don't be embarrassed, my friends, if you should be put out in this way. The eructations could rise to the brain, and that would be the end of you. The emperor Claudius was accustomed to behave thus, and nobody would laugh. Better to be impolite than risk one's life.'

Again he pondered for a while; then he said:

'I cannot drive away my thoughts. When I think of death, I see before me all those persons I have seen dying. And if we were sure of our bodies, after everything is finished! But poor creatures, wretched as we are, there are mysterious powers that lie in wait for us – I swear to you by my soul that there are. They are to be seen in the streets and in the squares. They have the shape of old women, and at night they go under the guise of birds. One day, when I still lived in Strait Street, I all but vomited out my soul for terror: one of them was lighting a fire of dried reeds in a niche in the wall; she poured wine into a copper dish, with leeks and parsley; and she threw in filbert-nuts and examined them. Then she took broad beans from her bag and topped-and tailed them with her teeth, as nimbly as a tomtit picking hempseed; and she spat out the pods about her like the corpses of flies.

'I am in no doubt that she was a *striga;* and if she had caught sight of me, she would perhaps have paralysed me with her evil eye. There are men who go out at night and who feel themselves swept by gusts of wind; they draw their swords and strike out about them, battling against shadows. In the morning they are covered with bruises, and their tongue hangs out of the corner of their mouth. They have met the *strigae.* I have known strong men, and even mannerless boors that they have led astray.

'These things are true; I tell you they are. What is more, they are admitted facts. I would not speak of them, and I might well have been doubtful of them, had it not been that I had an experience that made my very hair stand on end.

'While one watches over the dead, one can hear the *strigae*: they sing airs that carry one away and which, despite oneself, one obeys. Their voices are suppliant and plaintive, sweetly piping, like birdsong, soft as the crying of a little child; nothing can resist them. When I was in the service of my master, the banker of the Via Sacra, he was so unfortunate as to lose his wife. I was woebegone then, for my own wife had just died – a beautiful creature, I declare, and nice and plump – though I loved her above all for her civility. Everything she earned was meant for me; if she had no more than an *as,* she gave me half of it. When I returned to the "villa", I saw white objects moving about the tombs. I was mortally terrified, especially since I had left a dead woman in the town: I rushed to the house in the country and, on the threshold I found – what? – A pool of blood, and in it a sponge steeping.

'And throughout the house there was wailing and weeping: for the mistress had died at nightfall. The serving-women were rending their garments and tearing out their hair. One lamp was to be seen, like a point of red, at the far end of the room. When the master had left, I lit a great torch of pinewood, close to the window; the flame crackled and fumed as the wind swirled the grey wreaths of smoke about the room; with the wind, the light rose and fell; the drops of resin oozed down the torch and crackled on the ground.

The dead woman was laid out on the bed; her face was green, and there was a multitude of little wrinkles at her mouth and at her temples. We had bound her cheeks with a linen bandage to prevent her jaws from dropping open. The night-moths fluttered jerkily about, closely circling the torch; their wings were yellow; the flies roved about on the bed; and each gust of wind blew in dead leaves that tumbled. For my part, I watched at the bed's foot and thought of all the stories that are told, of the straw mannikins that are found in the morning in place of the dead, and of the round holes the witches come and make in their faces to suck the blood.

'All at once a strident note, sharp and sweet, arose among the howling of the wind; it was like a little girl singing in supplication. The notes hung on the air and were borne in more strongly on the gusts that stirred the dead woman's hair: and I, meanwhile, was stricken with a stupor and did not stir.

'The moon commenced to shine with a paler light; the shadows of the furniture and the amphorae blended into the blackness of the ground. My wandering eyes took in the countryside and I saw the sky and the earth shining with a soft gleam in which the distant thickets merged and the poplar trees were no more than long grey lines. It seemed to me that the wind was dying down and the leaves were no longer moving; I saw shadows moving about behind the garden hedge. Then my eyelids felt heavy as lead, and they closed; I was conscious of tiny rustlings.

'Suddenly the crowing of the cocks startled me into wakefulness and an icy breath of morning wind agitated the tops of the poplars. I was leaning against the wall; through the window I saw that the grey of the sky was lighter, and in the east there was a streak of white and rose. I rubbed my eyes and, when I looked at my mistress – come to my aid, Oh gods! – I saw that her body was covered with black bruises; dusky-blue blotches the size of an *as* – yes, the size of an *as!* – spangled her whole skin. I ran to the bed: the face was a waxen mask beneath which the flesh could be seen, hideously gnawed: no more nose, no more lips, nor any cheeks, no more eyes; with their keen beaks the night-birds had pecked them away like plums. And each blue blotch was a funnel-shaped hole at the bottom of which glistened a driblet of congealed blood; and there were no longer either heart, or lungs or any viscera, for the chest and belly were stuffed with straw bungs.

'The singing strigae had carried everything away while I slept. Man cannot withstand the power of sorceresses. We are the playthings of destiny.'

Our host began to weep, his head on the table between the silver skeleton and the empty winecups. 'Ah!' he wept, 'Ah! I the rich man, I who can go to my estates at Baiae, I who have my farm-accounts published, I with my troupe of actors, my dancers and my mimes, my silver tableware, my country houses and my metal mines, I am only a wretched body the *strigae* may soon come and make holes in.' The boy handed him a silver pot, and he retched.

Meanwhile the lamps were going out; the guests were blundering around, muttering vaguely; the silverware was clashing together and the oil from an upturned lamp was spreading a stain over the entire table. A mountebank entered on tiptoe, his face streaked with black lines; and between a double line of newly-purchased slaves whose feet were still white with chalk, we ran out through the open door.

Train 081

The great terror of my life seems far distant from the shrubbery in which I am writing. I am an old man in retirement, resting his limbs on the lawn of his little house; and I often ask myself if it is I – the same I – that lived the hard life of an engine-driver on the PLM line – and I am astonished not to have died, there and then, that night of 22 September 1865.

I can certainly say that I know that Paris – Marseilles line. I could drive the train with my eyes shut, uphill and down, taking in the intercrossings of the lines, the branches and the points, the curves and the iron bridges. From third-class fireman I rose to first-class driver; but promotion was very slow. If I had been better educated, I would have become a deputy stationmaster. But what am I saying! On the footplate one grows stupid; one sweats blood by night, and by day one sleeps. In our times work was not regulated as it is nowadays; teams of drivers had not been formed: we did not have regular working hours. How was a man to study? And me especially: a man would have to be thick-headed to withstand the shock I had.

My brother had joined the navy, on the transport side. He had joined before 1860 – the China campaign. And when the war was over, I don't know how it happened, but he stayed in the yellow country, near a town they call Canton. The slant-eyes had kept him on as a pilot for their steamships. In a letter I received from him in 1862 he told me he was married and had a little daughter. I was very fond of my brother, and it made me sad, not seeing him any more; and our old folk were not at all pleased about it. In their little shanty on the outskirts of Dijon, they were too much on their own; with their two boys gone, on winter nights they would sleep fitfully by the fireside.

Towards the month of May 1865 people in Marseilles began to be worried about what was happening in the Levant. The packet-boats arriving brought bad news from the Red Sea. They said cholera had broken out in Mecca. Pilgrims were dying by the thousand. Then the sickness reached Suez, Alexandria; then it leapt to Constantinople. It was the Asiatic cholera: the ships stayed in quarantine in the Lazaret; everybody was in a vague state of fear.

I had no great responsibility on that score; but I can say that the idea of conveying the sickness bothered me a great deal. To be sure it had to reach Marseilles; then the express would take it to Paris. In those days we had no communication-cords for passengers. I know that now they have installed very ingenious mechanisms. But nothing of the sort existed then. And I knew if a passenger had been stricken with Asian pestilence that stifles a man within an hour, he would have died without help, and I would have carried his blue-coloured corpse to Paris, to the Gare de Lyon.

June began, and the cholera reached Marseilles. Men were said to be dying like flies. They fell down in the street, by the docks, everywhere. It was a terrible sickness: two or three convulsions, a fit of coughing blood, and that was that. From the first attack one became cold as a lump of ice; and the faces of the dead were speckled with blotches the size of a five-france piece. Travellers left the fumigation-hall in a fog of stinking smoke that clung to their clothing. The company officials took note of the matter; and we, in our wretched job, had yet another worry.

July, August, mid-September passed: the town was deserted, but we regained confidence. Up till now, nothing in Paris. On 22 September, in the evening, I mounted the footplate of train 180 with my fireman, Graslepoix.

At night the travellers sleep in their carriages – but our job is to keep watch throughout the journey. During the daytime, because of the sunlight, we have big protective goggles fitted in our helmets. They are called mistral-goggles. The blue glass lenses protect us from the dust. At night we push them back over our foreheads; and, with our neckerchiefs, with the ear-flaps of our helmets turned back and our big pilot-jackets, we look like fiends mounted on red-eyed beasts. The light of the furnace illumines us and warms our bellies; the north wind slices our cheeks; the rain whips our faces and the vibration shakes up our innards until we are breathless. Dressed in this fashion we strain our eyes into the darkness, looking out for red signal-lights. You will find many men grown old in the service whom the colour red has driven out of their minds. Even now this colour takes hold of me and grips me with an inexpressible anxiety. I often wake at night with a start, a *red* glare in my eyes. Terrified, I peer into the darkness – it seems as if everything were breaking to bits about me – and a rush of blood mounts to my head; then I realise I am in my bed and I burrow beneath the sheets.

That night the humid heat hung heavy upon us. A tepid drizzle was falling. Graslepoix was mechanically pitching shovelsful of coal into the furnace; the locomotive lurched and swung at the curves. We were making sixty-five kilometres per hour – a tidy speed. The night was pitch-black. With Nuits behind us and approaching Dijon, it was one o'clock in the morning. I was thinking of our two old folk, who must have been sleeping peacefully when, all of a sudden, I heard the sound of an engine on the double track. At one in the morning, between Nuits and Dijon, we expect no trains, either on the up line or the down.

'What's that, Graslepoix?' I said to the fireman. 'We can't reverse steam.'

'Nothing to get worked up about', said Graslepoix. 'It's on a parallel track, we can lower the pressure.'

If we'd had, as they have now, a compressed-air brake... and suddenly, with an unexpected turn of speed, the train on the double track caught up with ours and ran alongside; my hair stands on end when I think of it.

It was entirely enveloped in a reddish mist. The brasswork shone. The steam silently condensed on the test-plate. In the mist, two swarthy figures were moving about on the footplate. They were alongside us and they reproduced our actions. The number of our train was written in chalk on a slate – 180. Across from us, in black on a large white board, the figures 081 stood out. The line of carriages extended into the night, and in every one the four windows were darkened.

'Now there's a rum do!', said Graslepoix. 'If ever I'd thought... You just wait a minute, and you'll see!'

And he stooped and took a shovelful of coal, and slung it into the fire. One of the men opposite likewise stooped and hurled his shovelful into the flames. I saw Graslepoix' image standing forth against the red glow of the mist.

Then a strange understanding filled my mind, and my thoughts gave place to an extraordinary fancy. I raised my right arm; and the other man raised his. I nodded in his direction; and he responded. And next, all at once, I saw him move towards the steps of the footplate; and I *knew* that I was doing the same. We slipped backwards along the moving train and, before our eyes, the door of carriage A.A.F. 2551 opened of its own volition. I saw the spectacle opposite us – and at the same time I *felt* that the same scene was being enacted in *my* train. A man was lying in this carriage, his face covered by a white velvet cloth:

a woman and a little girl, wrapped in silk embroidered with yellow and red flowers lay motionless on the cushions. I *saw myself* go to this man and draw aside the cloth that covered him. His chest was bare. There were bluish patches on his skin. His fingernails were livid and his tightly-clasped fingers were shrivelled. There were blue circles about his eyes. I saw all this in the twinkling of an eye; *and as quickly I realised that it was my brother I had seen and that he had died of cholera.*

When I regained consciousness I was at Dijon station. Graslepoix was mopping my brow – and he has told me that I never left the controls: but I know better. At once I cried out 'Run to A.A.F. 2551!' And I dragged myself to the carriage; I saw my brother there, lying dead, as I had seen him before. The staff were terrified. The only words to be heard in the station were 'The blue cholera!'

Graslepoix brought out the woman and the little girl – who had only fainted away from fear – and since no one would take responsibility for them, he laid them on the footplate, among the fine coal-dust, with their pieces of embroidered silk.

My brother's wife is Chinese; she has narrow, almond eyes and a yellow skin. I had some trouble in getting to like her; being a person of another race, she seemed odd. But the little girl was so like my brother! Now that I'm old and the vibration of the engine has done for my health, they live with me, and we live quietly, except that we remember that terrible night of 22 September 1865 when the blue cholera came from Marseilles to Paris by train 081.

Arachné

Her waggon-spokes made of long spinners' legs;
The cover of the wings of grasshoppers;
Her traces of the smallest spider's web;
Her collars of the moonshine's watery beams...
      Shakespeare, *Romeo and Juliet,* I, iv, 60–3.

You say I am mad, and you have locked me up; but I laugh at your precautions and your terrors. For, the day I desire it, I shall be free; I shall flee far from your warders and your bars along a silken thread thrown me by Arachné. But the hour has still to come – though it is close: increasingly my heart is enfeebled and my blood grows paler. You who now think me mad will believe I am dead: and I shall be swinging by Arachné's thread beyond the stars.

If I were mad, I should not be so clearly aware of what has happened, I should not recall with such precision that which you have called my crime, nor the pleas made in court by your advocates, nor the sentence of your red-robed judge. I should not laugh to scorn the reports of your doctors, I should not see on the ceiling of my room the clean-shaven face, the black frock-coat and the white cravat of the idiot who declared me unaccountable for my actions. No, I would not be so clearly aware – for the insane do not have clear notions; whilst I follow out my chains of reasoning with a lucid logic that I myself find astonishing. And the mad are troubled at the crown of their head: they believe – poor wretches! – that columns of smoke rise, swirling from their occiput. Whilst my own brain is so airily volatile that I often feel my skull is empty. The novels I have read, which formerly gave me pleasure, I now take in at a glance and judge for what they are worth; I see each fault in composition – and at the same time the symmetry of my own inventions is so perfect thay you would be dazzled were I to let you see them.

But I hold you in infinite contempt; you would not comprehend them. I leave you these lines as a final witness of my ridicule, and to bring home to you your own insanity, when you find my cell deserted.

Ariane, the pale Ariane at whose side you seized me, was an embroidress. This is what brought about her death. That is what will bring about my salvation. I loved her with an intense passion; she was tiny, dusky-skinned and nimble-fingered; her kisses were needle-pricks, her caresses palpitant embroideries. And embroidresses lead so thoughtless a life and are so fickle in their caprices that I very soon wished that she would quit her employment. But she resisted me: and I was enraged at the sight of the young men, pomaded and sporting cravats, that lay in wait for her as she left the workshop. My state of nervous irritation was such that I tried to re-immerse myself in the studies that had been my delight.

It was perforce that I took down volume XIII of *Asiatic Researches,* published in Calcutta in 1820: and mechanically I began to read the article on the *Phansigars.* This led me to the Thugs.

Captain Sleeman has had much to say of them. Colonel Meadows Taylor has ferreted out the secrets of their association. They were joined among themselves by mysterious bonds and served as domestics in country houses. In the evening, at supper, they would stupefy their masters with a decoction of Hemp. At night, creeping along the walls, they slipped in by the windows, open to the moon, coming silently to strangle the householders. Their cords too were made of Hemp, with a thick knot at the nape of the neck, to kill more speedily.

Thus, by means of Hemp, the Thugs linked sleep to death. The plant that yielded the hashish with which, as with alcohol or opium, the rich besotted them, thus served to avenge them. The idea came to me that, in chastening my embroidress Ariane with Silk, I would bind her to me wholly in death. And this assuredly logical idea became the bright focus of my thoughts. I did not long resist it. When she lay her head in the hollow of my shoulder, I surreptitiously passed about her throat the silken cord I had taken from her basket; and, gradually tightening it, I drank in her last breath with her final kiss.

You came upon us thus, mouth to mouth. You thought I was mad and she was dead. For you do not know that she is always with me, forever faithful, because she is the nymph Arachné. Day after day, here in my white cell, she has revealed herself to me, since the day I saw a spider spinning her web above my bed; she was tiny, brown and nimble-footed.

The first night, she came down to me by a thread; hanging above my eyes she wove over my eyeballs a silky and sombre tissue, with watery reflections and luminous purple flowers. Then I felt Ariane's compact and vigorous body at my side. She kissed my chest at the point above the heart, and I cried out at the burning sensation. And we embraced, long and silently.

The second night, she spread about me a phosphorescent veil, studded with green stars and yellow circles, traversed by brilliant points that glided about, sporting among themselves, waxing, waning and wavering in the distance. And kneeling on my chest, she shut my mouth with her hand; in a long kiss above the heart, she bit my flesh and sucked the blood to the point of drawing me towards the nothingness of insensibility.

The third night, she bound my eyes with a band of Mahratta silk, patterned with dancing, glinting-eyed spiders. And she tightly laced my throat with an endless thread; and she violently drew my heart towards her lips through the wound her bite had left. Then she slid into my arms to whisper in my ear: 'I am the nymph Arachné!'

By no means am I mad; for I at once understood that my embroidress Ariane was a mortal goddess, and that I had from all eternity been selected to draw her by her silken thread out of the labyrinth of humanity. And the nymph Arachné was grateful for my having delivered her from her human chrysalis. With infinite care she has enmeshed my heart, my poor heart, in her sticky thread: she has entwined it in a thousand coils. Every night she draws closer the meshes between which this human heart shrivels like the corpse of a fly. I had eternally bound myself to Ariane by throttling her with her silk: now Arachné has eternally bound me to her with her thread by constricting my heart.

At midnight, by this mysterious bridge, I visit the Spiders' realm of which she is queen. I must pass through this hell to swing, later, in the starlight.

The woodland spiders hasten there with luminous bulbs at their feet. The trapdoor spiders have eight terrible, scintillating eyes; bristling with hairs, they pounce upon me where the roads bend. Beside the ponds where water spiders tremble on long legs like those of harvest spiders, I am drawn into the dizzy rounds the tarantulas dance. The garden spiders watch for me at the centre of their grey circles traversed with spokes. They fix on me the innumerable facets of their eyes, like a suit of mirrors set to trap larks, and they fascinate me. As I go through the copse, tacky webs brush against my face. Crouched in the thickets, swift-footed, hairy monsters wait for me.

Now Queen Mab is not as powerful as my Queen Arachné, for she has the power to have me ride in her marvellous car that travels along a thread. Her car is made of the hard shell of a gigantic trapdoor spider, begemmed with facetted studs cut from its black-diamond eyes. The axletrees are the articulated legs of giant harvest spiders. Transparent wings with rosettes of veins bear it aloft, rhythmically beating the air. In it we swing, hour upon hour: then, abruptly, I faint away, worn out by the wound in my chest in which Arachné ceaselessly forages with her pointed lips. In my nightmare I see bellies starred with eyes bent over me, and I flee before wrinkled legs hung with filaments.

Now I distinctly sense Arachné's two knees grasping my sides, and the guggling of my blood rising towards her mouth. My heart will very soon be sucked dry; then it will remain swathed in its prison of white filaments – and I shall flee beyond the Spiders' Realm towards the refulgent lattice of the stars. Thus, by the silken cord Arachné has thrown me, I shall escape with her. And I shall bequeath you – poor madmen – a pallid corpse with a tuft of blond hair stirring in the morning breeze.

The Veiled Man

Of the combination of circumstances that have been my undoing I can say nothing; certain accidents of human life are as artistically contrived by chance or by the laws of nature as by the most demoniacal invention: one cries out in wonder before them as before a painting by an impressionist who has captured a singular and momentary truth. But if my head should fall, I trust that this narrative will survive me and that in the history of human lives it might be a true oddity, as it were a lurid opening on to the unknown.

When I entered that terrible carriage, two persons were occupying it. One facing away from me, enveloped in a travelling-rug, was fast asleep. His covering was flecked with spots on a yellowish ground, like a leopard-skin. Many such are sold in travel-goods departments: but I can say at once that, touching it later, I realised that this was really the skin of a wild animal. Likewise the sleeper's bonnet, when I observed it with the especially acute power of vision that came to me, seemed to me to be of an infinitely fine white felt. The other traveller, who had a pleasant face, appeared just into his thirties. Beyond that he had the insignificant appearance of a man who readily sleeps on railway-trains.

The sleeper did not show his ticket, nor did he turn his face while I was installing myself opposite him. And once I was seated on the bench I ceased to observe my fellow travellers so as to reflect upon the various matters that preoccupied me.

The movement of the train did not interrupt my thoughts, but it directed their current in a curious fashion. The song of the axle and the wheels, the grip of the wheels on the rails, the crossings of the points with the juddering that periodically shakes badly-suspended carriages transformed itself into a mental refrain. It was a species of vague thought that broke in regular intervals upon my other ideas. After a quarter of an hour the reiteration bordered on the obsessive. By a violent effort of will I rid myself of it; but the vague mental refrain took on the form of a musical notation which I anticipated. Each jolt was not a note, but it was the echo in unison of a note conceived in advance, at once feared and desired; to such an extent that these eternally similar shocks ran the most extended gamut of notes corresponding, in truth, in its superimposed octaves beyond the compass of any instrument, to the layers of suppositions that are often piled up by the mind in travail.

In the end, to break the spell, I took up a newspaper. But, once I had read them, entire lines detatched themselves from the columns and, with a sort of plaintive and uniform sound, reintroduced themselves to my view at intervals I anticipated but could not modify. I leaned back against the seat, experiencing a singular sensation of disquiet and of emptiness in my head.

It was then that I observed the first phenomenon that plunged me into the realms of the uncanny. The traveller on the far side of the carriage, having raised his bench and adjusted his pillow, stretched out and closed his eyes. Almost at the same moment the sleeper facing me silently rose and drew about the globe of the lamp the little spring-loaded blue shade. In this operation I should have been able to see his face – *and I did not see it.* I caught a glimpse of a confused blur, the colour of a human face, but of which I could not distinguish the least feature. The action had been accomplished with a silent rapidity that stupefied me. I had not had the time to take in the sight of the sleeper standing erect when, already, I saw only the white crown of his bonnet above the speckled cover. It was a trifling matter, but it disturbed me. How had the sleeper so quickly been able to grasp that the other had closed his eyes? He had turned his face in my direction and I had not seen it; the rapidity and the mysterious quality of his motion were inexpressible.

A blue obscurity now hung between the upholstered benches, now and then barely broken by the veil of yellow light projected from without by an oil-lamp.

The circle of thoughts that haunted me closed in as the train's pulsations increased in the darkness. The uneasy quality of the motion had fixed it; and, slowly modified in time to the monotonous sing-song of the rails, stories of murderers on trains welled up out of the gloom. A cruel fear contracted my heart, all the more cruel since it was vague, and incertitude augments terror. Visible, palpable, I sensed the image of Jud starting-up – a thin face with cavernous eyes, prominent cheekbones and a filthy goatee-beard – the face of Jud the murderer, who killed at night in first-class carriages and who, after his escape, had never been recaptured. The darkness aided me in painting with the features of Jud the confused blur I had seen in the lamplight, to imagine beneath the speckled covers a man crouched, ready to spring.

I was violently tempted to hurl myself to the far end of the carriage, to shake the sleeping traveller, to cry aloud to him my peril. A sense of propriety held me back. Could I explain my disquiet? How could I respond to that well-intentioned man's astonished glance? He was sleeping comfortably, well wrapped-up, his head on the pillow, his gloved hands crossed on his chest: by what right was I to awaken him because another traveller had shaded the lamp? Was there not already a symptom of madness in my mind, which persisted in linking the man's action with the consciousness he must have had of the other's sleep? Were these two not different events, belonging to different series, linked by a simple coincidence? But at this point my fear stood pat and became insistent; so much so that, in the train's rhythmical silence, I sensed my temples throbbing; a tumult in my blood, which contrasted painfully with my outward calm, set things swirling round me, and events vague and still to come, but with the conjectured precision of things that are about to happen, marched through my brain in endless procession.

And suddenly a profound calm established itself within me. I felt the tension of my muscles relax in a complete abandon. The swirling of my thoughts was stilled. I experienced the inward slackening that precedes sleep and swooning and, with eyes open, I was in fact swooning. Yes: with eyes open and endowed with an infinite power of which they availed themselves without effort. And this relaxation was so complete that I was incapable of governing my senses, or of taking a decision, or even of representing to myself any thought of action of my own devising. Those superhuman eyes were of themselves directed upon the mysterious-faced man and, whilst seeing through obstacles, at the same time saw them. Thus I *knew* that I was looking through a leopard-skin, and through a flesh-coloured silken mask, a *crépon* covering a swarthy face. And my eyes immediately met with other eyes, eyes that shone with an insupportable blackness: I saw a man dressed in yellow, with buttons seemingly of silver, enveloped in a brown overcoat; I knew he was covered in a leopard-skin, but I saw him. I also heard (for my hearing had just taken on an extreme acuity) his breathing, urgent and panting, like that of a man making a considerable effort. But it must have been an inward effort, for the man was moving neither arms nor legs: it was indeed such – for his will annihilated my own.

One last resistance manifested itself in my being. I was aware of a struggle in which, in reality, I played no part, a struggle carried on by that deep-seated egoism of which one is never aware and which governs one's self. Then ideas came drifting into my mind – ideas that were not mine, that I had not created, in which I recognised nothing in common with my substance, perfidious and attractive as the black waters over which one leans.

One of these was murder. But I no longer conceived it as an act filled with dread, accomplished by Jud, as the issue of a nameless terror. With a certain glimmer of curiosity and an infinite prostration of everything that had ever been my will, I experienced it as possible.

Then the veiled man rose and, regarding me fixedly through his flesh-coloured veil, went with gliding steps towards the sleeping traveller. With one hand he seized him by the nape of the neck, firmly; and at the same time he stuffed a silken pad into his mouth. I felt no distress, nor had I any desire to cry out. But I was there, and dull-eyed I watched. The man drew a narrow, sharp-pointed Turkestan knife, the hollow-ground blade of which had a central channel and he cut the traveller's throat as one would bleed a sheep. The blood spurted up to the luggage rack. Drawing it sharply towards him, he had thrust in his knife at the right side. The throat gaped open. He uncovered the lamp and I saw the red gash. Then he emptied the man's pockets and dabbled his hands in the bloody pool. Next he came towards me and, without revulsion, I endured his smearing my inert fingers and my face, of which not a wrinkle twitched.

The veiled man rolled up his travelling-rug and threw on his overcoat; whilst I remained next to the *murdered* traveller. The terrible word made no impression upon me – until suddenly I found myself desolate of support, without the will to make up for the lack of my own, empty of ideas, befuddled. And coming to myself by degrees, gummy-eyed, phlegmy-mouthed, my neck stiff, as if held in a leaden grip, I found I was alone, in the early grey dawn, with a corpse that tossed about like a bundle. The train was threading its way through an intensely monotonous stretch of open country dotted with clumps of trees – and when, after a long-drawn-out whistle that echoed on the clear morning air, it stopped, I blundered stupidly to the carriage door, my face striped with clotted blood.

A Skeleton

I once spent a night in a haunted house. I dare not tell too much of this story, because I am convinced that no one would believe it. That house was most certainly haunted, but things did not happen there as they do in haunted houses. It was not a castle tottering into dilapidation, perched on a wooded hillock beside a gloomy precipice. It had not ages-since been abandoned. Its last owner had not died in a mysterious manner. The peasants did not, as they passed it, cross themselves for fear. When midnight sounded from the village belfry, no wan light was seen at its ruined windows. The trees in the grounds were not yews and, at nightfall, no frightened children caught sight of white forms looming through the hedges. I did not arrive at an inn where all the rooms were taken. The landlord did not, candle-in-hand, scratch his head for a long time and, at length, and hesitantly, offer to make up a bed in the remotest room of the keep. He did not add, with a scared expression, that of all the travellers who had slept there, none had returned to recount his terrible end. He did not tell me of fiendish sounds heard at night in the old manor-house. I felt no inner sense of bravura that impelled me to go through with the adventure. And I did not have the ingenious idea of providing myself with a pair of candlesticks and a flintlock; no more did I firmly resolve to watch until midnight, reading an odd volume of Swedenborg, and I did not, at about three minutes to midnight, feel a leaden sleep weighing down on my eyelids.

No; nothing transpired as it invariably does in those terrifying tales of haunted houses. I alighted from my train and stayed at the *Hôtel des Trois Pigeons*: I had an excellent appetite, and I put away three slices of roast, some *sauté* chicken and a first-rate salad; I drank a bottle of Bordeaux. Then I took my candle and went upstairs to my room. My candle did not go out; I found my grog on the mantelpiece, and no phantom had dipped his spectral lips therein.

But when I was on the point of getting into bed, and when I went to take my grog and put it on the night-table, I was a little surprised to see Tom Bobbins at the fireside. It seemed to me that he had lost a good deal of weight; he had not taken off his stovepipe hat, and he wore a very respectable frock-coat; but his trouser-legs flapped about in a most lamentable fashion. I had not seen him for more than a year; with the result that I went up to him, offering my hand and saying: 'How goes it with you, Tom?', in the most concerned way. He stretched out his sleeve and offered to my grip something I at first took for a nutcracker; and when I was about to make plain to him my disapproval of this stupid prank he turned to face me, and I saw that his hat was set atop a bare skull. I was all the more astonished to see him as a death's-head since I had positively recognised him by his way of *winking with his left eye.* I asked myself what terrible malady could have so disfigured him; he no longer had a hair to call his own; his eye-sockets were devilishly hollow, and what remained of his nose was not worth talking about. To tell the truth, I felt a sort of embarrasment in questioning him. But he began to chat in a friendly way and asked me about the latest prices on the Stock Exchange. After this he expressed his surprise at not having received my card in answer to his funeral invitation. I told him I had never received any communication – but he assured me that he had inscribed my name on the list and had expressly given all the names to the undertaker.

I saw then that I was conversing with Tom Bobbins' skeleton. I did not throw myself on my knees, and I did not exclaim: 'Begone, phantom, be you whom you may, soul troubled in your repose, expiating doubtless some crime committed here below, come not to haunt me!' No; but I looked more closely at my poor friend Bobbins, and I saw he was very much the worse for wear. There was about him, above all, a melancholy air that touched my heart; and his voice was the very echo of the dismal whistling sound of a wet-smoking pipe. I thought to comfort him by offering him a cigar – but he excused himself on account of his teeth which suffered cruelly from the humidity of his subterranean quarters. Naturally I enquired solicitously about his coffin; and he replied that it was of the finest pinewood, but there was a little draught in it that was in the process of of giving him rheumatism in the neck. I advised him to wear flannel and promised my wife would make him a knitted waistcoat.

The next moment, Tom Bobbins the skeleton and I were conversing as comfortably as could be, our feet on the mantelshelf. The only thing that bothered me was that although he had no eyes whatever, Tom Bobbins persisted in winking his left eye. But I reassured myself by recalling that my other friend, Colliwobbles the banker, was in the habit of giving his word of honour, although he no more had any than Bobbins had a left eye.

After a few minutes, gazing into the fire, Tom Bobbins launched into a kind of soliloquy. He said: 'I know of no race more despised than us poor skeletons. The coffin-makers accommodate us wretchedly. We are fitted out in our lightest garments, as if for a wedding or a *soirée*: I was obliged to go and borrow a suit from my process-server. And then there's a mob of poets and other clowns who go on about our supernatural powers, and of the fantastic way we have of flying through the air, and of the sabbats to which we abandon ourselves on stormy nights. One of these days I'd like to take my thighbone and crack a few heads a bit, just to give them some idea of a witches' sabbath. Not to speak of their having us dragging chains that clank diabolically. I'd dearly love to know how the cemetery-keeper would let us out in such a get-up. And then they come looking for us in old hovels, in owls' lurking-places, in holes stopped-up with nettles and wallflowers, and everywhere they make a great song and dance with stories of phantoms frightening people and letting out the howls of the damned. I really don't see what there is about us that's terrifying. All it is, is that we're very lean and we can no longer issue bills on the Exchange. If we were properly dressed, we could still make a good showing in the world. I've seen men who were even more threadbare than we are carry off some charming prizes; whilst, with our tailors and our quarters, we certainly don't do so well.' And Tom Bobbins stared in discouragement at his shinbones.

At this I started to weep over the fate of those poor old skeletons. And I pictured to myself all their sufferings as they mouldered in their nailed-up boxes and their limbs languished after a *schottische* or a *cotillon*. And I presented Tom Bobbins with a pair of old fur-lined gloves and a flowered waistcoat which I found rather on the tight side.

He thanked me coldly, and I noticed that as he grew warmer, so, in proportion, he was becoming more vicious. In an instant I saw that this indeed was Tom Bobbins; and we exploded in the jolliest skeletal laughter possible. Bobbins' bones tinkled most cheerfully, like sleighbells. I saw then that, in this excessive hilarity, he was becoming human, and I began to be frightened. Tom Bobbins hadn't had an equal, while he was alive, when it came to palming-off on you a bundle of shares in the Rostocostolados Tinted Guano Mining Company, and half a dozen comparable issues had likewise found no difficulty in swallowing up people's revenues. He also had a way of inviting you to a friendly game of *piquet* and then fleecing you at *rubicon*. With an easy and elegant grace he would relieve you of your *louis* at poker. If you were not content he would happily take your nose off, and then proceed by degrees to slice you up with his bowie knife.

I observed that strange phenomenon, then; and contrary to all those pale tales of phantoms, how fearful I was to see Tom Bobbins returning to life! For I recalled having been taken in a couple of times; and my old-time friend Tom Bobbins was a remarkable knife-fighter. In fact, in an unguarded moment, he had taken a strip of flesh off the rear part of my right thigh. So when I saw that Tom Bobbins was Tom Bobbins, and that he no longer had the air of a skeleton, my pulse commenced to beat so fast that it was no longer a beat; I was quite covered in gooseflesh, and I no longer had the courage to say a word.

Tom Bobbins planted his bowie knife on the table, as was his custom, and suggested a game of *écarté*. I humbly acquiesced in his wishes. He set to, playing with a gallows-bird's luck – I don't, for all that, believe Tom had ever danced at a rope's end; he was far too fly for that. And, contrary to the horror stories told about spectres, the gold I won from Tom Bobbins did not change into oak-leaves or cinders, simply because I won nothing whatever and because he made a clean sweep of the contents of my pockets. Afterwards he began to curse like one of the damned; and he told me appalling stories and entirely corrupted what innocence remained to me. He stretched out a hand to my grog and downed it to the last drop; and I dared not make a move to stop him. For I knew that, the next moment, I would have had his knife in my belly, and I could not beat him to it, precisely because *he* had no belly. Next, with a terribly vicious grimace, he asked after my wife and, for a moment, I felt inclined to smash what he had of a nose. I curbed this reprehensible instinct; but I inwardly resolved that my wife would not knit him a waistcoat. Then he took my correspondence out of my overcoat pockets, and with various ironic and disobliging remarks, started reading my friends' letters. Really, Bobbins the skeleton was supportable; but, dear God, the flesh-and-blood Bobbins was perfectly terrifying.

When he had done reading, I gently reminded him that it was four in the morning, and I asked whether he was not afraid of being late. He answered in a completely human way that, if the cemetery-keeper were to permit himself the least remark, he would 'lead him a fine dance'. Then he looked lecherously at my watch, winked his left eye, asked me for it and coolly slipped it into his watch-pocket. Immediately afterwards he told me he had 'business in town', and took his leave. Before going he thrust two candlesticks into his pocket, coldly unscrewed the head of my cane and, without a shadow of remorse, asked if I couldn't lend him one or two *louis*. I replied that, sadly, I no longer had anything about me, but that it would give me pleasure to send them to him. He gave me his address; but it was such a jumble of gratings, tombs, crosses and vaults that I have completely forgotten it. Thereupon he made an attempt on the clock; but, for all his efforts, it was too much for him. When he informed me that he was inclined to go by way of the chimney, I was so happy to see him reverting to truly skeletal ways that I made no move to keep him. It was with a joyous tranquillity that I listened to him kicking and clambering his way up the flue: only they charged me for the quantity of soot Tom Bobbins had dislodged in his passage.

I have had my fill of the society of skeletons. There is something human about them that I find profoundly repulsive. The next time Tom Bobbins comes, I shall have drunk my grog; I shall not have a *sou* of ready cash; I shall extinguish my candle, and the fire. Perhaps he will revert to the customs proper to phantoms, howling and rattling his chains. Then we shall see.

The Fat Man

A parable

Seated in his easy chair of supple leather, the fat man looked about him in delight. He was truly fat; about his neck there was great fatty collar; he had a barded chest, a well-covered belly; his arms were knotty at the joints, like sausages, and his hands lay round and white on his knees like big plucked quails. His feet were miracles of ponderousness, his legs pillars and his thighs fleshy capitals. His skin was as shiny and close-textured as bacon rind; his eyes were puffy with fat and his quadruple chin solidly propped up his overflowing face.

And, all about him, everything was solid, round and fat; the solid oak table, firmly set on its large feet, polished at the edges; the old armchairs with their rounded backs, their bulging seats and their big, spherical nailheads; the footstools, crouching low like fat toads, and the heavy carpets with their thick and tangled pile. The clock sprawled on the mantelshelf, the keyholes opening like eyes in its convex dial and the glass that enclosed it was domed like the porthole of a diver's helmet. The candelabra were like the knotty branches of a brazen tree, and the candles dripped lard. The bed was bloated as a padded paunch; plump and crackling, the logs on the fire were bursting their bark; the decanters on the sideboard were dumpy, the glasses knobbly; thick-necked, the bottles, half-filled with wine, were embedded in their circles of felt like vermilion bombs of glass. And, above all, in this substantial and portly room, warm and cheerful, there was a fat man, laughing bountifully, opening a wholesome, blubbery mouth, smoking and drinking.

The arched door with its bulky knob that made a comfortable handful, opened onto the kitchen where this man spent the greater part of his life. For, from morning on, he would prowl among the casseroles, dunking bread in the sauces, mopping the dripping-pans with the butt-end of a roll, sniffing at the bowls filled with *bouillon;* and, while the fire purred under the hotplate, he would plunge a dripping wooden spoon into the cooking-pots to compare his *ragouts.* Then opening the little door of the furnace, he would fill the room with the red glow that spread over his flesh. Thus, in the half-light he had the air of an enormous lantern, his face its window, lit by the blood and the glow of the embers.

And in the kitchen the fat man had a chubby niece, pink and white, who, her sleeves rolled up, would stir the vegetables, a smiling niece, all dimples, whose little eyes were lively with good humour, a niece who would rap his fingers when he filched from the plate, a niece who would toss hot pancakes for him when he was minded to turn the pan, and who made him all sorts of dainties, sugared, glazed, or simmered to the turn, with delectable *croûtons*.

Under the great deal table dozed a swag-bellied cat whose tail was as thick as that of a fat-tailed sheep and, as he leant against the brickwork of the range, blinking in the heat, the thick folds of the poodle's shorn skin hung down.

In his room the fat man was gazing voluptuously at a glass goblet into which he had just gently poured some *Konstanz*, the 1811 vintage, when the street door silently swung open. The fat man was so surprised that he opened his mouth and remained motionless, his lower lip pendulous. Before him stood a thin man, dark and tall, with a nothing of a nose and a lipless mouth; his cheekbones were pointed, his skull was bony and, whenever he made a movement, one expected to see splinters of bone sticking through his sleeves or his trouser-legs. He had hollow, gloomy eyes, his fingers were like wires, and his expression was so serious it saddened one to look at him. He carried a spectacle-case in his hand and, as he spoke, from time to time he put on a pair of blue glasses. Of all his person, his voice alone was beguiling and engaging, and he expressed himself with such charm that tears came to the fat man's eyes.

'Hey!' he cried, 'Marie! We have a gentleman here, come to dinner. Look sharp about it, lay the table; here's the key to the linen cupboard; find a tablecloth, fetch the table-napkins; have the wine brought up – the bottles at the bottom, on the left – perhaps you like Burgundy, monsieur? – hey, Marie, bring some Nuits; keep an eye on the fowl – the one we had the other day was rather overdone. Have just a little *Konstanz*, monsieur. You must be hungry; we eat too late. Make haste, Marie, the gentleman's dying of hunger. Have you put the roast on? You must cut up some bread for the soup. Don't forget the little glasses. And the thyme – did you remember it? I thought as much. Put a sprig in, right away. Perhaps the gentleman likes fish; I'm so sorry monsieur, the very thing we haven't got. Do hurry, Marie – decant this wine – put the chairs up to the table – get the tureen – see to the butter – skim this sauce – give us some bread. This soup is excellent, don't you think? One ought to live well. Would you like some of this sugar with your shrimps? It's first-rate.'

'Do you know what sugar is?' the thin man asked in a placid tone.

'Yes', the fat man replied, surprised, again letting his lower lip drop, stopping short, his spoon at his mouth. 'That is, no – I eat it with certain dishes – it's all one to me, sugar. Sugar is good. What have you got to say about sugar?'

'Goodness, nothing!' said the thin man, 'or next to nothing. You're perfectly well aware that you can absorb sucrose, or cane sugar; and you derive starches and carbohydrates from other sugars which you transform into animal sugar, invert sugar or glucose...'

'And you want me to worry my head about that?' the fat man said, laughing. Sucrose or glucose, sugar is good. I like sweet dishes.'

'Quite so', said the thin man, 'but if you generate too much glucose, my dear friend, you'll get diabetes; good living gives you diabetes; I shouldn't be surprised if you already had some traces. You ought to be careful with that sharp knife.'

'And why?' the fat man enquired.

'Good lord!' the thin man replied, 'for this simple reason: you probably have diabetes, and if you should cut yourself or prick yourself, you'll be running a great risk.'

'A great risk!' the fat man said. 'Bah! What nonsense! let's eat and drink!... What's the risk, then?'

'Oh!' replied the thin man, 'generally all the nutritive reserves are eliminated with the overplus of glucose; one cannot replace tissue; the wound fails to cicatrise, and one gets gangrene. The hand decomposes (the fat man dropped his fork), then the arm rots (the fat man stopped eating), and then the rest of the body follows suit (on the fat man's face could be seen an expression that had never appeared there before – that of fear). Oh dear! (the thin man continued) what troubles there are in this life!'

The fat man reflected for a moment, his head bowed; then he said wearily: 'Are you a physician, monsieur?'

'Yes, at your service, a doctor of medicine. Yes. I live at the Place Saint-Sulpice, and I came...'

'Monsieur', the fat man broke in beseechingly, 'can you prevent me from having diabetes?'

'With God's help, my dear monsieur, we can try', said the thin man.
The fat man's face filled out anew, and his mouth widened in a smile:

'Let's shake on it; and be my friend. You shall stay here with me; we shall do as you say, and you will have nothing to complain of.'

'All right', said the thin man. 'And I shall regulate your life.'

'Agreed', the fat man replied. 'Come now, have some fowl.'

'I beg your pardon', the thin man exclaimed. 'Fowl! That's not at all good for you. Get yourself an egg, with some tea and a slice of toast.' The fat man's features were a picture of desolation. 'Lord!' poor Marie sobbed, 'who'll eat the fowl?' And then, with a catch in his voice, the fat man said to the thin man: 'Doctor, I beg you, eat!'

Thenceforth it was the thin man who was in command. A progressive and general emaciation commenced. The furniture grew thin and angular; the footstools creaked on their feet; the waxed floorboards smelled of old wax; the curtains became limp and mildewed; the logs seemed to shiver with cold; the pans in the kitchen went rusty; the hanging casseroles were spotted with verdigris. The range sang no more, nor did the joyous stewpot; from time to time a dead coal could be heard dropping onto a bed of extinct ashes. The cat was lean and mangy; it squalled disconsolately. The dog turned snappish; one day, bolting with a scrap of cod, it broke a windowpane with its bony spine.

And the fat man went the way of the house. Little by little the fat collected in yellow deposits under his flesh; his bull neck had all but vanished, and his throat was as puckery as a turkey's; his face was covered in interlacing wrinkles, and the skin of his belly rippled like the lace on a waistcoat. His bony frame, which had grown in proportion, balanced on two thin staves that had been his thighs and his legs. Flaps of skin hung about his calves. And he was haunted by the fear of diabetes and of death. The thin man urged upon him his danger, from day to day more cruel, and exhorted him to look to his soul. And the poor fat man cared for his diabetes and his soul.

But he wept over his former joy, over Marie, his niece, who was now small-boned and waxen-faced. One day as he was warming before the fire the miserable, shivering stems that had been his fingers, slumped on a hard wooden chair, a little leather-bound book on his spindly knees, Marie placed a hand on his arm and whispered in his ear: 'Just you have a look at your friend, uncle – he's putting on weight.'

Surrounded by that desolation, the thin man was gradually filling out. His skin was taking on a rounded smoothness, becoming roseate.

His fingers were starting to plumpen. And his air of sweet satisfaction was constantly growing.

Then the man who had been fat piteously lifted the covering of skin that drooped from his knees – and let it drop.

The Dom

Sashuli, the jester of a maharaja who lived in the reign of Vikramaditya, one day said to him: 'Master, how do you regard life?'

'What question is this you put to me?' the Raja replied. 'Life is the gift of the gods: it is not for us to appraise it. They bestow it and withdraw it at their will; every man is content with what is his; and I praise the divinities for permitting me to live and to do good.'

'Do you believe that every man, even of the lowest caste, might be satisfied with life and do good?' the fool said.

'To be sure', the Maharaja answered, 'if he is pious and grateful to the gods.'

'Excellent', Sashuli responded; 'thou art the incarnation of the seven virtues.'

The Maharaja was extraordinarily pious. He had a great respect for the sacred seers. He did not drive in his chariot in the forests where the hermits dwelt and, when hunting, he did not kill the antelope they favoured. He protected the fakirs among his people, and when he encountered them on the roads, enveloped in mud and filth, covered in grass that had been growing on their skin for a dozen years, he washed them devotedly so that when they awoke their bodies were white and purified and they went off, spreading abroad in divers countries the blessings of heaven.

He possessed riches so vast that he could not number them. The tables of his bondsmen were made of solid gold. His serving-maids' beds were cut out of diamond. The face of his wife, the Rani, was adorned with stars and her hands with moons. His son was the paragon of celestial graces. The kings of the most distant realms came to him in procession, laden with the most precious products of their countries. In his land there were neither tigers nor demons, nor even the rakshasas who, by night, come and lay open men's breasts to gnaw at their hearts.

But when the jester had spoken as he did, the Raja fell into a state of gloomy meditation. He thought of those who tilled the soil, of the workmen, of men of low caste. He thought of the gift of life, so unevenly distributed by the gods. He thought that perhaps true piety lay not in doing good whilst being great, but being able to do good whilst of no account. He asked himself whether that piety sprang up like an immense flower from the heart of the rich, or whether it opened gently like a small and humble flower of the fields on the earthen heart of the poor.

The he assembled his princes and made a solemn declaration. He renounced his kingship and all its privileges. He distributed among them his lands and his fiefs, he opened the vaults where his treasures were stored and scattered them abroad, he disembowelled the bags of silver and gold coins and poured them forth for the people in the public squares, he threw to the winds the sumptuous manuscripts of his libraries. He had the Rani summoned and repudiated her in the presence of his advisers; she was compelled to depart with his son and return to the country whence she had come. Then, when the princes, his wife, his child, his retainers were gone, he shaved his head, stripped himself of his clothing, wrapped himself in a piece of coarse cloth and set fire to his palace with a torch. The conflagration rose red above the trees of the royal residence; the inlaid furniture and the ivory chambers could be heard crackling; the hangings of woven metal dropped down black and burnt.

Thus the Raja set out by the light of his burning treasures. He walked from one sun to the next, from one moon to the next, until his sandals fell from his feet. Then he went barefoot over the thorns, and his skin ran with blood. The parasitic animals that live by divine grace on the bark of trees and the surface of leaves entered into the soles of his feet and made them swell. His legs became like two full leather bottles that dragged after him as he went on his knees. The winged creatures, so small that they cannot be seen and that live in the air, fell with the rainwater on his head; and the Raja's hair dissolved in ulcers, and his scalp erupted in sores and gleaming nodes. And his whole body became bloody because of the small beasts of earth, water and air that came to live there.

But the Maharaja patiently supported the will of the gods, knowing well that everything that breathes has a soul and that one must not kill living beings, nor let them die. Although he was suffering fearful torments, he still felt pity for all the souls that surrounded him. 'Most certainly', he said to himself, 'I am not yet a fakir; renunciation must be still harder, and the struggle more terrible. Now I have renounced my riches, my wife, my son, my bodily health; what more is needed to achieve the pity that flourishes among the poor?'

The Raja had never dreamed that one of the blessings of earthly life was liberty. When he had thus meditated he saw that liberty is the condition of the kings of this world and that it was necessary he abandon it to experience true piety. The Raja resolved to sell himself to the first poor man he met.

Travelling through a black country where the soil was rich and oozy, where the birds of the heavens flew in circles and swooped in clouds, the Maharaja saw a hut of branches and mud, the most wretched work of human hands, that stood by a murky pond. In the door stood a dark-skinned old man with a dirty beard and bloodshot eyes; his whole body was covered in silt and aquatic plants; his appearance was repulsive and impure.

'What ails you?' asked the poor king, who was dragging himself along on hands and knees.

He sat down by the hut, stretched out his legs, swollen like leather bottles, and rested his enormous head against the mud-coloured wall.

'I am a Dom', the impure being replied; 'I am the lowest caste; I throw the corpses men bring me into that pond: men's bodies bring me in a rupee, children's bodies half of that; when people are too poor, they bring me a scrap of cloth.'

'So be it!' said the Raja. 'I shall sell myself to you, venerable Dom.'

'You are not worth very much', the corpse-sinker answered, 'but I shall buy you for this ounce of gold here. You can do my work if I am away. Sit yourself down there: if your legs are diseased, smear them with mud; if your head is bloated, cover it with the leaves that grow in the water and you will be refreshed. I am very poor, as you see. I have given you the last ounce of gold I possess, so as to keep you here as a companion – for the loneliness is horrible, and the snapping of the crocodiles' jaws wakens me in the night.'

The Raja stayed with the Dom. They lived on berries and roots, for they rarely had a corpse to sink. And those who reached the Dom's pond were so poor that often they could give no more than a piece of cloth or half a rupee. But the Dom was very kind to the Raja; he cared for his horrible sores as if he were performing a natural duty.

And it happened that there came about a time of great prosperity for the country. The sky was blue, the trees in flower. Men were no longer minded to die. The Dom lamented miserably in his hunger, half buried in the dried mud.

It was then that the Raja saw an old woman advancing towards the pond, carrying the corpse of a small boy. The Raja's heart started – and he recognised his son, who was dead. The corpse was gaunt and bloodless; one could count the ribs along its chest; the cheeks of the Raja's son were hollow and earthen-coloured; it was clear that he had died of hunger.

The Rani recognised the king and said to herself: 'He will commit his son's body to the water and take no fee.'

The poor Raja dragged himself on his knees to the lifeless corpse and wept over its head. Then he took pity on the Dom and said to the Rani: 'You must give me half a rupee for committing my son to the water.'

'I am poor', said the Rani. 'I cannot.'

'It is of no account', the Raja answered. 'Go and gather a few handfuls of rice. I shall watch over the body of my son.'

Grain by grain the Rani gleaned rice for a week to earn the half-rupee, and the Raja wept all the while over his child. And when he had the half-rupee he immersed his son in the murky pond and gave the money to the Dom to save him from dying. And then a resplendent light filled his eyes and he saw that he had truly attained to the great renunciation and the true pity of the poor.

Then he went into a thicket to pray. And God made him motionless; the wind covered him with earth; grass grew over his body; his eyes oozed out of their sockets and wild plants sprouted in his skull. The tendons of his emaciated arms, lifted up to the heavens, were like dried lianas entwined about dead branches. Thus the king attained eternal repose.

The Amber-trader

The glaciers had still not invaded the Alps; the brown-and-black mountains were less snow-capped; the corries did not glitter with so dazzling a whiteness. Where today one sees desolate moraines, uniformly frozen snowfields with, here and there, the fissures of liquid crevasses, there were occasional flowering clumps of heather and less sterile heathlands, still-warm earth, blades of grass and the winged creatures that alighted there. There were the round and flickering sheets of blue lakes, their basins hollowed in the high plateaux; whilst today they have the disquieting and bleak gaze of those enormous and glassy mountain's-eyes where the foot, fearing the abyss, seems to slide over the frozen depths of fathomless dead pupils. The rocks encircling the lakes were of basalt, a vigorous black in colour; the beds of granite were moss-covered and the sun lit up all their flecks of mica; today, like stone eyebrows, the ridges of blocks, obscurely piled-up, confusedly thrown together, under the seamless mantle of rime, protect their eye-sockets, filled with sombre ice.

In the hollow of a high massif, between two very green flanks, ran a long valley with a sinuous lake. Along the banks, and to the very centre, rose strange constructions, some leaning together, two-by-two, others isolated in the middle of the water. They were like a multitude of pointed straw hats on a forest of sticks. On all sides, at a certain distance from the bank, the heads of poles could be seen rising above the water, forming a pilework – rough trunks, many of them rotten, stripped of their bark, that held back the lapping of the little waves. Set immediately on top of the tree-trunks, the huts were fashioned of branches and the dried mud of the lake. Because of the smoke-holes – so that the wind might not blow the smoke back into the interior – the conical roofs could be turned in all directions. Some barnlike structures were more spacious; there were rungs of a sort leading down into the water, and narrow catwalks joining many of the pile-islets.

Large beings, heavy jowled and silent, moved about among the huts, descending to the water, dragging nets weighted with polished stones bored with holes, snapping up fish and sometimes guzzling the raw fry. Others, patiently crouched at a wooden frame, threw from their left to their right hand a hollowed, funnel-shaped flint, olive-shaped, with two longitudinal grooves, carrying a shaggy thread bristling with twigs. With their knees they gripped two fluted uprights that slipped over the frame; thus, by an alternating movement, a web was made in which the strands crossed at intervals. Of those who worked stones, splitting them with scraper-blades of hardened wood, none were to be seen there, nor were there any of the polishers who used a flat grindstone with a central depression for the palm of the hand, nor were there any of the skilful hafters who travelled from place to place with perforated antlers and who, using reindeer-leather thongs, would fix therein beautiful basalt axe-heads or elegant blades of jade or serpentine brought from the lands where the sun rises. There were no women skilled in threading the white teeth of beasts and beads of polished marble to make necklaces and bracelets, nor were there any of the craftsmen with a sharp burin who engraved curved lines on scapulae and carved the leaders' staves of office.

Living far from the lands that engender useful skills, the pile-villagers were an impoverished people, lacking tools and ornaments. They procured those they wanted by bartering them for dried fish with the wandering traders who came in dug-out canoes. They clothed themselves in the skins they purchased; they were obliged to wait for the arrival of those who provided them with weights for their nets and stone hooks; they had neither dogs nor reindeer; living isolated, with their swarm of mud-spattered children splashing about among the piles, they existed miserably in their dens that were open to the skies, protected by the water.

As night fell, the summits of the mountains about the lake still palely lit, there was a sound of paddles and the shock of a boat was felt against the piles. Standing out against the grey mist, three men and a woman advanced towards the ladders. They had hunting-spears in their hands and the father swung two stone balls on a stretched cord from which they hung by two hollowed grooves. In a canoe which she moored to a plunging tree a stranger-woman stood up, richly garbed in furs, holding aloft a basket woven of reeds. Vaguely, in the distance, they saw that the basket had in it a heap of yellow things, and shining. It seemed heavy, for in it were also to be glimpsed worked stones. The stranger-woman nonetheless climbed up nimbly, the basket clinking, held in her sinewy arms; then, like a swallow entering its nest under a roof, with a bound she was in the hut and crouched by the turf fire.

She was utterly different in aspect from the people of the pile-village.

They were stocky, ponderous, with enormous muscles between which furrows ran the length of their arms and legs. They had oily black hair that hung to their shoulders in hard and straight locks. Their heads were large, coarse, with a flat forehead, distended at the temples and with massive jowls, whilst their eyes were small, deep-set and ill-humoured. The stranger-woman had long limbs and a graceful carriage, a shock of blonde hair and clear eyes of a provocative freshness. Whereas the pile-village people were almost mute, sometimes murmuring a syllable, but observing everything persistently and with a wandering gaze, the stranger-woman prattled endlessly in an unknown tongue, smiled, gesticulated, caressed the objects and the hands of others, fumbled them, prodded them, jokingly shoved them aside and, above all displayed an insatiable curiosity. She had a wide and open smile; the fisher-people had only a narrow grin. But they looked covetously upon the blonde trader-woman's basket.

She pushed it to the centre of the group and held the objects to the light of an ignited chip of resin. They were rods of worked amber, marvellously clear, like yellow translucent gold. She had spheres in which milky veins wandered, berry-sized pieces cut in facets, necklaces of rods and of little balls, bracelets cut from a single piece, large, through which the arm could be thrust to below the shoulder, flat rings, ear-rings with a little bone, hemp-hackles, sceptre-heads for the chiefs. She tossed the objects into a sounding, cup-shaped vessel. The old man, whose white beard hung in plaits to his belt, looked closely and ardently at that singular vessel, which must have been magical since it had the sound of an animated thing. The bronze goblet, offered in trade by a people who knew how to smelt metal, shone in the light.

But the amber too sparkled, and its price was inestimable. The yellow richness filled the darkness of the hut; and the old man kept his little eyes riveted upon it. The wife turned about the stranger-woman and, more familiar now, held the bracelets against her hair to compare the colours. As he cut the torn meshes of a net with a flint blade one of the young men shot furiously lustful glances at the blonde girl: he was the younger son. On a bed of dried herbs that creaked at his movements the elder son groaned piteously. His wife had just given birth; having tied her child to her back she was dragging a sort of trawl-net for night-fishing among the piles while her husband, laid low, cried like a sick man. Leaning his head to one side, turning his face, he regarded the basketful of amber every bit as avidly as his father, and his hands trembled with covetousness.

Before very long, with calm gestures they invited the amber-trader to cover her basket, huddling about the fire and feigning to take counsel. The old man spoke very urgently; he addressed his elder son, who blinked rapidly. This was their sole sign of the understanding of language; living closely in the dismal proximity of aquatic creatures had fixed the muscles of their faces in a bestial placidity.

At the extremity of the chamber of branches there was an unoccupied space, two balks of timber better squared than the rest. By signs they gave the amber-trader to understand that, after she had nibbled at some dried fish, she could sleep there. A simple bag-net close by must have served, by night, under the habitation, to capture the fish that followed the lake's very feeble current. But it seemed they were going to make no use of it. Reassuringly they placed the amber-filled basket at the sleeper's head, but not on the two planks upon which she was stretched out.

Then, after some grunting, the resin light was put out. The water could be heard moving beneath the poles. The current slapped languidly against the tree-trunks. Rather anxiously the old man spoke a few interrogative phrases; his two sons replied affirmatively, the younger, to be sure, with some hesitation. And then and there, amid the watery sounds, silence was established.

Suddenly, at the far end of the chamber there was a short struggle, a rustling of two bodies, groans, a few sharp cries and a long expiring breath. The old man rose gropingly, took the bag-net, threw it and, abruptly sliding in their grooves the planks where the amber-trader lay, he uncovered the aperture made for the night-fishing. A hole gaped; there was a double falling sound; a brief splashing; when it was lit and waved above the hole, the resin light revealed nothing. The old man seized the basket of amber and, on the elder son's bed, they divided the treasure, the woman scrabbling after the beads that rolled, scattered.

They did not retrieve the net until morning. They cut the hair from the amber-trader's corpse, then threw her body among the piles to feed the fish. As for the drowned man, the father cut a disc from his skull with a flint blade to serve as an amulet for the future life, and this he pressed into the brain. Then they laid him outside the hut, and the women scratched their cheeks and tore their hair, uttering solemn ululations.

Mérigot Marchès

We had scoured the country of the Auvergne for three months without coming upon anything there worth the having, for the earth was desolate. All there is there are high forests where the ferns grow in swathes as far as the eye can see; and the grazing is poor, so that the people of the flatlands make only as much cheese as they can eat; all the beasts, even the wild beasts, are skinny; all that can be seen on all sides are the few black birds that swoop crying over the red rocks. There are places where the the terrain splits open among the grey stones, and the sides of the chasm seem stained with blood.

But on the twelfth of July of that year of 1392, as we were leaving Saignes, which is in the direction of Mauriac to get to Arches, we found company in a mountain tavern. It was a hostelry where both welcome and board were niggardly, at the sign of 'Le Pourcelet'; and the mug of wine they served you there was rough enough to take the skin off your mouth. Eating a morsel of cheese and a slice of black bread, we had a few words with a fellow who was there. He had the look about him of having served in the great wars, and perhaps against the King: we knew him by his *basilarde* of the English sort which seemed well worn by dint of beating on bastnets of oiled leather and twisted straw. His name – as he told us – was Robin le Galois and, he being from Aragon, he had a strange way of speaking. He told us he had been in the *Compagnies* breaking their way with scaling-ladders into towns, where they would roast the burgesses over fires to know where their hoards were hidden: and his captains had been Geoffroy Tête-Noire and Mérigot Marchès from the Limousin. This Mérigot Marchès had been beheaded the year before in the Halles in Paris; and his last torments so notable that we had seen his head at the end of a lance on the scaffold; a leaden-coloured head, with congealed blood at the nose and the skin of the neck hanging down in flaps.

We took heart at this account and asked him if there was any resource in the uplands for men at arms. At which he told us that there was not, by reason of the great plunder done by the *Compagnons* for ten years past and more; in company with whom he had stoutly levied contributions on market-towns and roved the surrounding farmsteads to such an extent that there was not so much as a pig's tail left for the roasting. And since it seemed he had drunk enough of the sour wine of the Auvergne country, his brains became overheated and he made his complaint to us. He said that in this world there is no time, no merriment and no glory but in waging war after the fashion of the *Compagnons*. 'Every day', he said, 'we had some more money. The villeins of Auvergne and Limousin catered for us and brought us grain, flour, freshly baked bread, hay for the horses and for bedding, the best wines, oxen, ewe lambs and fat sheep, poultry and all sorts of fowl. We were cherished and stuffed full like kings. When we rode out the whole country trembled before us. Everything was ours, on the outward and the homeward journey. The captains took possession of great quantities of silverware, of ewers, of goblets and of silver plate. They packed their iron-bound chests full with the riches. When our *captal* Mérigot Marchès set out to take Le Roc de Vendes he left behind him ample provision. Where? Take my word for it, I may well know something of this... See here now, friends; God's blood, but you yourselves have been about the highways as men at arms; and you are seeking to join a *compagnie*. We might come to an arrangement. I assure you, France is at our disposal; it is a paradise for men at arms. Since there is no longer any war, the time has come for us to take our money. I offer you a share – all done with due discretion – of Mérigot Marchès' silverware and plate; it is in a certain river not far from here: I have great need of you to recover it.'

I looked at Jehannin de la Montaigne, who was tippling: he winked at me. Our beloved Museau de Bregis had pressed us so hard we no longer had a *denier* in our purses. We must at all costs make some money to live well on our return. So I spoke out openly with that *Compagnon* Robin le Galois, testifying for myself and for Jehannin de la Montaigne. And we made a compact that the division would be equitable if half the treasure went to him, Robin, and we each had a quarter. A mug of wine sealed our pact; and we left the inn, more or less about the time the sun was going down behind the screen of mountains that lies to the west.

As we were marching we heard behind us a calling, as of a hunting-horn; when he heard that calling Robin turned aside, saying that he recognised the signal of his *compagnie*. Indeed a very ragged man appeared at the roadside, dressed in a green greatcoat, pale-faced and with his fur cap pulled down about his eyes; whereof Robin told us he was named Le Verdois, and that he had better come along with us some part of the way, lest he discover anything. Night came on quickly, as it is wont to do in mountain regions and, the gloom thickening, there came another silent companion, dressed in a black jerkin with many a hole in it, and having a little beard, which surprised us. He throwing back his hood by way of greeting, I saw that he was tonsured like a clerk. But I think he was no clerk, for the one time he broke silence he swore a foul oath. Of him Robin said nothing, save that he nodded his head and suffered the Silent Companion to march at his side. We were making our way over sharp stones, among bushes that rendered our way hard, a cold blast lashing our faces when a bony hand seized me by the arm – whereat I quickly backed away. The new man had a look about him that was terrifying; both his ears were cropped off close, and he had no left arm; a blow from a *basilarde* had split open his mouth so that his lips were drawn back like those of a dog gnawing at a bone. This man held me close against him, with a ferocious laugh, and he said nothing.

We marched thus for about two hours over the high track to Arches. Robin le Galois was still jabbering on, saying he knew the way, having followed it many times with Mérigot Marchès in the days when they used to hang the peasants from the trees so as not to deprive the birds of the air of their harvests, or when they gave them red hats for their heads with cudgels of sorbwood. And so Mérigot Marchès had been dismembered in the Halles like an ox and, he being noble, the son of monseigneur Aimery Marchès de Limousin, his four quarters were exposed before the justices of the King; whereas he, Robin, a simple soldier, would have had to make faces at the moon from our master's gibbet.

In the approaches of the market-town of Arches there is a river that flows in the bottom of a ravine. It is called the Vanve, and it widens a league above the town. Midnight had already come, and we were following the bank of the Vanve, which is here half sand, half mud. On either side are clumps of black bushes that extend into the distance, with clusters of broom, to the foothills. The moon gave a pale light and our long shadows reached to the bushes as we passed. Then we suddenly heard the air trembling to a shrill voice that cried: 'Mérigot! Mérigot! Mérigot!', which we might easily have taken for a strange bird of the Auvergne country, hooting and complaining in the night. For that voice was plaintive, cut through, so it seemed, with sobs – too much like the sorrowful cries of women weeping for those who had died in the great wars with the English.

But Robin le Galois halted when he heard the cry of 'Mérigot!', and I saw his limbs trembling. For my part, I dared go no further; for I was certain it was Mérigot Marchès; I seemed to see his leaden coloured head rising up amid the mists of the Vanve, with the flaps of skin hanging down from the neck.

Le Verdois, the Silent Companion and the Armless One continued on their way and entered the river; they plunged in up to their knees, among the reeds. Robin le Galois, having taken heart, ran to the water: there was a single channel there, easy to make out. They were thrusting their cudgels into the mud; Jehannin and myself were digging with our *basilardes.* Jehannin suddenly yelled out: 'I have the chest!' Then we hauled in the mud on a wooden chest, bound with iron, whose lid nonetheless seemed by the feel of it to be staved in. And, dragging it into the moonlight, that lit up our muddy garments and our pale faces, we saw that the chest was empty of silverware, filled only with silt, with flat stones and soft creatures and the fry of eels.

Suddenly looking up we saw a woman wearing a bluey-grey tunic, who was weeping. And Robin le Galois cried out that this was Mariote Marchès, the wife of Mérigot, and that she had annexed the silverware; cursing under their breaths, Le Verdois and the Armless One went towards her. But she called 'Mérigot!' and, fleeing into the bushes, shouted to us that it was the twelfth of July. Now it was a year since Mérigot Marchès had been brought to his last torment. Wherefore the others said we had scant hope of finding his treasure on such a night, for the spirits of those put to death come gladly to haunt their earthly goods on the days and at the hours when they died, in the years that follow. And we came together again by the Vanve, which river murmurs gently as it flows. And all at once we saw, Robin, la Montaigne, le Verdois, the Armless One and myself, that the Silent Companion had vanished among the bushes. Then Robin began to lament; and we all of us thought that Mariote Marchès had led him quietly away among the thickets to live with her in another country with the plates, the dishes, the covered cups, the comfit-boxes, goblets, tankards and bowls of silver Mérigot Marchès had buried in the River Vanve and which were worth, all in all, fully six or seven thousand marks.

The 'Papier Rouge'

I was in the Bibliothèque Nationale, leafing through a fifteenth-century manuscript, when my attention was caught by a strange name. The manuscript contained 'lays', almost all copies from the *Jardin de Plaisance,* a farce with four characters, and an account of the miracles of Sainte Geneviève; but the name that struck me was inscribed on two leaves inserted into the text with a bookbinder's strip. It was a fragment of a chronicle dating from the first half of the fifteenth century. And this is the passage that caught my eye:

'In the year fourteen hundred and thirty-seven the winter was cold, and there was a notable famine by reason of the harvests destroyed by great and fierce hailstorms.

'*Item:* numerous persons from the flatlands entered Paris about the Feast of Our Lord, saying there were devils in the countryside or foreign thieves. Captain Baro Pani and his henchmen, as many men among them as women, robbing men and carrying off their goods. The which, so they say, come from the land of Egypt and have their own language, and their women have wiles wherewith they beguile the simple. And these latter are to the furthest degree felons and murderers. And they are exceedingly unruly.'

The margin of the leaf bore the following annotation:

'The said captain of the bohemians and his people were taken on the orders of *monseigneur le prévôt* and brought to execution after torture, exception made of one of their women who escaped.

'*Item:* it should here be mentioned that this same year maître Etienne Guerrois was appointed criminal clerk to the *prévôté* to take the place and fill the post of maître Alexandre Cachmarée.'

I cannot say what it was aroused my curiosity in this short note – whether it was the name of Captain Baro Pani, the appearance of 'Bohemians' in the region of Paris in year 1437 or the curious parallel drawn by the author of the marginal note between the execution of the 'Captain', the escape of a woman and the replacement of the clerk to the *criminel.* But I felt an invincible urge to know more of the matter. So there and then I left the Bibliothèque and, reaching the quais, I followed the Seine, aiming to go and search the Archives.

As I walked through the narrow streets of the Marais, skirting the railings of the government buildings, under the dark porch of the

ancient edifice I had a moment of discouragement. Little is left to us of
the criminal records of the fifteenth century . . . Would I find my men
in the Registre du Châtelet? Had they perhaps appealed to the
Parlement? . . . Perhaps I would find only a sinister note in the Papier
Rouge. I had never consulted the Papier Rouge, and I decided to
exhaust the other records before turning to it.

The reading-room of the Archives is small; the high windows have
minuscule panes; those who sit there taking notes are bent over their
bundles of papers like precision-workers; at the far end, at a desk
raised above the room on a dais, the keeper works and keeps watch.
Despite the lighting, the atmosphere is dim, on account of the
reflection of the old walls. The silence is profound; no sound rises from
the street: nothing is heard but the rustling of leaves of parchment
being turned and the squeaking of pens. When I turned the first leaf of
the register for 1437 I felt that I, in my turn, had become the criminal
clerk of *monseigneur le prévôt*. The proceedings were signed AL.
CACHMARÉE. The hand of this clerk was well-formed, upright, firm. I
pictured myself a vigorous man of a suitably imposing aspect to
receive the last confessions of criminals before execution.

But I searched in vain for the affair of the 'Bohemians' and their
chief. There was only an action for sorcery and theft brought against 'a
woman called Princess of Cairo'. The body of evidence made it plain
that this was a girl belonging to the band. She was accompanied, the
verbal evidence declared, by a certain 'Baron, a captain of cutpurses'.
(This Baron must be the Baro Pani of the manuscript chronicle.) He
was 'a most cunning and sharp-witted man', lean and with black
moustaches, with two knives in his belt, the hafts of which were
ornamented in silver; 'and ordinarily he had about him a canvas bag in
which he kept *droue,* which is a poison for cattle, of which oxen, cows
and horses quickly die, that have eaten *droue* mingled with grain, in
strange convulsions'.

The Princess of Cairo was taken, and she was brought prisoner to
the Châtelet in Paris. From the questions of the *lieutenant criminel* it
would seem she was 'some twenty-four years old or thereabouts'; she
was dressed in a tunic of cloth decorated somewhat with flowers, with
a belt of braided wire, having the appearance of gold; she had black
eyes of a singular fixity, and her words were accompanied by emphatic
gestures of her right hand which she constantly opened and closed,
working the fingers before her face.

Her voice was harsh and her pronunciation sibilant and, answering their questions, she coarsely abused the magistrates and the clerk. They wished to have her undressed so as to put her to the question, 'in order to know of her crimes by her own admission'. The lesser rack being made ready, the *lieutenant criminel* ordered her to strip herself naked. But she refused and it was necessary to use force to divest her of her surcoat, her tunic and her *chemise,* 'which appeared to be of silk and was marked with the seal of Solomon'. Then she threshed about on the tiled floor of the Châtelet: and then, suddenly standing erect, she stood stark naked before the astonished magistrates. She stood erect, like a statue of gilded flesh. 'And when she was bound to the lesser rack, and they had thrown some water over her, the said Princess of Cairo pleaded that she be spared that question, saying she would tell what she knew.' They brought her to be heated before the fires of the prison kitchens 'where, lit by the red fires, she appeared most diabolical'. When she was 'quite ready', the examining magistrates being transported to the kitchens, she would say no more and drew her long black tresses across her mouth.

They brought her back to the chamber with the tiled floor and attached her to the greater rack. And 'before they had thrown any great quantity of water over her or had forced her to drink, she instantly solicited and supplicated that she be untied, saying that she would confess the truth of her crimes'. She chose not to dress herself again, save for her magic *chemise.*

Some of her companions must have been tried before her, for maître Jehan Martinet, examiner of the Châtelet, told her it would not profit her if she lied, 'for her friend, the *Baron* had been hanged, and many more besides'. (The register of the Châtelet does not contain his trial.) At that point she flew into a noisy rage, saying that 'this Baron was her husband (or much the same thing) and Duke of Egypt, and that he bore the name of the great blue sea from whence they had come'. (*Baro Pani* is the Romany for 'great water' or 'sea'.) Then she lamented and swore vengeance. She stared at the clerk as he wrote and, supposing in accordance with the superstitions of her people that this clerk's writings were the formula that destroyed them, she wished upon him *all the crimes he might have 'painted or otherwise figured by artifice' against her people on the paper.*

Then, before they could seize her wrists and fasten them, she suddenly advanced on the examiners and touched them both in the region of their hearts and on their throats. She told them they would suffer fearful torments in the night, and that their throats would be cut by act of perfidy. Finally she broke down in tears, calling upon 'the Baron' again and again, 'and piteously'; and when the *lieutenant criminel* continued the interrogation, she admitted to numerous thefts.

She and her people had pillaged 'and robbed' all the small towns of the region of Paris, notably Montparnasse and Gentilly. They travelled the countryside, setting up camp, in summer among the hayricks and in winter in the limekilns. Following the hedgerows, they 'stripped them of their blossoms', that is to say they slyly made away with the linen hung out there to dry. When the sun was high, encamped in the shade, the men mended kettles or killed their lice; there were those among them, the more religious, who cast these creatures aside: and in fact, although they have no beliefs, there exists among them an ancient tradition that after their death men live in the bodies of beasts.

The Princess of Cairo instigated the sacking of henhouses, the bearing away of the pewter vessels from inns, the digging-up of storepits to plunder the grain. At her orders the men would return by night to the villages from which they had been expelled to scatter *droue* in the mangers and throw packets the size of a fist, tied in linen cloth, into the wells to poison the water.

After this confession the examiners, consulting together, were of the opinion that the Princess of Cairo was 'a thoroughgoing thief and a murderess, and that she well deserved to be put to death; and *monseigneur le prévôt* so condemned her; and he ordered this to be done according to the custom of the realm, namely that she be buried alive in a trench'. The case of sorcery was held over for the next day's hearing, it having to be followed, if need arose, by a further sentence.

But a letter by Jean Mautainct to the *lieutenant criminel,* copied in the register, makes it clear that terrible things happened in the night. The two examiners the Princess of Cairo had touched awoke in the darkness, their hearts pierced with sharp, throbbing pains; until dawn they writhed in their beds, and, at first light, the servants of the house found them cowering in the corner, where the walls met, their faces shrunken with great wrinkles.

The Princess of Cairo was immediately sent for. Standing naked before the racks, dazzling the clerks and the judges with the golden lustre of her skin, twisting her *chemise* marked with the seal of Solomon, she declared that those torments had been sent by her. Two

'botereaux' or toads were concealed in a secret place, each at the
bottom of a large earthenware pot; they were nourished on
breadcrumbs steeped in women's milk. And the sister of the Princess
of Cairo called them by the names of the men in torment, thrusting
long pins into their bodies; while the toads foamed at the mouth, each
wound was echoed in the hearts of the bewitched.

The *lieutenant criminel* then delivered over the Princess of Cairo to
the clerk Alexandre Cachmarée, with the order to bring her to
execution without further ado. The clerk signed the proceedings with
his customary flourish.

The register of the Châtelet contained nothing more. Only the
Papier Rouge could tell me what had become of the Princess of Cairo. I
asked for the Papier Rouge, and they brought me a register bound in
leather that seemed coloured with congealed blood. It was the
executioner's account-book. Along its whole length bands of linen
adorned with seals hung down. The register had been kept by
Alexandre Cachmarée. It listed the payments made to maître Henry,
torturer. And against some lines commanding execution, maître
Cachmarée had drawn a gibbet with a grimacing corpse.

But beneath the note of the execution of a certain 'Baron of Egypt
and a foreign thief', where maître Cachmarée had scrawled a double
gallows with two hanged men, there was a break, and the handwriting
changed.

Thereafter there were no more drawings in the Papier Rouge; and
maître Etienne Guerrois had inscribed the following note: 'Today 13
January 1438 was maître Alexandre Cachmarée delivered over to the
Official magistrate and, by order of *monseigneur le prévôt,* brought to
execution. The which being criminal clerk and keeping this Papier
Rouge, figuring by way of pastime hanging-gallows, became suddenly
crazed. Wherefore he rose and went to the place of execution to
disinter a woman who had been buried there this morning and was not
dead; and I do not know whether this was of his own instigation or
otherwise, but by night he went to their chambers to cut the throats of
the two examiners of the Châtelet. The woman is called the Princess of
Cairo; she is now at liberty and they have not been able to lay hold of
her. And the same Al. Cachmarée confessed his crimes, if not however
his design, whereof he was not minded to speak. And this morning he
was taken forcibly to our master's gallows and there saw an end of his
days.'

The Firebrands

The year before the King was taken at Pavia, everywhere terrible things occurred. For, on the night of New-year's-eve, between nine and ten, the sky turned the colour of blood; and it seemed as if it were split open. Everything was bathed in a red glow; the beasts hung their heads and the plants lay close to the earth. Then there was a gust of wind and men saw in the firmament a great comet; it had the appearance of a burning dragon or of a fiery serpent. And shortly after it moved towards the fortifications of Saint-Denis and was seen no more.

But the same evening, when midnight was gone, men having already been four hours abed, because in December the nights are long, a commotion was heard in the streets. And indeed there was cause for commotion; for messengers from Troyes in Champagne had come saying that the town was almost wholly burnt down. Now this is how they spoke, in the night, on the Place de Saint-Jean-de-Grève, before the church. Some little lads, still asleep, restrained their horses; and, in the lamplight, their belts, their spurs and their swords glittered. The fire, they said, was still burning after two days; the Marché au Blé was destroyed, and the Rue du Beffroi, along with the great cast bell, and the Etape au Vin and the inn called *Le Sauvage* where men used to eat chitterlings, fat and firm, with light red wine. With their infernal concoction of powder, pitch and sulphur, the firebrands had set fire to everything. No one had been able to set eye on them, or to lay hands on them; and it was to be assumed they were from Naples and had come, under cover of great secrecy, to burn all the fine towns of the realm. It was said that, about Christmas, Paris was swarming with Italian marrabais who covertly took little children and killed them for their blood. And likewise the firebrands were of the same sect and denomination.

The prefect and the magistrates, dressed in their parti-coloured robes, together with the municipal councillors, the citizen officers of the guard, the tipstaffs, the constables of the watch, the crossbowmen, the harquebusiers with their yeomen, came out forthwith, bearing lanterns. And then and there it was enjoined and publicly proclaimed that a night watch be set on the streets – which was done. And the next day a man was led to the scaffold who, it would appear, had denied

God before an innkeeper of the Rue Saint-Jacques, and who was not inclined to say anything in the presence of the lieutenant of the provostry or before the Parlement. He was set on a mule at the Conciergerie, dressed in a haircloth coat and a coster's jerkin, and his case was cried three times before the men of the watch, mounted and on foot, and the people of Paris. As is customary, he was provided with bread and wine outside the church of the Filles-Dieu; and they put in his hands a cross, painted in red. Then the bonnet was taken from him, so that he mounted the gallows bare-headed.

And this execution carried out to Our Lord's pleasure, they made haste to set up lanterns, lamps and candles hanging in the doorways and had a watch established of five or six hundred men of the town, on foot and mounted. Men did not know where to turn for fear. It not being the custom to have the streets and the alleys lit, the porches, embrasures and stone passageways seemed the darker. And soon constables of the watch moved about, waving their torches. Candle-ends burnt in the little windowpanes after curfew, which was a great novelty. The images of Our Lady were illuminated with a lamp and had a special guard, certain members of a heretical sect having mutilated the holy images in divers places.

The next day it was said, about the streets and in the shops, in the barbers' especially, that four or six men had come into the town who were not to be recognised, for they changed their clothing daily. One day they were dressed as merchants, and then like sharpers, and the next like peasants. Sometimes they had hair on their heads, and sometimes they had not. And all men said that they would carefully watch these persons, being certain that they were none other than the firebrands, come to bring great evil and danger. But whatever their diligence, many houses were found marked with great Saint Andrew's crosses, put there in the night by unknown men.

The whole town was bewildered. And, on the King's command, at every street-corner it was cried abroad to the sound of the trumpet that all sharpers, low-born men of little account, false mendicants and street-idlers should quit the place on pain of the gallows. Many of the common sort of people fled before the criers; and, in the upshot, it was a good number that was expelled onto the highway by the Porte Baudoyer.

Among this rabble there were three, Colard de Blangis, Tortigne de Mont-Saint-Jean and Philippot le Clerc who, doubting the rigour of the royal justice, remained on the road outside the town. They were of no great repute, and were worse in appearance and feared, the people being unquiet and stirred-up by fear of the firebrands, that they might be murdered along the roads. And nor for that matter had they clear consciences concerning divers *testons* and *florins au chat* struck in surroundings that were not royal – for which they had with some difficulty escaped being boiled at the Marché aux Porceaux.

These gallants then, having been thus some few days in the fields, began to suffer from hunger, thirst and cold; the more so since the land was lying fallow and the birds (such as remained) were falling frozen-dead from the skies. There were neither the fruits of the earth nor the game of the heavens. The gallants then took sticks in their hands and set off in martial fashion, saying that they were going to the King's wars or, otherwise, in the Guyenne marches, that they were constrained, for lack of pay, to live off the land and off wayfarers.

'It's true', Tortigne would say, 'that I am going to the wars; that I have at my heels twenty or twenty-five men of the watch, bowmen or crossbowmen – or else I'll make off. And they have no aim but to join me and march with me, or have me march with them. They are very polite men and obliging; they have already had me sit, very comfortably, in those chairs of theirs they call the stocks.'

'Have you not', said Colard, 'been turned in the pillory? It's a new way of finding women; they come to look at you, and the serving-man turns you so that you face each and all of them.'

'A signal pleasure!' Philippot broke in. 'I knew it three times; and the last time I chose a fashionable lady, dressed in the Spanish style. She wore a silk brocade of crisped gold, on her head was a snood of cloth in golden butterfly-knots, in which her hair hung down behind to her heels, entwined in ribbons. She had on a bonnet of crimson velvet and a dress of the same, with a white taffeta lining in place of a chemise, with full sleeves, the sleeves covered with gold embroidery. Her petticoat was of white satin, set with beaten silver and with many jewels.'

'And you had the leisure', said Colard, 'to examine these divers garments and commit them to memory? By the bloody crucifixion you're lying!'

'Indeed', Philippot answered, 'you should not swear but for good reason. For the hangman's assistant held me most carefully before that lady, so that the page of the fair lady of my choice could conveniently spit in my face.'

Thus conversing in their pleasures, and swindling their way as they went, they came to the lower marches of Poitou. There they feigned to be soldiers until they came to a parish church, close to Niort. They went in, shouting and swearing. Dressed in his alb, the priest was saying a low mass. Despite his remonstrances they took the vases of copper, of pewter and of silver. Then they ordered him to go up to the altar and fetch the holy ciborium, or at least the chalice, which was of silver gilt. This the priest refused to do. Therewith Tortigne tied his alb about his mouth, while Philippot took the ciborium from the altar. And finding in the chalice the *Corpus Domini,* all three solemnly ate it, claiming they were hungry and, communicating, they were remitting the sin they had just committed.

Then they went down to a mean inn where the men turned aside at the fork of two roads. But wishing to drink, Colard vomited the wine; Tortigne stood as if amazed, his glass in his hand; and Philippot let his fall. They became very pale and, saying they were drunk upon what they had eaten in the church, they fell about the table in various ways. And suddenly threads of smoke, grey, thick and stinking were seen to burst from Colard's mouth, from Tortigne's back and Philippot's belly; at which it was plain they were burning, and very soon they were wholly consumed, their faces and limbs being black as coal. This was remarked in different ways by the natives of the place: but it is beyond doubt that these three gallants having been marked down for punishment on account of fire-raising, fell by divine grace into their sacrilege; for they were burnt.

from
LE ROI AU MASQUE D'OR
1892

The King in the Golden Mask

to Anatole France

The king wearing a mask of gold stood up from the black throne upon which he had been seated for hours and demanded to know the cause of the tumult. For the guards at the doors had crossed their pikes and the clash of steel was heard. Gathered about the bronze brazier, to the right there also rose the fifty priests and, to the left, the fifty jesters; and the women, in a semi-circle before the king, waved their arms. The rose and purple glow that shone through the bronze grille of the brazier illuminated the masks on their faces: at the example of the emaciated king, the women, the jesters and the priests wore immovable masks of silver, iron, copper, wood and cloth. And the jesters' masks were open-mouthed with laughter, whilst the masks of the priests were black with care. Fifty hilarious faces beamed on the left, and on the right fifty dismal faces scowled. And the light fabrics stretched over the heads of the women portrayed eternally gracious faces animated by an artificial smile. But the king's golden mask was majestic, noble and truly royal.

Now the king stood silent and, in his silence he was at one with the line of kings of which he was the last. The city had once been governed by princes who left their face uncovered; but long since there had arisen a protracted succession of masked kings. No man had ever seen the face of any of these kings, and for this not even the priests knew the reason. Meanwhile, in the olden time, long ago, the order had been given that those who approached the royal residence should cover their faces; and that line of kings knew only men's masks.

And whilst the pikes of the guards at the doors clashed and their arms resounded, the king enquired in a grave voice: 'Who dares trouble me during the hours in which I sit among my priests, my jesters and my women?'

And, trembling, the guards replied: 'Most imperious king, golden mask, it is a poor man dressed in a long robe; he seems to be one of those pious mendicants who roam the countryside, and his face is uncovered.'

'Let this mendicant enter', said the king.

Then the priest whose mask was the gravest turned towards the throne and bowed.

'O king', he said, 'the oracles have predicted that it is not good for your line to look upon men's faces.'

And the jester whose mask was split open with the widest-gaping hilarity turned his back on the throne and bowed.

'O mendicant I still have not seen', he said, 'no doubt you are more royal than the king in the golden mask, since it is forbidden to look upon you.'

And the woman whose false face had the silkiest down joined her hands, spread them, and cupped them as if to lay hold of the sacrificial vases. Now the king, looking in her direction, feared the revelation of an unknown face.

Then an evil desire crept into his heart.

'Let the mendicant enter', he said.

And from among the quivering forest of pikes, among which flashed sword-blades like brilliant leaves of steel splashed with green or red gold, an old man with a bristling white beard advanced to the foot of the throne and lifted towards the king a bare face in which wavering eyes trembled.

'Speak', said the king.

'If he to whom I address my words is the man in the golden mask, I shall certainly reply; and I think it is he. Who would dare raise their voice before him? But I cannot judge of this by sight – for I am blind. However I know there are women in this hall by the sleek rubbing of their hands on their shoulders; and there are jesters – I can hear laughter; and there are priests – they are whispering gravely. Now the men of this country have said that you go masked, and that you, king in the golden mask, have never beheld faces of flesh. Listen: you are a king, and you do not know the common people. These ones here on my right are the jesters – I can hear them laughing; these ones here on my left are the priests – I hear them weeping. And I perceive that the muscles of these women's faces are grimacing.'

Now the king turned towards those the mendicant called jesters, and his gaze fell upon the masks of the priests, black with care; he turned towards those the mendicant called priests, and his look fell upon the wide-mouthed, laughing masks of the jesters; he lowered his eyes to the crescent formed by his seated women and their features seemed to him beautiful.

'You are lying, stranger!', said the king. 'And you are yourself the laugher, the weeper and the one who grimaces; for your horrible face, incapable of fixity, has been made mobile to dissimulate. Those you have called my jesters are my priests, and those you have called my priests are my jesters. And how can you, whose features crease at your every word, judge of the immutable beauty of my women?'

'Neither of that, nor of yours', said the mendicant quietly, 'for being blind I can know nothing of them, and you yourself know nothing either of others or of your own person. But I am superior to you in this: I know that I know nothing. And I can conjecture. Now perhaps those who seem to you jesters weep behind their masks; and it is possible that those who seem to you priests have their true faces distorted with the joy of deceiving you; and you do not know whether, under the silk, your women's cheeks are not ashen-coloured. As for yourself, king in the golden mask, who knows if you are not hideous despite your adornments?'

And the jester whose laughing mouth was the widest-split with cheerfulness let out a chuckle that sounded like a sob; and the priest with the most sombre brow uttered a supplication that might have been a nervous laugh; and all the women's masks shuddered.

The golden-faced king gave a sign; the guards seized the barefaced man by the shoulders and cast him out by the great door of the hall.

The night passed and the king was unquiet in his sleep. And in the morning he wandered about the palace, because an evil desire had crept into his heart. But neither in the bedchambers, nor in the high, tiled festival halls did he find what he was seeking. In all the royal residence there was not one mirror; for thus, for long years, the command of the oracles and the decree of the priests had appointed.

The king on his black throne did not laugh at the jesters, nor did he listen to the priests or pay attention to his women: for he was thinking of his face.

When the setting sun cast its metallic, blood-red light on the palace windows, the king left the hall of the brazier, dismissed the guards, quickly crossed the seven concentric courts enclosed in seven gleaming walls and slipped obscurely out into the countryside by a low postern-gate.

He was trembling and curious. He knew that he was about to see other faces, and perhaps his own. In his inmost being he wished to be assured of his own beauty: why had that wretched beggar slyly implanted doubts in his breast?

The king in the golden mask came to the woods that clustered about the banks of a river. The bark of the trees was shiny and smooth. There were trunks that shone white. The king broke a few branches. Some of them exuded a little frothy sap at the broken place, and the interior remained marbled with brown stains; others had parts that were quietly mouldering, and black fissures. The earth was dark and humid under the varicoloured carpet of grasses and little flowers. With his foot the king turned a heavy, blue-veined stone, embedded with flecks that glittered in the sun's last rays; and a soft pouchy toad escaped from its muddy hiding-place with a startled leap.

At the edge of the wood, at the top of the river-bank, emerging from the wood, the king halted, charmed. A young girl was seated on the grass; the king saw her hair caught up in knot, the graceful-curved nape of her neck, her supple haunches from which her body swung to the shoulders; for between two fingers of her left hand she was turning a thickly-wound spindle and the point of a heavy distaff was unravelling close to her cheek.

She stood up, speechless, showed her face and, in her confusion, took between her lips the thread she was shaping: thus her cheeks seemed as if traversed by a pale dividing line.

When the king saw her restless black eyes, her delicate palpitating nostrils, the trembling of her lips and the rounded curve of her chin descending to the throat caressed by the rosy light, he ran forward enraptured and violently grasped her hands.

'I wish, for the first time', he said, 'to adore an unclothed face; I wish to take off this golden mask since it separates me from the air that kisses your skin; and, carried away in wonder the two of us shall go and see ourselves in the river.'

With the tips of her fingers the young girl wonderingly touched the metallic plates of the king's mask. And meanwhile the king was impatiently unfastening the golden clasps; the mask fell among the grass and the young girl, holding her hands over her eyes, let out a cry of horror.

The next instant, clasping the hemp-entwined distaff to her breasts, she fled into the darkness of the forest.

The young girl's cry echoed sorrowfully in the king's heart. He ran down the bank, leant over the waters of the river, and from his own lips there burst a harsh groan. At the moment the sun was vanishing behind the hills on the horizon he had seen a whitish face, tumified, covered with scales, the skin puffed-up in hideous swellings and, from the memory of books he had read, he knew at once that he was a leper.

The moon rose, like a yellow aerial mask above the trees. From time to time a flapping of damp wings could be heard from the branches. A thread of mist hung above the river. The shimmering of the water lingered on into the far distance and was lost in the horizon's blue-tinged depths. Scarlet-headed birds rippled the water with slowly-fading wings.

And the king, standing erect, held his arms away from his body, as if he were disgusted at his own touch.

He retrieved the mask and placed it over his face. Walking as in a dream he set off towards the palace.

He struck the gong at the gate in the outer wall and the guards came rushing forth with a great noise, carrying their torches. They lit up his golden face; and the king's heart was wrung with anguish, thinking that they saw white scales on the metal. He crossed the moonlit court: seven times his heart was wrung with the same anguish at the seven gates at which the guards held their red torches towards his golden mask.

His sorrow was meanwhile growing with his rage, like a black plant twined about a tawny-coloured plant. And the sombre and obscure fruits of affliction and rage rose to his lips and he found their taste bitter.

He entered the palace: and at his left the guard turned on the toes of one foot, the other leg extended, and with shining, circular movements whirled their sabres above their heads; and the guard on his right turned on the toes of the other foot, with the other leg extended, raising above their heads a glittering pyramid formed by the rapid twirlings of their diamond-bright maces.

And the king did not even recall that these were the nocturnal ceremonies; he went on his way shuddering, believing the men at arms wished to smash or cleave open his hideous swollen face.

The great rooms of the palace were deserted. A few solitary torches were burning low in their rings. Others had gone out and were dripping cold drops of resin.

The king traversed the festival halls where cushions embroidered with red tulips and yellow chrysanthemums were still strewn about, and there were ivory swings and seats of mournful ebony embellished with golden stars. Brightly-dyed hangings on which were painted birds with varicoloured feet and silver beaks were suspended from the ceiling in which were set the muzzles of beasts carved in coloured woods. There were flambeaux of greenish bronze, made in a single piece and pierced with prodigious holes,lacquered in red, in which a wick of unbleached silk passed through the centre of squat, oily disks. There were long reclining chairs, low and arched, upon which one could not lie down save with one's hips raised, as if borne up by hands. There were vases cast of near-transparent metals which, under the touch of a finger, gave out a piercing sound, as if they were wounded.

At the far end of the hall the king took up an iron cresset that darted its red tongues into the darkness. The flaming drops of resin fell upon his silken sleeves. But the king paid them no heed. He made his way to a tall, dark gallery where the resin left a perfumed trail. There, on the walls cut by crossing diagonal decorations, there were portraits, shining and mysterious: for the paintings were masked and sur-mounted by crowns. Only the portrait of the most ancient among them, hung in a place apart, represented a pale young man, his eyes dilated with terror, the lower part of his face concealed by regal ornaments. The king halted before this portrait and, raising the cresset, threw the light upon it. Then he sighed and said: 'O first of my line, O my brother, how pitiable we are!' And he kissed the portrait on the eyes.

And before the second painted face, which was masked, the king stopped and tore the cloth of the mask, saying: 'This is what must be done, my father, second of my line.' And in this way he tore the masks of all the other kings of his line, down to himself. Beneath the torn masks could be seen the sombre bareness of the wall.

Then he came to the banqueting-halls where the shining tables were still laid. He held the cresset above his head and lines of purple winged away into the darkness of the corners. In the centre of the table was a lion-footed throne about which hung a spotted animal-skin. The glass vessels were as if heaped up in the corners along with pieces of silverware and perforated lids of smoky gold. There were certain bottles that reflected violet lights; others were plated on the inside with thin layers of precious metals. Like a terrible presentiment of blood, a burst of light from the cresset set a square cup, cut from a garnet, into which the cupbearers customarily poured the king's wine, glistening. And the vermilion light also caressed a basket woven of silver in which crusty bread-rolls were neatly stacked.

The king crossed the banqueting-halls, turning aside his head. 'They were not ashamed', he said, 'to bite, under their masks, into the healthful bread and to touch the blood-red wine with their white lips. Where is the man who, knowing his sickness, banned mirrors from this house? He is among those whose masks I have torn: and I have eaten bread from his basket and drunk wine from his cup...'

The bedchambers are reached by a narrow gallery paved with mosaics, and there the king slowly went, bearing his blood-red torch before him. A guard advanced, seized with disquiet, and his belt of wide rings shone on his white tunic: then, recognising the king by his face, he prostrated himself.

A pale light from an iron lamp suspended in the centre illuminated a double row of state beds; the silken coverings were woven of silk threads of ancient colours. An onyx spout dripped monotonously into a polished stone basin.

The king first considered the apartment of the priests; and the grave masks of the sleeping men were alike in sleep and immobility. And in the jesters' apartment their sleeping mouths gaped just as widely in laughter. And the immutable beauty of his women's faces was not marred when they were at rest; their arms were crossed over their breasts, or they pillowed their head on one hand, and they did not seem to be concerned for their smile, which was quite as gracious when they were unaware of it.

At the farthest point of the innermost chamber was a bronze bed with high-reliefs of women making obeisance and of giant flowers. The yellow cushions bore the imprint of a restless body. There, at that hour of the night, the king in the golden mask would have to sleep; there, down the years, his ancestors had slept.

And the king turned away from the bed: 'They were able to sleep', he said, 'with that secret on their face, and sleep came to kiss their brows, as it has come to me. And they did not shake their masks in the black face of sleep, to terrify it. And I have brushed against this metal. I have touched those cushions where once lay the limbs of those shameful...'

And the king went to the chamber of the brazier, where the rose and purple flames still danced and swiftly flickered over the walls. He struck a blow on the great copper gong, so sonorous that all the metal objects about vibrated. The frightened guards rushed forward, half-dressed, with their axes and their steel maces bristling with points; the priests appeared, still asleep, their robes trailing; the jesters forgot their customary bounding entrances and the women's smiling faces were seen peering around the doors.

The king now mounted the black throne and commanded: 'I struck the gong to bring you here for an important purpose. The mendicant spoke the truth. Every one of you is deceiving me. Take off your masks.'

A rustling of limbs,and of garments and of arms was heard. Then slowly, those who were present made up their minds and took off their masks.

The king in the golden mask then turned towards the priests and scrutinised fifty coarse, humorous faces with little eyes gummy from sleep; and, in turning to the jesters, he studied fifty wan faces lined with sorrow, their eyes bloodshot from insomnia; and bending towards the crescent of his seated women he laughed mirthlessly – for their faces were filled with boredom and ugliness, and overlaid with stupidity.

'So', said the king, 'you have deceived me concerning yourselves and concerning the whole world. Those I thought were serious and who gave me counsel as to things divine and human are like goatskin bottles puffed-up with wine and wind; and those whose constant gaiety was my amusement were melancholy to the depths of their hearts; and you women – your sphinxlike smiles signified nothing whatever! You are miserable; but I am the most miserable among you. I am king, and my features seem royal. Now, in reality, look: the most wretched man in my kingdom has nothing to envy me.'

And the king took off his golden mask: a cry rose from the throats of those who saw; for the rosy light of the brazier lit up his white leper's scales.

'It was they who deceived me', cried the king. 'I mean my forefathers, who were lepers as I am, and who have transmitted their sickness to me with the royal heritage. They have deceived me, and they have bound you to lies.'

At the great opening at the end of the hall, the waning moon showed its yellow mask.

'That moon', said the king, 'which always turns towards us the same golden face may perhaps have another face, dark and cruel; thus my royalty has spread out over my leprosy. But I shall no longer see the appearances of this world, and I shall turn my gaze on dark things. Here before you I punish myself for my leprosy and for my lying, and my line with me.'

The king picked up his golden mask: and, standing upon the black throne, amidst the uproar and the supplications, with a cry of pain he forced the clasps at the side of the mask into his eyes. For the last time a red light burst before him; and a surge of blood ran down his face, onto his hands, onto the black steps of the throne. He rent his garments and, staggering, he descended the steps: the guards were struck dumb with horror; fumblingly he thrust them aside and went out alone into the night.

Now the leprous and blind king journeyed through the night. He blundered against the concentric walls of the seven courts and against the ancient trees of the royal residence, and he tore his hands in touching the thorns of the hedges. When he heard the sound of his steps he knew he was on the highway. He journeyed for hours and hours, without even feeling the need to take any nourishment. He knew the sun was shining by the heat that clung about his face, and he recognised the night by the cold of the darkness. The blood that had coursed from his gouged-out eyes covered his skin with a dry and blackish crust. And when he had been journeying a long time, the blind king felt weary and sat down by the roadside. He lived now in a world of darkness, and his gaze was always turned inwards.

As he was wandering in this sombre plain of thought, he heard the sound of little bells. At once he pictured the return of a flock of dense-fleeced sheep, led by rams whose fat tails hung down to the ground. And he held out his hands to touch the white fleeces, not feeling any shame before animals. But his hands met with other, soft hands, and a gentle voice said: 'What is it you want poor blind-man?'

And he recognised the pleasant voice of a woman.

'You must not touch me', the king cried. 'But where are your sheep?'

Now the young girl who stood before him was a leper, and for that reason she had little bells hanging from her garments. But she dared not admit it and, lyingly, she answered the king: 'They are following a little behind me.'

'Where are you going thus?' the king asked.

She replied: 'I am returning to the City of the Wretched.'

Then the king remembered that, in a place apart in his realm, there was a refuge for those who had been driven from life on account of their sicknesses or their crimes. They lived out their lives in huts they built for themselves, or else in dens hollowed out of the ground. And their solitude was extreme.

The king resolved to go to that city: 'Take me there', he said.

The young girl took him by the sleeve.

'Let me wash your face', she said, 'for the blood has run down your cheeks for perhaps a week.'

And the king trembled, thinking she would be horrified by his leprosy and abandon him. But she poured some water from her gourd and washed the king's face. Then she said: 'Poor man! How you must have suffered, having your eyes put out!'

'How much I suffered before, without knowing it!', the king said. 'But let us be on our way: will we reach the City of the Wretched before evening?'

'I hope so', said the young girl.

And she led him, speaking to him pleasantly. Meanwhile the blind king heard the bells and, turning, wished to caress the sheep; and the young girl feared he would guess her sickness.

Now the king was worn out with tiredness and hunger: she took a piece of bread out of her bag, and she offered him her gourd. But the king refused, fearing to taint the bread and the water. Then he asked: 'Do you see the City of the Wretched?'

'Not yet', said the young girl.

And they went on further. She gathered blue-lotus roots for him, and he chewed them to refresh his mouth. The sun went down over the great ricefields that shimmered on the horizon.

'I smell a meal cooking', said the blind king. 'Are we not getting closer to the City of the Wretched?'

'Not yet', said the young girl.

And, while the bloody dusk of the sun still stood out against the violet sky, the king fainted away with lassitude and inanition. At the end of the road a thin column of smoke trembled above thatched roofs; a marsh-mist hovered.

'There's the city!' the young girl said. 'I can see it.'

'I shall enter another city on my own', the king said, 'in just a little while. I have only one more desire. I should have liked to rest my lips on yours, so as to refresh myself at your face, which must be beautiful. But I would have sullied you, for I am a leper.'

And the king fell dying.

The young girl fell to sobbing, seeing that the blind king's face was pure and without blemish, and knowing well that she herself had feared to pollute him.

Now out of the City of the Wretched there came an old mendicant with a bristling white beard, whose wavering eyes trembled.

'Why are you weeping?' he asked.

The young girl said that the blind king was dead, having had his eyes put out, and thinking he was a leper.

'And he did not wish to give me the kiss of peace', she said, 'so as not to pollute me; and it is I who, in truth, am really a leper.'

And the old mendicant replied: 'Doubtless his heart's blood, that gushed from his eyes, cured his sickness. And he is dead, thinking he wore a mask of wretchedness. But now he has laid aside all masks, whether of gold, of leprosy, or of flesh.'

The Death of Odjigh

to J.-H. Rosny

In those days the human race seemed on the point of extinction. The sun's orb was as cold as the moon. An eternal winter cracked the earth into fissures. The mountains that had arisen, vomiting the earth's burning entrails to the sky, were grey with frozen lava. Parallel or radiating cracks traversed the regions; subsidences, suddenly opening huge crevasses, swallowed things up and long files of erratic blocks were to be seen slowly sliding towards them. The gloomy air was spangled with a transparent lacework of ice-crystals; the universally-spreading silver appeared to be sterilising the world.

Save for some traces of pale lichen on the rocks, there was no longer any vegetation. The world's bones were stripped of their flesh, which is made up of the earth, and the plains lay extended like skeletons. And the wintry death attacking first life of the lower kinds, the fish and the sea-creatures had perished, imprisoned in the ice, then the insects that swarmed on the creeping plants, and the animals that carried their young in ventral pouches, and the semi-aerial creatures that had haunted the great forests; for, as far as the eye could see, there were no longer any trees or any greenery, and no living creatures were to be found but those that lived in caverns, grottoes or dens.

Thus, from among the descendants of men, two races were already extinct; those who had lived in nests of lianas at the tops of great trees and those who, in floating houses, had lived retired in the middle of lakes: the forests, woods, copses and thickets that had bestrewn the glittering earth, and the surface of the waters were as hard and gleaming as polished stone.

The Beast-hunters who knew the use of fire, the Troglodytes who could burrow into the earth to reach the interior heat, and the Fish-eaters who had laid up stores of marine oil in their holes in the ice, still held out against the winter. But animals were becoming rare, caught by the frost the moment their muzzles touched the ground; and firewood had all but been exhausted and the oil was solid, like a yellow rock with a white crest.

Nevertheless a wolf-hunter called Odjigh, who lived in a deep den and possessed an immense axe of green jade, heavy and redoubtable, had pity on living creatures.

Living on the shores of the great inland sea whose furthermost reach expands to the east of Minnesota, he turned his gaze to the northern regions where the cold seemed to be gathering. In the depths of his grotto of ice he took the sacred pipe, hollowed from a white stone, packed it with fragrent herbs from which the smoke rises in curls and blew the divine essence onto the air. The curls mounted upwards, and the grey whorls inclined to the north.

It was to the north that Odjigh, the wolf-killer, commenced to march. He covered his face with a furry raccoon-skin, pierced with holes, the tail of which waved above his head like a plume; from a leathern thong about his waist he had hung a pouch filled with dried meat mixed with fat: and, swinging his green-jade axe, he set out towards the thick clouds piled up on the horizon.

He went on his way, and about him life was dying out. The rivers had long been silent. The opaque air carried only muffled sounds. The masses of ice, blue, white and green, resembled pillars flanking a great road.

In his heart Odjigh grieved for the wriggling of the mother-of-pearl coloured fish among the meshes of fibre-woven nets, and the serpentine swimming of the sea-eels, and the ponderous gait of turtles, and the sidelong running of gigantic, squint-eyed crabs, and the lively sighing sounds of terrestrial beasts, shaggy beasts with a flat beak and clawed paws, beasts covered in scales, beasts speckled in various fashions pleasing to the eye, beasts fond of their young, agile in their leaping or strange in their gyrations, or venturesome in their flights. And above all animals he mourned the passing of the fierce wolves with their grey fur and their familiar howling, being accustomed by the red light of the moon on foggy nights, to hunt them with club and stone axe.

On his left there now appeared a beast of the sort that lives in a den dug deep in the soil and lets itself be drawn backwards from its burrow, a skinny, mangy Badger. Odjigh saw it and rejoiced, without a thought of killing it: keeping its distance, the Badger advanced abreast of him.

Then, on Odjigh's right, a wretched hollow-eyed Lynx suddenly emerged from a gully among the ice. It looked sidelong at Odjigh, fearful and slinking in its anxiety. But again the wolf-killer rejoiced, marching between the Badger and Lynx..

As he advanced, his pouch of meat slapping against his side, he heard behind him a feeble, hungry howling; and turning to the sound of a voice he knew, he saw a bony Wolf miserably treading in his footsteps. Odjigh took pity on all those creatures whose skulls he used to split. The Wolf hung out his steaming tongue, and his eyes were red.

Thus the slayer continued on his way with his animal companions, the subterranean Badger on his left and the all-seeing Lynx on his right, and behind him the famished Wolf,

They reached the centre of the inland sea which was to be distinguished only by the endlessly green colour of its ice. And there Odjigh, the wolf-killer, seated himself on a boulder and placed before him the stone pipe. And before each of his companions he placed a block of ice which he hollowed out with the blade of his axe, after the manner of the sacred censer breathing forth smoke. He packed fragrant herbs in the four pipes: then he struck the fire-making stones together, and the herbs caught fire, and the four meagre columns of smoke arose.

Now the grey whorl that arose before the Badger bent towards the west, and that which rose before the Lynx bent towards the east, and that which arose before the Wolf curved to the south. But the grey whorl from Odjigh's pipe rose to the north.

The wolf-killer started once more on his way. And looking to the left he was saddened, for the Badger that can see below ground, was going off towards the west; and looking to the right, he regretted the all-seeing Lynx that was making off to the east, although in fact he thought that, each in its way, those two animal companions were prudent and well-advised.

Nevertheless he went steadily on, behind him the red-eyed, starving Wolf on which he had taken pity.

The mass of frozen clouds to the north seemed to reach the sky. The winter was becoming still more cruel. Cut by the ice, Odjigh's feet bled, and his blood froze in black crusts. But for hours, for days, for weeks, for months perhaps, he continued, sucking at a little dried meat and throwing the leavings to his companion, the Wolf that followed him.

In a vague hope, Odjigh continued on his way. He felt pity for the world of men, for the dying animals and plants, and he felt himself filled with strength for the fight against the cold.

And, in the end, his path was blocked by an immense barrier of ice that, like a chain of mountains whose peaks were lost to view, sealed the sombre dome of the sky. As they tipped into the solid expanse of the frozen ocean the great ice-floes were a limpid green; then, in their congested heaping-up, they grew cloudy; and, as they rose higher, they appeared an opaque blue, like the sky in the summers of times past: for they were composed of fresh water and of snow.

Odjigh took his green-jade axe, and he cut steps in the escarpment. In this way he climbed to a great height, where it seemed to him that his head was enveloped in clouds and that the earth had fallen away. And on the step just below him, the Wolf sat and confidently waited.

When he thought he had reached the summit, he saw that it was formed of a glistening, vertical blue wall, and it was impossible to go further. But he looked behind him and he saw the living, hungry beast: pity for the living world gave him strength.

He plunged his jade axe into the blue wall and hewed away the ice. Multicoloured, the fragments flew about him. He hacked for hours and hours. His limbs were yellow and wrinkled from the cold. His pouch of meat had long since been shrunken and empty. To appease his hunger he had chewed the fragrant herbs he smoked in his pipe and, all at once disbelieving in the Superior Powers, he had thrown the pipe and the pair of fire-making stones into the void.

He dug on. He heard a sharp grating sound, and he cried out, for he knew that this sound had come from his jade axe-blade that was about to split with the great cold. Then he picked it up and, no longer having the means to warm it, thrust it fiercely into his right thigh. The green axe was tinged with warm blood. Sitting behind him, the whimpering Wolf lapped up the red drops as they fell.

And suddenly the polished wall burst open. There was a great blast of heat as if, on the far side, the warm seasons were stored up at the bar of heaven. The aperture enlarged and the powerful blast engulfed Odjigh. He heard all the little shoots of spring rustling and he felt the summer's blazing heat. It felt to him as if in the great tide that lifted him off his feet, all the seasons were returning to the world to save life from extinction. The tide bore with it the white rays of the sun, and the caressing breezes and the clouds laden with fecundity. And in the breath of warm life the black clouds gathered and engendered fire.

With the clap of thunder there was a long bolt of flame, and the resplendent shaft, like a red blade, pierced Odjigh to the heart. He fell against the polished wall, his back turned to the world towards which the seasons were returning in the river of the storm: and the hungry Wolf, climbing up timidly, set his paws on Odjigh's shoulders and began gnawing at the back of his neck.

The Embalming-women

to Alphonse Daudet

That there may still be in Libya, on the confines of Ethiopia where there live very old and wise men, witcheries more mysterious than those of the sorceresses of Thessaly, I cannot doubt. It is terrible, to be sure, to think that the incantations of women can cause the moon to descend into a mirror-case or plunge it, when it is full, into a silver bucket along with the drenched stars or, while the Thessalonian night is black and men who can change their skins are free to roam about, cause it to fry in a pan like a yellow medusa of the sea: but I would be less fearful of these things than to meet again in the blood-coloured desert those Libyan embalming-women.

We had traversed, my brother Ophelion and I, the nine circles of different sands that surround Ethiopia. There are terrestrial dunes which, in the distance, appear glaucous as the sea or azure-coloured as lakes. The pygmies do not extend to these regions; but we had left them in the great dark forests, where the sun never penetrates; and the copper-coloured men who feed upon human flesh and recognise one another by the sound their jawbones make are further away to the west. The red desert we were entering to travel towards Libya was to all appearances bare of cities and of men.

We marched for seven days and seven nights. In that country the night is transparent and blue, cool, and dangerous to the eyes, so that sometimes that blue nocturnal light dilates the pupils in the space of six hours and the man thus afflicted does not again see the rising of the sun. Such is the nature of the malady that it attacks only those who sleep on the sand and do not cover their eyes; but those who march night and day have nothing from which to apprehend danger save the white powder of the desert that irritates the eyelids in the sun.

On the evening of the eighth day we perceived some white cupolas of no great size, disposed in a circle on the blood-red plain; and Ophelion was of the opinion that it would be worth while to examine them. As is usual in the land of Libya, the night fell rapidly, and when we approached the darkness was very deep. The cupolas emerged from the earth, and we could not at first detect any opening in them: but when we crossed the circle they formed, we saw that they were pierced by doors having the height of a man of middle stature and were all pointed towards the centre of the circle. The openings of those doors were dark; but through the narrow fissures about them rays escaped that marked our features with long red fingers. We were surrounded, also, by an odour that we did not know, and that seemed compounded of perfumes and corruption.

Ophelion halted me and told me that someone was making signs to us from one of the cupolas. A woman we could not see distinctly was standing in the doorway and beckoning to us. I hesitated, but Ophelion drew me towards her. The entry was gloomy, as was the circular room under the cupola: and no sooner were we there than she who had summoned us disappeared. We heard a gentle voice pronouncing words in a savage tongue. Then the woman was again before us, bearing a smoky clay lamp. We greeted her, and she bade us welcome in our own Greek language, which she spoke with a Libyan accent. She showed us beds of baked earth, decorated with figures of naked men and of birds, and she had us be seated. Next, saying that she was going to fetch us our meal, she vanished again without our being able to see, by the feeble light of the lamp which was placed upon the ground, by which way she had made her exit. The woman's hair was black, and her eyes were of a dark colour; she was dressed in a linen tunic; a blue girdle supported her breasts, and she smelled of earth.

The supper she served us on clay plates and in cups of dusky glass consisted of circular loaves with figs and preserved fish; there was no flesh other than pickled locusts. She ate with us, but she touched neither fish nor locusts. As long as I was under that cupola, I never saw her put any flesh in her mouth: she contented herself with a little bread and fruits in conserve; as to the wine, it was pale and rosy, seemingly mixed with water, and of an exquisite flavour. The reason for her abstinence was, no doubt, a distaste you will readily comprehend by this account; and it may be that the perfumes among which that woman lived relieved her need of nourishment and appeased it with their subtle particles.

She questioned us little and we scarcely dared speak to her; for her ways appeared strange. After supper, we lay down on our beds; she left us a lamp and prepared another, smaller, one for herself; then she left us, and I saw that she went below ground through an opening situated on the far side of the cupola. Ophelion seemed little inclined to respond to my conjectures and towards the middle of the night I fell into a troubled sleep.

I was awakened by the lamp's sputtering sound, for the wick had burned down to the oil: and I no longer saw my brother Ophelion next to me. I rose and called to him in a low voice, but he was no longer in the cupola. Then I went out into the night and it seemed to me that, from below the earth, I heard the lamentations and the cries of mourning-women. This echo of a sound rapidly died away: I made a round of the cupolas without discovering anything. But there was a kind of quivering, as of a murmuration in the earth, and in the distance the dismal calling of a wild dog.

I approached one of the orifices from which the red rays were streaming, and I contrived to climb up on one of the cupolas so as to look within. Then I grasped the strangeness of the country and of the city of cupolas. For the place I saw, lit by cressets, was strewn with corpses; and, among the mourning-women, other women were busying themselves with vases and instruments. I saw them opening at the side newly-dead bellies and drawing out the yellow, brown, green and blue entrails which they plunged into amphorae; forcing a silver hook into noses so as to break the delicate bones at the base and draw out the brains with a spatula; washing the bodies with tinted waters, rubbing them with the perfumes of Rhodes, with myrrh and cinnamon; plaiting their hair, conglutinating the eyelashes and eyebrows with colour; painting the teeth and hardening the lips; polishing the nails of the fingers and toes and circling them with a line of gold. Then, the belly being flattened, the navel hollowed, they straightened the white and puckered fingers of the dead, encircling them at the wrists and ankles with rings of electrum, and binding them in long linen bandages.

All those cupolas were apparently a settlement of embalming-women, where the dead were brought from the towns round about. And in certain of the habitations the work was carried out above, and in others below the ground. The sight of a corpse the lips of which remained clamped shut, and between which was thrust a twig of myrtle, just as with women who cannot smile and would accustom themselves to display their teeth, filled me with horror.

I resolved, as soon as day had dawned, to flee the city of the embalming-women with Ophelion. And on re-entering our cupola, I put a new wick in the lamp, and I lit it at the fire under the dome: but Ophelion had not returned. I went to the farther end of the chamber and I shone a light into the opening of the subterranean staircase; and from below I heard the sound of love-making. I smiled then to think that my brother was spending a night of love with a corpse-handler. But I was at a loss what to think on seeing the woman who had received us enter the cupola by an opening that led, no doubt, to a tunnel cut in the wall of cement. She went to the staircase; and she listened, as I had done. Then she turned in my direction, and her face filled me with fear. Her eyebrows were drawn together so that they met: and she seemed to draw back into the wall.

I fell again into a deep sleep. In the morning Ophelion was lying in the bed next to mine. His face was ashen. I shook him and urged him to depart. He looked at me, without recognising me. The woman came in and, when I questioned her, she spoke of a pestilential wind that had blown upon my brother.

The whole day he turned from one side to the other, racked by the fever and, eyes fixed, the woman stared at him. Towards evening he moved his lips, and he died. Wailing, I embraced his knees, and I wept until two in the morning. Then my soul was carried away in dreams. The sorrow of having lost Ophelion troubled me and caused me to awaken. His corpse was no longer at my side. And the woman had vanished.

I cried out then, and I turned hither and thither about the chamber: but I could not find the staircase. I left the cupola and, climbing towards the red ray, I applied my eyes to the opening. Now this is what I saw:

The corpse of my brother Ophelion was stretched out among the vases and the jars; and they had drawn out his brains with the hook and the silver spoons, and his belly was laid open.

His nails were already gilded, and his body had been rubbed with bitumen. But, what is more, he lay between two embalming-women who so strongly resembled one another that I could not distinguish which was the one who had received us. Both were weeping, and lacerating their faces with their nails, and kissing my brother Ophelion and clasping him in their arms.

And I called out through the aperture of the cupola, and I searched for the entrance to the subterranean chamber, and I ran to the other cupolas; but I received no response, and I wandered helplessly in the blue and transparent night.

And it was my belief that those two embalming-women were sisters, and sorceresses, and jealous, and that they had killed my brother Ophelion to mummify his beautiful body.

I covered my head with my mantle and, in a frenzy of fear, I fled that sorcerers' country.

The Plague

CCCCI e mille l'an corant
Nella città di Trento Rè Rupert
Volle lo scudo mio essere copert
De l'arme suo Lion d'oro rampant
Cronica del Pitti

to Auguste Bréal

I, Bonacorso de Neri de Pitti, son of Bonacorso, *gonfaloniere di giustizia* of the commune of Florence, whose escutcheon was covered in the year fourteen hundred and one, by order of King Rupert in the city of Trento, with the golden Lion rampant, would recount for my ennobled descendants what befell me when I commenced to rove the world seeking adventure.

In the year MCCCLXXXIV, being a young man without money, I fled the city of Florence by the highways, with Matteo for companion. For the plague was devastating the city. The malady was sudden and struck men down in the streets. The eyes became burning and red, the throat hoarse; the belly swelled. Next, the mouth and the tongue were covered with little blisters, filled with an irritant fluid. One was possessed by thirst. For many hours the sick were convulsed by a dry cough. Then the limbs grew stiff at the joints; the skin was studded with swollen red spots that some called buboes. And finally the faces of the dead were pale and distended, and the mouth gaped wide like that of a trumpet. The public fountains, almost exhausted in the heat, were crowded about by bent and emaciated men who sought to plunge their faces in the water. Many leapt into them, and they were drawn out with hooks on chains, black with mud and their skulls smashed. The corpses, turning brown, piled up in the middle of the streets where, in the season, the rainwater flowed in a torrent; the stench was insupportable, and the fear was terrible.

But Matteo was a great dice-player. We rejoiced together, once we were clear of the town, and at the first hostelry drank mixed wine to our salvation from mortality. There were merchants there from Genoa and Pavia; we challenged them, dice-cups in hand, and Matteo won twelve ducats. I, for my part, invited them to a game of tric-trac in which I had the pleasure of winning twenty golden florins, with which florins and ducats we bought mules and a load of wool: and Matteo, who had resolved to go to Prussia, laid in a stock of saffron.

We roved the highways from Padua to Verona, we returned to Padua to furnish ourselves more amply with wool, and we journeyed as far as Venice. Thence, crossing the sea, we entered Slavonia and we visited fine towns up to the border of Croatia. At Buda I fell sick with the fever and Matteo left me alone in the inn with twelve ducats, returning to Florence where certain affairs called him, and where I was to rejoin him. I lay on a sack of straw in a dry and dusty room, without a physician, and the door open upon the tap-room. On Saint Martin's night a company of fife-players and flutists entered with some fifteen or sixteen Venetian and Teuton soldiers. Having emptied many flagons, flattened the pewter cups and smashed the jugs against the wall, they began dancing to the sound of the fife. Thrusting their grogblossomed faces over the threshold, and seeing me lying on my sack, they set about dragging me into the tap-room, crying: 'Either you drink or you die!', then buffeting me, whilst my head throbbed with the fever; finally they shoved me among the straw of my sack, tying the opening about my neck.

I sweated mightily, and my fever was no doubt thereby dissipated; but at the same time I was put in a rage. My arms were pinioned, and they had taken my poniard, otherwise I should have flung myself, bristling as I was with straw, upon the soldiers. But at my belt, under my hose, I wore a little dirk in a scabbard. I succeeded in reaching it with my hand and, by this means, I slit the canvas of the sack.

Perhaps the fever was still inflaming my brain; but the memory of the plague we had left in Florence, and which had since spread to Slavonia, merged in my mind with a sort of notion I had conceived of the face of Sulla, the dictator of the Latins of whom the great Cicero speaks. His face, the Athenians said, was like a mulberry besprinkled with flour. I made up my mind to terrify the Venetian and Teuton men-at-arms: and since I found myself in the middle of the closet in which the inn-keeper kept his provisions and the preserved fruits, I rapidly ripped open a pouch filled with maize-flour. I rubbed my face with this dust and, when it had taken on a colour that was neither yellow nor white, I scored my arm with my dirk, drawing from it blood enough to irregularly spatter the floury coating. Then I got back into the sack, and I waited for the drunken scoundrels. They came in, laughing and lurching: they had scarcely set eyes on my white and bloody face than, blundering one against another they bellowed: 'The plague! The plague!'

The hostelry was empty before I had recovered my arms. Feeling myself cured on account of the sweating those ruffians had imposed on me, I set off for Florence to rejoin Matteo.

I found my companion Matteo wandering about the Florentine countryside and in a fairly miserable condition. The plague continuing to rage there, he had not dared to enter the city. We turned about and we started for the states of Pope Gregory, there to seek our fortune. Going up towards Avignon, we met with bands of armed men bearing lances, pikes and *vouges;* for the citizens of Bologna has just revolted against the Pope at the request of those of Florence (of this we knew nothing). There we had great pleasure in gaming, as much at tric-trac as at dice, with the men of both sides; and thus we won three hundred ducats and eighty gold florins.

The city of Bologna was all but empty of men, so we were received in the stews with cries of joy. The rooms there are not strewn with straw, as in many Lombard cities; there is no shortage of truckle beds there although, for the greater part, their straps are broken. Matteo met a Florentine girl he knew, Monna Giovanna; as for me, I did not think to ask mine her name, but I was content with her.

There we drank abundantly of the muddy wine of the region and of beer, and we ate of preserves and tartlets. Matteo, to whom I had recounted my adventure, feigning to visit the privy, went down into the kitchens and returned in pestilential guise.Squealing, the girls of the stews fled in all directions. Then, taking courage, they came and touched Matteo's face. Monna Giovanna was not inclined to go back with him and remained, trembling, in a corner, saying that he smelled of the fever. Meanwhile, drunk, Matteo laid down his head among the pots on the table that shuddered at his snoring, and he looked like one of the gaudily-painted figures quacks display on platforms.

We finally left Bologna, and after divers adventures we came close to Avignon, where we learned that the Pope was having all the Florentines clapped in gaol, and having them and their books burned to avenge himself for the rebellion. But the warning came too late; for in the night the officers of the Papal Marshal took us and threw us in the prison of Avignon.

Before being put to the question, we were examined by a magistrate and provisionally condemned to imprisonment in a bottle-dungeon, pending enquiries, with, as is the custom of the ecclesiastical justice, a diet of dry bread and water. I managed, nonetheless, to conceal under my robe our canvas bag, which contained a little polenta and some olives.

The floor of the dungeon was waterlogged; and all the air we had was by a barred vent that opened onto the courtyard of the conciergerie. Our feet were fixed in very heavy wooden stocks, and our hands shackled with rather weighty chains, in such manner that our bodies touched from knee to shoulder. The gaoler was sufficiently thoughtful to inform us that we were under suspicion of being poisoners; for the Pope had learned from certain ambassadors that the *gonfalonieri* of the commune of Florence were minded to have him killed.

So there we were in the prison's darkness, hearing no sound, not knowing the hour, whether by day or by night, in great danger of being burned. Then I remembered our stratagem; and the idea came to me that, out of fear of the malady, the Papal justice would order us expelled. With difficulty, I laid on my polenta, and it was agreed that Matteo should smear his face with it and bespot himself with blood, whilst I would raise a clamour to summon the guards. Matteo made ready his mask and began roaring hoarsely, as if his throat were being compressed. Shaking my chains, I called upon Our Lady. But the dungeon was deep, the door was thick, and it was night. For hours we supplicated uselessly. I ceased my cries: nevertheless Matteo continued to whimper. I shoved him with my elbow, conveying to him that he should rest until daylight: his groans became louder. I touched him in the darkness: my hands reached only his belly, which seemed to me swollen like a water-skin. And then fear took hold of me – I was pressed close against him! And while in a rasping voice he caterwauled 'Water! Water!', until it seemed to me I heard the desperate crying of a pack of unleashed hounds, the pale disk of dawn fell from the vent. And then the cold sweat ran down my limbs; for under the powdery mask, under the blotches of dried blood, I saw that his face was livid and I recognised the white scabs and the red oozing of the Florentine plague.

The Milesian Virgins

to Edmond de Goncourt

Suddenly, without anyone knowing the reason, the virgins of Miletus began hanging themselves. It was a sort of moral epidemic. Pushing open the doors of the gynaeceum, one would strike against the still-quivering feet of a white corpse hanging from a beam. People would be taken unawares by a harsh gasp and a tinkling of rings, bracelets and anklets rolling on the floor. The hanged girls' breasts heaved like the palpitating wings of a throttled bird. Their eyes seemed full of resignation rather than horror.

In the evening the young girls retired, silently as is proper, remained in a seated position, dressed in modest garments, not pressing their knees together. In the middle of the night wails rang out and, at first believing them troubled by oppressive dreams, the night-birds of the mind, their parents rose and visited their chambers. They thought to find them lying face downwards, loins convulsed with terror, or with their arms crossed over their breasts, their fingers pressed upon the place where the heart beats. But the young girls' beds were empty. Then they heard rocking sounds from the rooms above. They were hanged, lit by the moon, white tunics trailing, hands entwined to the roots of their fingers, and their distended lips were turning blue. At dawn the household sparrows flew onto their shoulders, lightly pecking at them and, finding their flesh cold, took flight with little cries.

Scarcely had the first breeze of morning set the curtains stretched in the inner courtyards trembling than it carried from the neighbouring houses the low chant of the mourning-women.

And in the market place, among the early purchasers, before the light clouds took on their rosy tint, they would read out the list of the night's dead. The heralds ran hither and thither. Like the others, the daughters of magistrates and archons, barely nubile, on the eve of taking the yellow nuptial veil, mysteriously hanged themselves. The men who came to the assembly, each of them distinguished by the red cord that indicates the latecomer, neglected the affairs of the people and wept into their hands. The trembling judges handed down sentences of banishment, no longer daring to condemn a man to death.

A large number of old crones who shunned the light of day were hounded out of the obscure alleys where the women drug-peddlers lived. The painted women whose gait was too slow and whose eyes were too-much blackened were expelled from the city. Those who taught unknown doctrines under the porches, those who discoursed to the young men, the priests who paraded about images of the goddess on beasts of burden, the initiates of the mysteries and the lovers of Cybele were expelled beyond the city boundaries.

They took up residence in caves hollowed in times immemorial in the rockface of the nearby mountains. There they slept in stone chambers; and some served for the prostitutes, others for the philosophers – with the result that, at nightfall, the young men of Miletus would leave the city to spend the night below ground. Thus, from the first watch of the night, on the slopes of the foothills, one could see lights glimmering from the openings cut in the mountainside; and everything that in the city of Miletus had appeared strange or impure continued its life under the earth.

Then the archons of the colony issued a decree whereby the young girls that were hanged be entombed in a new manner. They were to be exposed to the populace, naked, the cord about their neck, and carried thus to the grave. And they hoped that in this way modesty would prevail over voluntary death when, the evening after the promulgation of this law, the Milesian virgins' secret was uncovered.

Some priests that tended the sacred fire at the temple of Athena rose shortly before midnight to add twigs to the fire and pour oil into the lamps. In the darkness of the central hall they saw a troop of virgins advancing, who seemed to have been warned by a dream. For, in the shadows, they were making their way towards a certain flagstone, close to the altar, which was raised. A young boy, whose habit it was to carry the goddess's baskets veiled his head and went with the virgins below the temple.

The vault was lofty, barely illuminated from a feebly luminous point at the summit. The wall at the far end appeared to shine, being made of a single mirror of metal. At first this polished surface was cloudy, then images floated within it. It was of a gracious colour, like the eyes of the owls that are sacred to Pallas Athene.

The first of the Milesian virgins advanced towards the immense mirror, smiling, and she undressed. The veil attached at her shoulder fell, then the veil which covered her breast, then that which fastened at her throat: her body appeared in its splendour. And she loosened the knot of her hair which fell about her shoulders to her heels. The other young girls at her sides smiled to see her admiring herself. Nevertheless, no image appeared in the mirror to those who stood beside her. But the young girl, her eyes horribly dilated, wept with the cry of a terrified animal. She fled, and they heard the sound of her naked feet on the stone floor. Then, when some minutes had passed, in the terror of silence, echoed the howling of the mourning-women.

And the second contemplated the polished surface and uttered the same cry over her nudity. And when, in her flight, she had climbed the steps of the temple, again the distant plaints made it known that she had hanged herself in the cold light of the moon.

The young man stood directly behind the third, and his look followed hers; and the cry of horror burst from his lips at the same time. For the image in the sinister mirror was deformed in accordance with the natural order of things. As she might see herself in a mirror, the Milesian girl saw her brow seamed with wrinkles, her eyelids cracked, the film of age on the eyes running with rheum, the ears flabby, the cheeks fallen-in, the nostrils reddened and hairy, the chin greasy and divided, the shoulders hollowed, the breasts withered and the nipples obliterated, the belly sagging towards the ground, the thighs gone brown, the knees flattened, the tendons standing out on the legs, the feet swollen with nodes. The image had no hair and opaque blue veins ran under the skin of the head. Her hands, which she held out, were horny and the nails a leaden colour. Thus the mirror showed the Milesian virgin the spectacle of what life held in store for her.And in the features of the image she found every sign of resemblance – the movement of the forehand, the line of the nose, the curve of the mouth, the distance of the breasts and, above all, the colour of the eyes that gave the impression of profound thought. Terrified of her body, ashamed of the future, before having known Aphrodite she hanged herself from the rafters of the gynaeceum.

Now the young lad ran after and chased the other virgins before him. But he arrived too late and the Milesian girl's body was already bucking in the last agony. He laid her out on the ground and, before the mourning-women came, he gently caressed her limbs and kissed her eyes.

Such was this young lad's answer to the mirror of future truth, to Athene's mirror.

The Sabbat at Mofflaines

to Jean Lorrain

Returning home one night from the town of Arras where he had drunk late of honeyed hippocras at the Hôtel du Cygne, Colart, Lord of Beaufort and knight, took the road by the cemetery. There, by the light of the moon which, being wrapped in mists seemed red, he saw three *filles de joie,* hand in hand. They muttered slyly and smiled a crafty smile. They took him most civilly by the arm, and two of them told him their names were Blancminette and Belotte; and the third, who was a Fleming, shook her blonde locks and spoke to him in her jargon. The others called her Vergensen.

Drawing closer, the Chevalier de Beaufort saw that they were dancing about a white flagstone. And the three *filles de joie* laughed at him when he fell back; for they were pouring *aqua regia* over the stone from a green bottle – and the stone commenced to make a spluttering sound, like quicklime. And they threw eviscerated lizards upon it, and frogs' legs, the whiskery muzzles of rats, the claws of nocturnal birds, rock arsenic, black blood from a copper bowl, strips of soiled linen, mandrake roots, and the long-shaped flowers of digitalis that are called dead-men's fingers. And in the meantime all the while they were saying: 'Besom-riders, besom-riders, besom-riders.'

Colart saw then and there the predicament he was in: but Belotte, Blancminette and Vergensen led him to an old limekiln that stood open, close by the cemetery. He stood in the shelter of the white door and a woman came out, without petticoat or shoes, or ornaments: she appeared to be dressed only in a long shift decorated with lunulae, and her face was half covered with a black hood. The three *filles de joie* clapped their hands, crying 'Demiselle, Demiselle, Demiselle!'

Now this Demiselle held in her hands a small earthenware pot and some little bundles of birch-twigs. She anointed five bundles with a black unction that was in the pot, and the three *filles de joie* placed the bundles between their legs, bestriding them as they would a horse. And Demiselle had the Chevalier de Beaufort do likewise. And with her finger she anointed the palms of their hands: so that, suddenly, Colart found himself flying through the night air with the four women. For it seemed to him that the anointed besom between his legs was transformed into a wayward horse flying silently through the night, and his hands, stained with the unction, into clawed membranes like wings.

While they were flying over the city of Arras, the Chevalier Colart questioned the three girls. And they told him they were going to their Master in the wood at Mofflaines, which is in the countryside a league distant. And Vergensen, in the air, still shook her head and laughed.

They descended in a feebly-lit clearing. The masses of fóliage were fluttering. There was a prodigiously long table, the end of which was lost to sight among the forest trees, flanked by high-playing fountains. It was piled high with meat, red, brown and white, with quarters of mutton, breast-cuts of beef, haunches of venison and boars' heads. There were mounds of fowl, with pockets of fat under their fine skins, surmounted by great geese on spits. The sauce-boats were filled to the brim with verjuice and sugared broth. The plates glittered like silver and gold under the flans, custard tarts and rounds of fried pastry. The tankards were steaming, for they were red with warmed wine, and there were jugs of foaming golden hydromel. And along each table, as far as could be seen, among the glassware and the pots of mottled porcelain and enamelware, were naked women bathing their heels in oval bowls. But at the centre, seated half on the women and half on the viands, was a huge black dog, his feet spread wide, bloody-muzzled, baying the moon.

Now the dog bayed in the direction of Demiselle, and Colart stood shuddering between Blancminette and Belotte for, stripping herself naked, Vergensen had darted to the table and kissed the great dog's dark muzzle. And it seemed to the Chevalier that, in reciprocation, the dog bit the Flemish girl on the throat, on which she retained a red triangle, as if she had been marked with a hot iron. Nevertheless Colart seated himself between Belotte and Blancminette and, in a vessel of singular form, they gave him a hot liquor to drink, that tasted of ink. And thereupon he saw that what had seemed to him like a black dog was a green ape with a lashing tail, crouching, with a jaw that cracked and eyes of fire. Many of the guests went to kiss his paw, and he scratched them with his claws about the mouth. Colart de Beaufort recognised there Jehanne d'Auvergne, a well-born lady of Arras, and Huguet Camery, barber, called Patenôtre, and Jehan Le Fevre, *Sergent d'echevins,* and many other magistrates, noblemen, clerks and notables of the city, even to an old painter, Jean Lavite, whom he knew well, who must have been seventy years old, and whose beard was white.

The old painter seemed to be held in great esteem there, and the others called him the Abbé de Peu-de-Sens, and by way of greeting he pulled his cap to the right or the left. Being skilled in rhetoric, he recited many maxims and fine ballades of the carefree life, and one in praise of the Virgin Mary at the end of which he bared his head and said: 'With due deference, Master!' This made Vergensen laugh, and the ape pulled his hair under his hood.

The Abbé de Peu-de-Sens came to the Chevalier, greeted him with respectful zeal under the style of 'fine sir', and told him he wished to bring him to his Master, to do homage, commanding him nevertheless to spit as he went. And Colart, following him, was struck senseless with fear; for on the earth there was a long crucifix upon which the guests set their feet and which they were commanded to defile. Then he went before the green ape and recognised that he had been mistaken, seeing that the ape was in fact a goat with cloven hooves, having, to be sure, a long tail as does an ape. The Abbé de Peu-de-Sens placed two lighted candles in his hands and told him that he should go thus, on his knees, to kiss the goat's rump, which is the fashion of doing him homage. And, Colart bearing the two lighted candles, all the male riders on the left cried out 'Homage! Homage!', and the female riders on the right, 'Our Master! Our Master!' The goat turned about, and Colart obeyed, feeling that his mouth had become burning hot and gave forth smoke.

And that done, the goat summoned the male riders on the left and the female riders on the right and praised Colart for his fidelity; and the Abbé brought forward other neophytes, grasping two candles in their hands, and they kissed the goat in the same manner as the Chevalier. Then, with the naked women and the Abbé, who recited *lais,* they set to, eating and drinking. And suddenly there was a gust of cold wind, and the sky grew grey between the leaves. The riders, male and female, took their besoms between their legs, and Colart found himself once more flying through the morning air. And first Demiselle vanished, then Belotte and Blancminette; but Vergensen had remained with the goat in the wood at Mofflaines.

All these things were confessed by Colart, Chevalier, Seigneur de Beaufort, after which the Bishop of Arras had him put to the question in his prison. For before him Demiselle, Belotte and Blancminette, *filles de joie,* along with the Abbé de Peu-de-Sens, had been delivered to the secular arm. Mitres were placed on their heads on which the

Devil was figured, surrounded by flames, and they were burned at the stake, although the Abbé had cut out his tongue with a small knife so as not to give any answer under torture. As for the blonde Fleming who laughed as she rode to the sabbat, Colart never saw her again. For the Chevalier was not burned. The Duke of Burgundy sent his favourite herald, Toison d'Or, from Brussels to hear his confession. Toison d'Or implored the mercy of the ecclesiastical court. Colart de Beaufort had a mitre upon which the Devil was painted placed upon his head, and he was confined for seven years on bread and water in one of the Bishop of Arras' prisons, called the *Bonnel*.

Blanche the bloody

to Paul Marguerite

After Guillaume de Flavy grew weary of wars and politics he determined to augment his patrimony and take a wife. He was a tall man, and strong, broad in the shoulders, with a hairy, full-breasted chest; setting his two hands on two armed knights, he would force them both to the ground. He would put on his leather leggings and himself make his way over the fields, through the mire, clapping on the back the muddied men that bent among the furrows. His square-set face was red with the blood that constantly pulsed at his temples and, as he ate, he would crack the bones of his meat between his teeth.

One day, near Rheims, riding the confines of his lands, he saw the fields that belonged to Robert d'Ovrebreuc. He dismounted and entered the great hall of the house. Set along the walls, large enough each to hide a man, the great bread-bins were a wretched spectacle; the dining-table was rickety; the fire-irons were rusty; the spit was caked with an inch of filth. Scattered about could be seen a cobbler's apron, awls, some flat-faced hammers; and, in a corner, seated crosslegged, a man was sewing a coarse linen shirt. But squatting on the hearth-stones, her gaze bright and astonished, her golden hair straggling about her pale face, a little girl turned her head towards Guillaume de Flavy. She must have been ten years old; she was flat-chested; her limbs were thin; her hands were small; and her mouth was that of a woman, slashed in her pale features like a bloody wound.

It was Blanche d'Ovrebreuc; a few days previously her father had by succession become vicomte d'Acy. Hump-backed, long-bearded, his hands grown apt only for tools, as regards his fiefs he had the surprised and uneasy look of a man handling a dangerous object. The English squire, Jacques de Béthune, who served under Luxembourg, had already come to demand his daughter and her father, undecided, did not know whether he should expect any better; the estates to which he had succeeded were burdened with debts of three hundred thousand *écus;* the former vicomte d'Acy himself owed fully ten thousand; perhaps the English or the Luxemburgers would take care of that.

But it was Guillaume de Flavy that carried off little Blanche. So as to keep the land, he paid the debts. Having married her according to the law, he gave his word to marry her in fact only after three years. Thus, as a man of impressive bearing, he had laid hands on the fiefs of d'Acy and on a frail, wild, childish creature. Three months later, scowling, with lack-lustre eyes, little Blanche was wandering about the castle like a sick cat, having known the cruel nuptials of Guillaume de Flavy.

She did not and she could not understand. She was completely different in age and in kind. The man treated her harshly, as he did his barber; when, at a table, he had wiped his mouth with the back of his hand, he would fling the food he no longer wanted in the face of the obsequious barber. He bawled and cursed ceaselessly, having retained the management of his wine and his victuals. He piled the plates up before him, leaving Blanche's father and mother at either end of the table – a mother whose head was already nodding and whose bones were already showing through the flesh: she lived on for a while, almost without eating, scarcely speaking, old, mumble-mouthed, grew wan and died. Having wasted away as if he had been taking poison the father, after drinking, signed the deeds in de Flavy's favour; he had surrendered the estates, loaded with debts and, humming a tune, rubbed his hands together over his fine life-annuity. But, no longer eating, he wanted money; the poor bewildered creature protested feebly and, in his trembling hand, composed a scroll of complaints to the king. Guillaume seized the papers in transit; the old man snivelled; the flunkeys placed him in a dungeon and, opening it a month later, found a dried corpse, its teeth fixed in a shoe the toe of which had been gnawed away by the rats.

Little Blanche became extraordinarily greedy. She would eat sweetmeats until she was replete, and she stuffed her blood-red mouth full with round pies and with custards. Elbows on the table, her eyes close to the food, her gaze always limpid, she ate rapidly; then throwing her head back, she would drink wine, *pinet* or *morillon,* in great gulps; one could see the wave of pleasure cross her features; she would upend a goblet of wine into her wide-open mouth below, hold it without swallowing, cheeks puffed-out, and squirt it, like a living fountain, in the faces of the guests. After the meal she would rise, staggering, and being in liquor would piss standing against the wall like a man.

The swarthy and malevolent bastard of Aurbandac, whose eyebrows met in a line above his nose, was taken with her ways. He often visited Flavy, whose relative he was and for whose lands he was impatient. Being supple, wiry, with steel-hard hams and strong wrists, he looked with cynical amusement upon Guillaume's lumbering form. But little Blanche was not roused. Consequently he subtly spoke to her of her clothes; he expressed surprise to see her still dressed in her wedding-outfit (for he saw she had grown in the meantime); he mentioned young *bourgeoises* who had dresses of scarlet, of Malines lace and of fine vair, lined with squirrel-fur – with a hood from the long peak of which a silken veil of red and green hung down to the ground. She listened as if he were speaking of dolls' clothing. Then, glass in hand, the bastard of Aurbandac answered her toast and had her at once drink and laugh, and gave her sweetmeats, scoffing at her husband, so that she sputtered the wine about like a bathing bird flapping its wings in a water-filled rut.

The barber, whose long face bore the marks of mutton-bones, leant between them, and he bent his head close to the bastard's. They plotted the taking of the castle; it would be the bastard's, the wife in her innocence being at the mercy of one and all provided she had the key of the cellar and the pantry.

One evening Guillaume de Flavy tripped at the threshold and fell on his face, laying open his nose and his cheek. He shouted for the barber who, almost at once, brought medicated cloths of a singular odour. In the course of the night Guillaume's face became bloated; the skin was white and taut, streaked with brown; the protruding eyes constantly ran, and the wound had the hideous aspect of gangrene.

All morning he remained in a chair, howling with pain; little Blanche appeared terrified, so much so that she forgot to drink; and from the far side of the room she watched Guillaume, her look fathomless, whilst her lips, bright red, stirred feebly.

Guillaume had scarcely gone upstairs to bed, guarded by the squire Bastoigne, than the castle echoed with countless faint sounds. An ear to the door, a finger to her lips, Blanche listened. The muffled impacts of coats of mail could be heard, and the dull clash of arms; the grille of the heavy postern gate creaked; in the courtyard there was an unaccustomed crackling sound, as of fire; the uncertain light of lanterns came and went. Meanwhile, in the great hall, where the lumps of meat were piled up, the resin torches burnt with an upright flame, leaving a long thread of smoke in the calm air.

With her childish gait Blanche quietly climbed the stairs to her husband's room: he was sleeping on his back, his bloated face, swathed in bandages, turned to the rafters. Bastoigne left since Blanche made as if to go to bed. Indeed she slipped into the bed and took the fearful head in her arms, caressing it. Guillaume was breathing with difficulty, in uneven gasps. Then little Blanche threw herself across him, took the pillow and held it firmly over the swaddled face; and she slid open a Judas, ordinarily closed, above the bed.

The bastard's swarthy head appeared cautiously in the opening. Then, with a leap, he was kneeling on Guillaume's chest, and he struck him twice, three times with the cleft cudgel he carried. The man struggled free of the sheets and a horrible cry burst from his swollen mouth. But the barber, emerging from beneath the bed-trestles, grappled with Bastoigne who had opened the door; and the bastard cut Guillaume's throat with a dagger shaped like a mason's trowel he had in his belt. The body sprang erect and rolled to the floor, carrying with it little Blanche; she remained on the floor, lying under the warm corpse, bathed in the warm blood that flowed from its throat, because her dress was caught beneath her dying husband and she was not strong enough to disengage herself.

While the bastard was making a dash for the window, the attentive barber helped little Blanche to her feet; and since Blanche d'Ovrebreuc, vicomtesse d'Acy, was religious, she wiped her mouth and her husband's face with her Picardy hood, laid it on his swollen face and in her childish voice, amidst the cries of the bastard of Aurbandac's men as they rifled the fodder-boxes, said three *Paters* and an *Ave*.

The Flute

to Rachilde

The storm had driven us very far from the parts where we had been accustomed to pursue our privateering. During those long, sombre days the ship had plunged headlong over masses of green water crested with foam. Even above our heads the black sky seemed to bear down on the Ocean; only the horizon was surrounded by a vivid line, and we wandered about on the deck like shades. Lanterns hung from each yard, and their glasses perpetually ran with raindrops so that what light they gave was uncertain. At the stern the portholes of the steersman's binnacle glowed a transparent and humid red. The tops were half-circles of darkness; the wan sails broke momentarily into view in the gusts of wind.Now and again the lanterns, as they swung, reflected coppery gleams in the pockets of water gathered on the tarpaulins that covered the cannons.

We had driven on before the wind since our last encounter. The grappling-irons still hung all along the hull; and the rainwater, slipping away, had washed and massed together all the debris of the fight. For dead bodies dressed in common cloth, with metal buttons, hatchets, sabres, whistles, loose ends of chains and ropes still lay in the confused agglomeration along with chain-shot; pale hands gripped the butts of pistols, the pommels of swords; faces torn with grapeshot, half covered with hooded cloaks tossed about in the rigging and we slipped on sodden corpses.

The sinister tempest had robbed us of the spirit to clear the decks. We were waiting for the light of day to distinguish our comrades and sew them into their sacks; and the vessel we had taken was laden with rum. A good many casks had been lashed to the foot of the masts, as many to the foremast as to the mizzen mast, and there were many among us, clinging on about them, who held out their mugs or their mouths to the brown jets that gushed out with a liquid gurgle at every pitch.

If the compass did not deceive us the ship was running to the southward; but the darkness and the empty horizon gave us no bearing on the chart. Once we thought we saw dark masses rising to the west; on another occasion, pale sandbanks: but we did not know whether these were mountains or cliffs, and the pallid shade of the sandbanks could have been the lurid sea breaking on rocks.

There were moments when, through the fine rain, we discerned misty-red flares; and the captain hailed the steersman, calling upon him to avoid them. For we knew we were marked out and being pursued; and these fiery points were perhaps fireships, or if we were to pass too close, without seeing them, inhospitable coasts where we might have cause to fear the treacherous signals of wreckers.

We traversed the channel of warm water that runs about the Ocean; for a while the spray was warm. Then, once again, we entered upon the unknown.

And it was then that the captain, not knowing what the future held in store for us, had an assembly piped. There in the night, some of the men bearing lanterns, our troop came together on the poop-deck, and the master-at-arms divided us into groups and dark mutterings could be heard. The purser drew numbers from a powder-bag and called out our shares. Thus each of us received his due from the booty of our voyage, be it of clothing, of provisions, of gold and silver, or of jewelry found on the hands, about the necks or in the pockets of the men and women of the vessels pillaged.

Then we were dismissed, and we departed in silence. It was not thus that the division of spoils was usually made; rather it was done close to our isle of refuge, at the end of an expedition, the ship crammed with riches and amid oaths and bloody disputes. For the first time nobody was knifed, no pistol was discharged.

After the division of the spoils the sky gradually cleared and the darkness began to lift. First some of the clouds rolled away and the mists parted; then the livid circle of the horizon took on a more glaring yellow tint; the Ocean reflected things in less sombre colours. A bright splash of light betokened the sun; in the distance a few rays spread fanwise. The sea-swell was orange-hued, violet and purple; and some of the men cried out in joy, for they saw seaweed floating.

Night fell, stiflingly hot and oppressive, and we were awakened by the pale and blue morning light of the southern seas. Our eyes, unaccustomed to the hot whiteness, pained us; and we were swinging in our hammocks, seeing nothing, when our look-out man cried: 'Land straight ahead!' An hour later, the sky being an intense blue, we discerned a brown line where the Ocean ended, with an edging of foam.

We turned our prow upon it. Red and white birds were skimming among the gear. Scraps of multicoloured wood drifted on the waves. Then a moving point appeared: on the utterly opaque sea, under the incandescent sun, it seemed pink-coloured; and when it drew closer we saw it was a canoe or pirogue. The craft had no sail, and it appeared to be without oars.

However it was moving on our beam; but when we hailed it, nothing could be seen in it. As we drew closer though, we heard a sweet and peaceable sound borne on the breeze, a sound so modulated that it could not be confused with the plaint of the sea or the vibration of the ropes stretched at our sails. The calm, sad sound attracted our comrades to the two sides of the vessel, and we gazed curiously at the pirogue.

When the forecastle went down into the trough of a great wave, the mystery of the craft was made plain: she was of coloured wood; the oars seemed to have broken adrift, and an old man lay in it, one foot resting on the bar of the rudder. His white beard and hair framed his whole visage; save for a striped cloak the two lappets of which were wrapped about him, he wore no clothing; and in his two hands he held a flute, into which he was blowing.

Without a move from him we made the pirogue fast. His eyes were vague, and perhaps he was blind. He must have been a great age, for the tendons of his limbs showed through the skin. We hoisted him up to the deck and laid him out on a tarred sail, next to the mainmast.

Then, still holding the flute to his lips with one hand, he stretched out an arm and gropingly felt all about him. And he fumbled at the confusion of weapons, of chain-shot and of corpses becoming tepid in the sun; his fingers moved over the cutting edges of axes and caressed the contused flesh of faces. And then he withdrew his hand and, his eyes pale and vacant, his face turned towards the sky, he played on his flute.

It was black and white: and as soon as it began to sound among us, it was like a bird of polished ebony, spotted with ivory, and the transparent hands, fluttering about it, were like wings.

The first sound was shrill and thin, tremulous as the old man's voice must have been, and our hearts were penetrated by the past, with the remembrance of the old women who had been our grandmothers and the innocent times when we were children. All the present subsided about us; and, smiling, we nodded our heads; our fingers made as if to play with toys and our lips were half-closed, as if for childhood kisses.

Next the sound of the flute filled out and was a cry of tumultuous passion. Yellow things, and red, flitted before our eyes, the colour of flesh, the colour of gold, and the colour of blood. Our hearts swelled, responding in unison, and the follies of the days that had seduced us into crime whirled around in our heads. And the sound of the flute mounted and was the sonorous voice of storms and the call of the wind to the breaking of the waves, the din of hulls burst open, the howling of men whose throats have been cut, the terror of soot-blackened faces boarding the enemy ship, sabres between their teeth, the whining of chain-shot and the explosion of air in the shells of ships going down. And we listened in silence, in the midst of our own life.

All at once the sound of the flute was a mewling cry; we heard the lamentation of children coming into the world, a cry so feeble and plaintive that there was a yell of horror. For in a single moment, our vision suddenly enlightened by the future we saw what we could no longer have and that which we were eternally destroying, the death of hope for those who roam the seas, and the future existences we had destroyed. We ourselves, without wives, red with murder, bloated with gold, could never hear the voices of newborn children: for we were damned to the rocking of the waves, whether the deck danced under our feet or our head, topped with a black cap, danced at the end of a rope hanging from a yard; our lives were lost, without the hope of creating other lives.

And Hubert, the master-at-arms, cursed vilely and snatched the ebony bird spotted with white from the old man: the sound perished, and Hubert flung the flute into the sea. The old man's unfocussed eyes jerked and his ancient limbs stiffened, without our hearing a sound. When we touched him he was already cold.

I do not know whether this strange man belonged to the Ocean, but the moment he touched it – when we sent him to join his flute – he sank and vanished along with his cloak and his pirogue; and never again did the cry of a child being born reach our ears, on land or on the sea.

The Sleeping City*

to Léon Daudet

Under the clear blue light of the dawn the coast was steep and sombre. The Captain of the pirate vessel gave the order to make landfall. Since the compasses had been smashed in the last storm, we no longer knew in which direction we were sailing, nor the name of the territory spread out before us. The ocean was so green that we might have believed ourselves, by the enchantment, sailing in deep waters. But the sight of that dark cliff troubled us; those who had spent the previous night over the tarot cards; those who had been drunk on the plant that grows in their native land; those who, though there were no women aboard, were dressed in an unaccustomed fashion; those who were mute, having had a nail driven through their tongue; and those who, having walked the buccaneers' narrow plank above the abyss, were still crazed with terror; all our comrades, black or yellow, white or red, leaning on the gunwales, regarded the new country with uncertain eyes.

Being of all nations, of every colour, speaking every language, not having even gestures in common, they were bound only by a like passion and common murders. For so many were the vessels they had sunk, so many the bulwarks they had reddened by the bloody blades of thier axes, the lockers they had burst open with their crowbars, the men they had silently strangled in their hammocks, the galleons they had taken by noisy assault, that they were one in action; they were like a colony of noxious and disparate animals inhabiting a little floating island, habituated one to the other, without conscience, but with a total instinct guided by the eyes of one alone.

They were ceaselessly active and they no longer thought. All day and all night they were crowded together. There was no silence in their ship, but the prodigious and continuous roaring; to them no doubt silence would have been baneful. In foul weather they had the struggle to steer the ship amid the waves; and in fair, resounding drunkenness and discordant songs; and when they encountered ships, there was the crash of battle.

All this the Captain of the pirate vessel knew, and he alone

---

*These pages were found in an oblong book with wooden covers; the greater part of the leaves were blank. A skull and crossbones were crudely carved on the upper cover and the book was found protruding from the sands of a hitherto unexplored desert.

understood it; he himself lived only in uproar, and his horror of silence was such that in the quiet of the night he would tug at the long robe of his hammock-neighbour in order to hear the inarticulate sound of a human voice.

The constellations of the far hemisphere paled. An incandescent sun pierced the great sheet of the sky, now a profound blue, and the Comrades of the Sea, having cast anchor, launched narrowboats towards a little cove that divided the cliff.

A rocky defile opened at that point, the vertical walls of which were so high that they seemed to meet in the air above; but instead of experiencing there a subterranean cool, the Captain and his companions suffered the oppression of an extraordinary heat, and the tiny streams of sea-water that filtered through the sand dried so quickly that the entire beach gave off a dry, crackling sound, as did the soil of the gorge.

This rocky passage opened out onto a flat and sterile country, surrounded at the horizon by low, rounded hills. A few clumps of grey vegetation sprouted at the cliff's edge; minute creatures, brown, squat or elongated, with fine, quivering, gauzy wings or high-stepping, jointed legs buzzed about the velvety leaves or, here and there, disturbed the soil.

Inanimate nature no longer had the moving life of the sea or the crepitous sound of the sand; the breeze of the open sea was cut short by the barrier of the cliffs; the plants were as if fixed in the rock and the brown creatures, winged or creeping, were confined to a narrow band beyond which there was no more movement.

Now if the Captain of the pirate vessel had not thought, despite his not knowing in which country they were, that the last bearings of the compasses had been taking the ship in the direction of Eldorado, where the Comrades of the Sea all desired to make landfall, he would not have pushed the adventure further, and the silence of those lands would have terrified him.

But he thought that unknown coast was the edge of Eldorado, and to his companions he spoke excited words that implanted various desires in their hearts. We marched with heads lowered, suffering from the calm; for the horrors of life gone by welled up tumultuous within us.

At the extremity of the plain we met with a rampart of glittering golden sand. From the already parched lips of the Comrades of the Sea a cry arose; an abrupt cry that died on the instant, as if choked in the air since in that land where silence seemed to augment itself there was no echo.

The Captain believing that beyond those sand-dunes the auriferous earth was richer, the Comrades scrambled painfully up; the earth slid away under our feet.

And on the far side we met with a strange surprise; for the sandy rampart was the abutment of the walls of a city, whence gigantic steps led down from the sentries' walkway.

No rumour of life arose from the midst of that immense city. Our steps sounded on the marble paving-stones as we went – and the sound fell away. The city was not dead, for the streets were filled with wagons, with men and with animals: pale bakers carrying round loaves; butchers bearing on their heads red briskets of beef; brickmakers bent over flat trolleys on which rows of scintillating bricks intercrossed; fish-dealers with their trays; women hawking salted goods, their skirts tucked up and with ragged straw hats set high on their heads; slave porters bent under litters draped with metallic cloths; runners arrested in mid pace; veiled women, still pushing aside with a finger the fold covering their eyes; horses, rearing or at draught in a harness of heavy chains; dogs, muzzle raised or fangs bared. Now all these figures were motionless, as if in the gallery of a sculptor who shaped waxen statues; their movement lay in the intense liveliness of their gesture, brusquely arrested; they were distinguished from the living only by their immobility and their colour.

For those whose faces had been high-coloured were grown completely red, the flesh bloodshot; and those who had been pale had grown livid, the blood having rushed to their hearts; those whose face had been of a sombre hue now showed the world rigid features of ebony; and those the sun had tanned had abruptly turned yellow-skinned and their cheeks were citron-coloured; so that among all those red men, white men, black men and yellow, the Comrades of the Sea were like living and active beings in the midst of an assembled multitude of the dead.

The terrible calm of that city caused us to quicken our pace, to thresh our arms about, to cry out confused words, to laugh, to weep, to toss our heads as madmen do; we thought the artificial agitation might hold in check our sinister reflections; we sought to deliver ourselves from the curse of silence; we thought that one of those men who had been living might have shown us some response. But the great abandoned gates gaped open upon our path; the windows were like closed eyes; the watchtowers on the roofs stretched indolently up towards the sky. The air, it seemed, had the weight of some corporeal thing. The birds, gliding above the streets, between the pilasters, the flies, suspended motionless, were like multicoloured creatures suspended in a block of crystal.

And the somnolence of that sleeping city spread in our limbs a profound lassitude. The horror of silence enveloped us. We who would seek in active life forgetfulness of our crimes, we who would drink the waters of Lethe, tinged with narcotic poisons and blood, we who on the sea's breaking waves would pursue an ever-new existence, were within a few moments made fast by invincible bonds.

Now the silence that took us in its thrall put the Comrades of the Sea in a frenzy. And from among the peoples of the four colours that stared at us immobile, they each chose in dismayed flight the memory of their distant land; those who were of Asia clasped the yellow men and took on the colour of impure wax; and those of Africa seized the black men and became dark as ebony; and those from the land situated beyond Atlantis embraced the red men and were statues of mahogany; and those from the land of Europe threw their arms about the white men and their faces became the colour of pure wax.

But I, the Captain of the pirate vessel, who have no country nor any memories that can induce me to tolerate silence as my thought keeps vigil, fled headlong, terrified, far from the Comrades of the Sea, beyond the sleeping city; despite the sleep and the fearful lassitude that are gaining on me, as I go on across the undulations of the golden sand, I am seeking the green sea that eternally moves and tosses its foam.

from
LES VIES IMAGINAIRES
1896

Introduction

Historical science leaves us in a state of uncertainty concerning individuals. It lays bare to us only the points by which they were attached to general events. It tells us that Napoleon was in pain on the day of Waterloo, that we must attribute Newton's excessive intellectual activity to the absolute continence of his temperament, that Alexander was drunk when he killed Klitos, and that certain of Louis XIV's shifts of policy may have been caused by his fistula. Pascal speculates about how things might have turned out had Cleopatra's nose been shorter, and about the grain of sand in Cromwell's urethra. All these individual facts are important only because they have influenced events, or because they could have influenced the order of events. They are real or possible causes. They must be left to scholars.

Art is opposed to general ideas, describes only the individual, desires only the unique. It does not classify: it *de*classifies. So far as we are concerned, our general ideas might be like those that obtain on the planet Mars, yet three lines that intersect form a triangle at whatever point in the universe. But take the leaf of a tree, with its capriciously-wandering veins, its colours varied by sunlight and shadow, the swelling raised by the fall of a raindrop, the perforation left by an insect, the silvery trail left by a little snail, the first mortal gilding that betokens autumn. Now look for a leaf exactly similar in all particulars: I defy you to find one in all the great forests of the earth. There is no science of the teguments of a foliole, of the filaments of a cell, of the curve of a vein, of the idiosyncrasy of a habit, of the oddities of a character. That such-a-one had a crooked nose, that he had one eye higher than the other, that he had rheumatic nodules in the joints of his arm, that at such-an-hour he customarily ate a *blanc-de-poulet,* that he preferred Malvoisie to Château Margaux – there is something unparalleled in all the world. Thales might just as well have said ΓΝΩΘΙ ΣΕΑΥΤΟΝ as Socrates; but he would not have rubbed his leg in the same way, in prison, before drinking the hemlock. The ideas of great men are the common patrimony of all mankind; all they possessed that was really their own was their eccentricities. The book that would describe a man in all his anomalies would be a work of art like a Japanese print in which one sees, for all eternity, the image of a little caterpillar, seen once, at a particular hour of the day.

History-books remain silent about these things. In the rough-and-ready compilation of materials furnished by the evidence there are not very many singular and inimitable breaks with convention. The ancient biographers above all were miserly. Holding scarcely anything in esteem but public life and grammar, they hand down to us great men's discourses and the titles of their books. It is Aristophanes himself who has given us the delight of knowing he was bald, and if Socrates' snub nose had not served the purpose of literary comparisons, if his habit of going barefoot had not been part and parcel of his philosophical system of contempt for the body, we would have conserved nothing of him beyond his moral questionings. Suetonius' tittle-tattle is nothing more than hate-inspired polemic. Plutarch's good genius sometimes made him an artist; but he could not understand the essence of his art, for he imagined 'parallels' – as if two men, properly described in all their details, could resemble one another! One is reduced to consulting Athenaeus, Aulus Gellius, some scholiasts, and Diogenes Laertius, who believed he had composed some species of history of philosophy.

The feeling for the individual is more developed in modern times. Boswell's work would be perfect if he had not judged it necessary to cite therein Johnson's correspondence and to include digressions on his books. Aubrey's *Brief Lives* are more satisfying. Aubrey had, beyond doubt, the biographer's instinct. How tiresome it is that this excellent antiquary's style should not measure up to his conception! But for this his book would be the eternal recreation of sagacious minds. Aubrey never felt the need to establish a relation between individual details and general ideas. It sufficed him that others should have marked for celebrity the men that took his interest. The greater part of the time one is not concerned whether he treats of a mathematician, a man of state, a clockmaker or a poet. But each of them has his unique trait that marks him off forever among men.

The painter Hokusai hoped, when he reached the age of a hundred and ten, to achieve the ideal of his art. At that moment, he said, every point, every line traced by the brush would be alive. For alive, read individual. There is nothing more alike than points and lines: geometry is founded on this postulate. Hokusai's perfect art demanded that nothing should be more different. Thus, the biographer's ideal would be infinitely to differentiate the aspect of two philosophers who had invented as near as may be the same metaphysical system.

This is why Aubrey, who was concerned only with men, did not achieve perfection, since he did not succeed in accomplishing the miraculous transformation of resemblance into diversity to which Hokusai aspired. But Aubrey did not reach the age of a hundred and ten. He is nonetheless much to be esteemed, and he realised the compass of his book. 'I remember one saying' he says in his preface to Anthony Wood, 'of General Lambert's, that "the best of men are but men at the best"; of this you will meet with divers examples in this rude and hastie collection. Now these Arcana are not fitt to lett flie abroad, till about 30 yeares hence, for the author and the Persons (like Medlars) ought to be rotten first.'

We may discover among Aubrey's predecessors some elements of his art. Thus Diogenes Laertius teaches us that Aristotle wore on his stomach a leather purse filled with heated oil, and that, after his death, a good number of earthenware vases were found in his house. We will never know what Aristotle did with all these pots. And the mystery is as pleasurable as the conjectures to which Boswell abandons us concerning the use Johnson made of the dried orange-peel he liked to keep in his pockets. Here Diogenes Laertius rises almost to the heights of the inimitable Boswell. But these are rare pleasures. Whilst Aubrey gives us such joys in every line. Milton, he tells us, 'pronounced the letter R (littera canina) very hard'. Spenser 'was a little man, wore short haire, little band, and little cuffs'. Barclay 'was in England *tempore regis Jacobi.* He was then an old man, white beard; and wore a hatt and a feather, which gave some severe people offence.' Erasmus 'loved not Fish, though borne in a Fish-towne'. As for Bacon, 'None of his servants durst appeare before him without Spanish leather bootes; for he could smelle the neates leather,which offended him.' Doctor Fuller had 'a very working head, in so much that, walking and meditating before dinner, he would eate-up a penny loafe, not knowing that he did it'. He remarked of Sir William Davenant: 'I was at his funerall. He had a coffin of Walnutt-tree; Sir John Denham sayd "'twas the finest coffin that ever he sawe."' Regarding Ben Jonson he wrote: 'I have heard Mr Lacy, the Player, say that he was wont to weare a coate like a coachman's coate, with slitts under the arme-pitts.' This is what struck him about William Prynne: 'His manner of studie was thus: he wore a long quilt cap, which came two or three, at least, inches over his eies, which served him as an Umbrella to defend his Eies from the light. About every three houres his man was to bring him a roll and a pott of Ale to refocillate his wasted spirits; so he studied and dranke, and munched some bread; and this maintained him till night, and then he made a good Supper.' Hobbes became very bald in his old age; nevertheless it was his custom, at home, to study bareheaded, and he said that he never caught a chill, but that his greatest trouble was in preventing the flies from landing on his bald pate. He says nothing of James Harrington's *Oceana,* but tells us that the author, 'Anno Domini 1661 ... was committed prisoner to the Tower: then to Portsey castle.His durance in these prisons (he being a Gentleman of high spirit and a hot head) was the procatractique cause of his deliration or madness; which was not outragious, for he would discourse rationally enough and be very facetious company, but he grew to have a phancy that his Perspiration turned to Flies, and sometimes to Bees; and he had a versatile timber house built in Mr Hart's garden (opposite to St James's parke) to try the experiment. He would turn it to the sun, and sitt towards it; then he had his fox-tayles there to chase away and massacre all the Flies and Bees that were to be found there, and then shut his *Chassees.* Now this experiment was only to be tried in Warme weather, and some flies would lye so close in the cranies and cloath (with which it was hung) that they would not presently shew themselves. A quarter of an hour after perhaps, a fly or two, or more, might be drawen out of the lurking holes by the warmeth; and he would cry out, Doe not you see it apparently that these come from me?'

This is all he tells us of Meriton: 'his true name was Head. He had been amongst the Gipsies. He looked like a knave with his gogling eies. He could transforme himselfe into any shape. Brake 2 or 3 times. Was at last a Bookseller in Little Britaine, or towards his latter end. He maintained himselfe by Scribbling: 20s per sheet. He wrote many bookes: *The English Rogue, The Art of Wheadling,* etc. He was drowned goeing to Plymouth by long Sea about 1676, being about 50 yeares of age.'

Finally we must cite his biography of Descartes:

M^{eur} Renatus Des Cartes

'Nobilis Gallus, Perroni Dominus, summus Mathematicus et Philosophicus, Natus Turonum, pridie Calendas Aprilis 1596. Denatus Holmiae, Calendis Februarii, 1650. (I find this inscription beneath his portrait by C. V. Dalen.) How he passed his time in his youth and by what means he became so learned, he tells the world in his treatise entitled *On Method*. The Societie of Jesus glorie in that their order had the educating of him.He lived many years at Egmont (close to The Hague), from where he dates many of his books. He was too wise a man to encumber himselfe with a Wife; but he was a man and had the desires and appetites of a man; he therefore kept a good conditioned hansome woman that he liked, and by whom he had some Children (I think 2 or 3). 'Tis pity but comeing from the Braine of such a father, they should not be well cultivated. He was so eminently learned that all learned men made visits to him, and many of them would desire him to shew them his Instruments (in those days mathematicall learning lay much in the knowledge of Instruments, and, as Sir Henry Saville sayd, in doeing of tricks) he would drawe out a little Drawer under his Table, and shew them a paire of Compasses with one of the Legges broken; and then, for his Ruler, he used a sheet of paper folded double.'

It is clear that Aubrey was perfectly aware of what he was about: do not suppose that he misapprehended the value of Descartes' or Hobbes' philosophical ideas. It was not there that his interest lay. He tells us very plainly that Descartes himself has explained his method to the world. He is not unaware that Harvey discovered the circulation of the blood; but he prefers to note that the great man spent his sleepless nights walking about in his shirt, that he wrote a very bad hand, and that the best physicians of London would not have given threepence for one of his prescriptions. He is convinced he had enlightened us about Francis Bacon when he explains that Bacon had a delicate, lively hazel eye, 'like that of a viper'. But he was not so great an artist as Holbein. He did not know how to fix an individual for eternity, by his special traits, against a background of resemblance to the ideal. He gives life to an eye, a nose, a leg, to his models' pouts: he does not know how to give life to the whole figure. The old Hokusai saw clearly that it was necessary to succeed in making individual that which was most general. Aubrey had not the same penetration. If Boswell's book took up ten pages it would be the book we were looking for. Doctor Johnson's common sense comprises the vulgarest of commonplaces; expressed with the bizarre violence that Boswell has the art to depict, it has a quality unique in this world. Only this ponderous catalogue resembles the doctor's dictionary; from it one could extract a *Scientia Johnsoniana*, with an index. Boswell has not had the aesthetic courage to select.

The art of the biographer consists precisely in choice. It is not for it to be preoccupied with veracity; it must create out of a chaos of human traits. In creating the world, Leibniz said, God chose the best among those possible. The biographer, like a minor divinity, has the capacity of choosing among human possibilities that which is unique. He must no more be mistaken as regards art than God is mistaken regarding goodness. It is necessary that, in both cases, the instinct be infallible. For the biographer, patient demiurges have assembled ideas, quirks of the physiognomy, events. Their work is to be found in the chronicles, the memoirs, the correspondence and the *scholia*. The biographer, in the midst of this wholesale assembly, sorts it over, seeking the wherewithal to put together a form unlike any other. Provided it be unique, like every other creation, there is no point in its being comparable to that already created by a superior god.

Unfortunately biographers have for the most part taken themselves for historians: and thus they have deprived us of admirable portraits. They have supposed that only the lives of great men should interest us. Art is alien to such consideration. In the eyes of a painter Cranach's portrait of an unknown man is every bit as valuable as the portrait of Erasmus. It is not thanks to Erasmus' name that this picture is inimitable. The biographer's art should be such as to set as high a price on the life of a poor actor as on that of Shakespeare. It is an abject instinct that makes us note with pleasure the foreshortening of the sterno-mastoid bone in the bust of Alexander, or the forelock in the portrait of Napoleon. The Mona Lisa smile, of which we know nothing (the face is, perhaps, that of a man) is more mysterious. A grimace drawn by Hokusai evokes profounder meditations. Were we to practise the art in which Boswell and Aubrey excelled we should, beyond doubt, not have to describe in minute detail the characteristics of the most celebrated men of the past but, with the same minuteness, tell of the *unique* existence of men, be they divine, mediocrities, or criminals.

Empedocles, reputed god

No one knew what was his birth or how he came upon earth. He appeared near the gilded banks of the River Acragas, in the very beautiful city of Agrigentum, a little after the time when Xerxes had the sea beaten with chains. Tradition reports only that his grandfather was called Empedocles; no one knew him. No doubt we must understand by this that he was his own son, as befits a god. But his disciples are certain that, before travelling the lands of Sicily in his glory, he had already lived four existences in our world, and that he had been plant, fish, bird and young girl. He wore a purple mantle upon which his long hair hung down; about his head he had a band of gold, on his feet were sandals of bronze, and he held garlands of wool woven with bays.

He healed the sick by the laying on of hands and, mounted on a chariot, he recited verses in the Homeric manner, in high-flown tones and with his head raised towards the heavens. A great crowd of people followed him and fell down before him to hear his poems. Under the pure sky that lights the cornfields, men came to Empedocles from all parts, their arms filled with offerings. He kept them spellbound and gaping open-mouthed, singing to them of the divine dome made of crystal, the mass of fire we call the sun, and love, which like a vast sphere contains all.

All beings, he said, were but disjunct morsels of this sphere of love, into which hate had crept. And that which we call love is the desire to unite ourselves, to merge and intermingle, to be as we once were in the depths of the globular deity that discord has sundered. He invoked the day when, after all the transformations of souls, the divinised sphere would inflate. For the world we know is the work of hate, and its dissolution will be the work of love. Thus he sang in the towns and in the fields. And his bronze sandals from Laconia rang at his feet, and before him cymbals sounded. Meanwhile a column of black smoke sprang up from Etna and cast its shadow over Sicily.

Like a king of heaven, Empedocles was wrapped round in purple and girt in gold, whilst the Pythagoreans trailed about in their tunics of thin linen and their shoes made of papyrus. It was said that he knew how to drive away bleariness of the eyes, to dissolve tumours and relieve pains in the limbs; they supplicated him to cause rains and hurricanes to cease; he conjured storms over a circle of hillocks; at Selinonte he expelled the fever, diverting two rivers into the bed of a third; and the inhabitants of Selinonte adored him, and raised a temple to him, and struck medals upon which his image was placed face-to-face with the image of Apollo.

Others claimed that he was a diviner and that he was taught by the magicians of Persia, that he possessed the arts of necromancy and the science of herbs that induce madness. One day when he was dining with Auchitos, a raving madman rushed into the hall, sword held aloft. Empedocles rose, extended his arms and chanted the verses of Homer on the herb nepenthe that brings insensibility. And immediately the power of nepenthe took hold of the madman and, forgetting all, he remained fixed, sword in the air, as if he had drunk the sweet poison blended in the sparkling wine of a mixing-bowl.

Outside the cities the sick came to him, and he was surrounded by a crowd of the poor. Some women mingled with his followers. They would kiss the hem of his precious mantle. One of them, the daughter of a noble of Agrigentum, was called Panthea. She was to be consecrated to Artemis, but she fled far from the cold statue of the goddess and dedicated her virginity to Empedocles. The signs of their love no one ever saw, for Empedocles maintained a divine in-appetency. He uttered words only in epic metre and in the dialect of Ionia, although the people and his followers employed only Dorian. All his gestures were sacred. When he approached men it was to pronounce blessings upon them or to heal them. The greater part of the time he remained silent. None of those who followed him ever came upon him asleep. They never saw him otherwise than majestic.

Panthea was clothed in fine wool and in gold. Her hair was dressed after the opulent fashion of Agrigentum, where life was lived leisurely. A red strophion supported her breasts, and the soles of her sandals were scented. For the rest she was beautiful, tall and slim, and of a most desirable colour. It is impossible to affirm that Empedocles loved her, but he had pity on her. It happened that a wind blowing from the east engendered the plague in the fields of Sicily. Many men were touched by the plague's black fingers. At the meadows' edges the corpses of cattle lay scattered, and here and there the bloated carcasses of sheep were to be seen, shorn and gaping to the skies, bare of their fleeces, their ribs poking through their sides. Panthea fell ill of that malady and languished. She fell at the feet of Empedocles and ceased breathing. Those who surrounded her lifted up her stiffened limbs and bathed them in wine and aromatic spices. They loosened the red strophion that bound her youthful breasts and wound her in bandages. And her open mouth was fastened with a cord, and her eyes no longer looked upon the light.

Empedocles looked closely at her, took off the band of gold that encircled his forehead, and placed it upon her. On her breasts he laid the garland of prophetic laurel; and he chanted unknown verses on the transmigration of souls, and three times he called upon her to rise and walk. The crowd was filled with terror. At the third call Panthea left the realm of shadows and her body, all enfolded in the funerary windings, took on life and she rose up on her feet. And the people saw that Empedocles was a raiser of the dead.

Psianacte, father of Panthea, came to adore the new god. Tables were laid out under the trees of his country to offer him libations. At Empedocles' sides slaves raised great torches. As at the celebration of the mysteries, the heralds proclaimed solemn silence. Suddenly, at the third watch, the torches were extinguished and night enveloped the worshippers. There was a great voice that called out 'Empedocles!' When it was light, Empedocles had vanished. Men never saw him again.

A terrified slave told how he had seen a red streak of fire in the darkness near the summit of Etna. In the dreary light of the dawn the faithful climbed the mountain's sterile slopes. The crater of the volcano vomited forth a shower of flames. On the lip of porous lava that encircles the fiery abyss they found a bronze sandal warped and twisted by the fire.

Herostratos, incendiary

The town of Ephesus, where Herostratos was born, stretched along the mouth of the Caÿster to the quays of Panormus whence, over the deep-tinted sea, one could see the hazy line of Samos. Since the time when the Magnesians with their war-dogs and their javelin-throwing slaves had been defeated on the banks of the Meander, since the laying in ruins by the Persians of the magnificent Miletus, it had overflowed with gold and cloth, with linen and with roses. It was a lax city where the courtesans were feted in the temple of Aphrodite Hetaera. The Ephesians wore transparent amorgine tunics, linen robes, spun on a spinning-wheel, violet-coloured, purple and saffron, sarapids of a golden-apple colour, and white and pink, Egyptian fabrics, hyacinth-coloured with blazes of fire and the shifting nuances of the sea, and closely-woven Persian calasiris, light,sprinkled on their ground with grains of fine gold.

Between Mount Prion and a high, scarped cliff, on the bank of the Caÿster could be seen the great temple of Artemis. It had taken a hundred and twenty years to build it. Austere paintings embellished the inner chambers, whose ceilings were of ebony and of cypress-wood. The heavy columns that sustained it had been daubed with minium. The hall of the goddess was small and oval. In the middle stood a prodigious black stone, shining and conical, marked with gilt moons; this was Artemis. The triangular altar too was cut from a black stone. Other tables, fashioned from black flagstones, were pierced with regularly-spaced holes to drain away the blood of the victims. Broad blades of steel with handles of gold, that served to cut throats, hung from the walls, and the polished floor was strewn with bloody bandages. The great dark stone had two hard and pointed breasts. Such was the Artemis of Ephesus. Her origin was lost in the night of Egyptian tombs, and it was necessary that she be worshipped according to the rites of the Persians. She possessed a treasure shut up in a kind of green-painted hive whose pyramidal door bristled with bronze nails. There, among the rings, the great coins and the rubies lay the manuscript of Heraklitos, who had proclaimed the supremacy of fire. The philosopher himself had placed it there, at the base of the pyramid, while it was being built.

Herostratos' mother was violent and proud. It was not known who was his father. Herostratos later declared that he was the son of fire. His body was marked, under the left breast, with a crescent; when he was tortured this appeared to blaze. Those who were present at his birth foretold that he would be under the governance of Artemis. He was choleric and remained a virgin. His face was etched with indistinct lines and his skin was a blackish colour. From his childhood he had loved to stand under the high cliff, close to the Artemision. He would watch the processions going by with offerings. Because his lineage was unknown, he could not become a priest of the goddess to whom he believed he was dedicated. Many times the priestly college had been obliged to forbid him entry to the *naos,* where he hoped to draw aside the heavy and precious cloth that veiled Artemis. He conceived a hatred for them and vowed to violate the secret.

Just as his own person appeared to him superior to all humanity, so Herostratos' name appeared to him incomparable to any other. He desired fame. At first he attached himself to the philosophers who taught the doctrine of Heraklitos; but they did not comprehend its secret part, for that was enclosed in the little pyramidal cell of the treasury of Artemis. Herostratos merely guessed at the opinion of the master. He grew hard in contempt of the riches that surrounded him. His disgust for the love of courtesans was extreme. Men thought he was preserving his virginity for the goddess. But Artemis showed him no mercy. To the college of the Gerousia who watched over the temple he seemed dangerous. The satrap granted permission for his exile to the suburbs. He lived on the slopes of Koressos, in a vault dug out by men of old. From there, at night, he would watch the lamps of the Artemision. Some believe that Persian initiates came there to converse with him. But it is more probable that his destiny was revealed to him in a moment.

In fact he admitted under torture that he had suddenly grasped the meaning of Heraklitos' words *'the way on high',* and why the philosopher had taught that the greatest soul was the driest and the most fiery. He attested that, in this sense, his was the most perfect soul, and that he wished to proclaim this. He gave no other cause for his action than the passion for fame and the joy of hearing his name uttered. He said that his reign alone would have been absolute, since they did not know who was his father and Herostratos would have been crowned by Herostratos, that he was the son of his deed and that his deed was the essence of the world: that, thus, he would have been all-in-one, king, philosopher and god, unique among men.

In the year 356, on the night of the 21st of July, the moon had not yet risen in the sky and, Herostratos' desire having assumed an unaccustomed strength, he resolved to break into the sacred chamber of Artemis. So it was that, by a winding mountain path he slipped down to the banks of the Caÿster and climbed the steps of the temple. The priests' guards were sleeping by the sacred lamps: Herostratos took one up and penetrated into the *naos*.

There was a powerful scent of oil of nard. The edges of the ebony beams glittered. The oval chamber was divided by a curtain of purple and cloth-of-gold that hid the goddess. Panting with delight, Herostratos tore it down. His lamp illuminated the terrible, erect-breasted cone. Herostratos seized the breasts in both hands and avidly embraced the divine stone. Then he turned about, and he saw the green pyramid where the treasure was. He grasped the bronze nails of the little door and loosened them. He dabbled his fingers among the virgin jewels. But he took only the papyrus roll upon which Heraklitos had inscribed his verses. By the light of the sacred lamp he read them, and he knew all.

He at once cried out: 'Fire! Fire!'

He took the curtain of Artemis and applied the lighted lamp-wick to the lower hem. At first the stuff burnt slowly; then, because of the perfumed vapours of oil with which it was saturated, the flame mounted, bluish, towards the ebony panelling. The terrible cone reflected the flames.

The flame lapped about the capitals of the columns, crawled along the vaulting. With a metallic clatter, one by one the plates of gold dedicated to the powerful Artemis fell upon the flagstones. Then the fiery sheaf burst out from the roof and lit up the cliff-face. The bronze tiles caved in. Herostratos stood erect in the glare, roaring out his name to the night.

The entire Artemision stood, a red heap in the midst of darkness. The guards laid hands on the criminal. To prevent him from crying out his own name, they gagged him. While the fire continued he was thrown, bound, into the cellars.

Artaxerxes immediately sent an order that he be tortured. He would admit only what has been said. Under pain of death the twelve cities of

Ionia forbade that the name of Herostratos be handed down to future ages. But rumour has brought it down to us. The night that Herostratos set fire to the temple at Ephesus, Alexander, King of Macedonia, was born.

Crates, cynic

He was born in Thebes, was a disciple of Diogenes, and also knew Alexander. His father, Ascondas, was rich and left him two hundred talents. One day, when he went to see a tragedy of Euripides, he was inspired at the sight of Telephos, king of Mysia, dressed in a beggar's rags and carrying a basket in his hand. He stood up in the theatre and announced in a loud voice that he would make over his two hundred talents inheritance to whoever should want them, and that henceforth Telephos' garments would suffice him. The Thebans laughed, and they thronged together outside the house; he, however, laughed even more than they did. He threw his money and furniture out of the windows, took a mantle of coarse cloth and a beggar's scrip, and went on his way.

When he reached Athens he wandered about the streets, resting among the excrement, leaning his back against the wall. He put into practice everything Diogenes preached. Diogenes' barrel he thought superfluous. According to Crates' view man was neither a snail nor a hermit-crab. He lived stark naked among the sweepings, and he collected crusts of bread, rotten olives and dried fishbones to fill his wallet. This scrip, he said, was a spacious and opulent town in which no whores or parasites were to be found and which produced for its king a sufficiency of thyme, garlic, figs and bread. Thus it was that Crates carried his realm on his back and nourished himself thereon.

He did not meddle in public affairs, even to make a mock of them, and he did not affect to insult kings. He did not approve of that characteristic behaviour of Diogenes who, having one day shouted out 'Come closer, men', laid about those who came with his stick and said, 'It was men I summoned, not shits.' Crates was kindly disposed towards mankind. Nothing bothered him. He was perfectly accustomed to sores; his great regret was that his body was not supple enough to allow of his licking them, like the dogs. He likewise deplored the necessity of taking solid food and drinking water. He thought man should be sufficient unto himself, without need of external aid. At all events he did not go out of his way to get water to wash himself. Having noted that the asses did so, he was content to rub himself against the walls, if his filth made him uncomfortable. He rarely spoke of the gods, and he did not concern himself with them. Whether or not they existed worried him little, and he knew well that they could not harm him. He reproached them, moreover, with having deliberately made men miserable by raising their gaze to the heavens and depriving them of the capacity common to most of the four-footed beasts; since the gods have decided that one must eat to live, they should have turned men's faces towards the earth, where the roots grow: men cannot feed on the air or on the stars.

Life was not kind to him. His eyes ran with rheum through exposure to the acrid dust of Attica. An unknown skin-disease covered him with swellings. He scratched himself with nails he never trimmed and remarked that from this he drew a double profit, since he wore them down and at the same time experienced relief. His long hair became like a thick covering of felt, and he arranged it on his head in such a way as to protect him from the rain and the sun.

When Alexander came to see him he did not favour him with any pointed remarks but looked upon him as he did upon the other spectators, without making any distinction between the king and the crowd. Crates had no views about prominent persons. He thought no more highly of them than he did of the gods. He was concerned only with men and with how to live one's life with the greatest possible simplicity. Diogenes' railing made him laugh, as did his claims to reform men's morals. Crates felt himself infinitely superior to these vulgar concerns. He modified the maxim inscribed on the pediment of the temple at Delphi and would say: 'Live thyself.' The notion of any knowledge whatever seemed to him absurd. His only study was the relation between his body and that which was necessary to it, seeking as far as possible to cut down these necessities. Diogenes used to bite like a dog; Crates lived like a dog.

He had a disciple whose name was Metrocles and who was a rich young man from Maronea. His sister, Hipparchia, beautiful and well-born, fell in love with Crates. It is an established fact that she was enamoured of him and that she went to him. The thing seemed impossible, but it is beyond doubt. Nothing disheartened her, neither the cynic's filth, nor his absolute poverty, nor horror of his public life. He forewarned her that he lived as dogs do, in the streets, and he searched for bones in the middens. He cautioned her that nothing in their life together would be hidden and that when the fancy took him he would have her publicly, as dogs do with bitches. All this Hipparchia expected. Her parents tried to hold her back; she threatened to kill herself. They took pity on her. Then she left the town of Maronea, quite naked, her hair hanging down, covered only in an old scrap of cloth, and she lived with Crates, dressed as he was dressed. It is said he had a child by her, called Pasicles, but in this matter we have no certain knowledge.

It seems this Hipparchia was kind to the poor and compassionate; she would caress the sick with her hands; being persuaded they were as a sheep is to a sheep or a dog to a dog, she would without repugnance lick the bloody wounds of the afflicted. When it was cold Crates and Hipparchia slept with the poor, clasping them close and seeking to impart some of the warmth of their bodies. They gave them the mute aid animals give to one another. They had no preference among those who came to them. It was enough that they were human.

This is all that has come down to us concerning Crates' woman; we do not know when she died, or how. Her brother Metrocles admired Crates and followed his example. But his life was not easy. His health was troubled by a constant flatulence which he could not restrain. He gave way to despair and resolved to die. Crates heard of his trouble and resolved to console him. He ate a choenix of lupin-seeds and went to visit Metrocles. He asked if it was the shame of his sickness that distressed him. Metrocles admitted that he could not bear the shame – whereupon, all blown up with the lupin-seeds, Crates loosed the wind in his disciple's presence and declared that all men were, by nature, subject to the same misfortune. Then he reproached him for being ashamed of other men and offered himself as a model; he then several times further broke wind, took Metrocles by the hand and led him away.

For a long while the two stayed together in the streets of Athens, no doubt in the company of Hipparchia. They did not speak much together. They were ashamed of nothing. Even though they were foraging in the same middens, the dogs appeared to respect them. One might think that, had they been pressed by hunger, men and dogs might have bitten each other – but the biographers have reported nothing of this sort. We know that Crates died an old man and that, at the end, he remained in the same place, lying under the lean-to roof of a shed in the Piraeus where the sailors stacked the newly-landed bales, that he ceased wandering about in quest of edible things to gnaw at, not having the wish even to stretch out an arm, and that he was found one day, wasted away with hunger.

Septima, enchantress

Septima was a slave under the African sun in the town of Hadrumetum. And her mother Amoena was a slave, and her mother too was a slave, and they were all beautiful, and unknown and lowly, and the gods of the infernal regions revealed to them philtres of love and death. The town of Hadrumetum was white, and the stones of the house where Septima lived were of a flickering pink. And the sands of the beach were strewn with the shells the warm sea carries from the land of Egypt where the seven mouths of the Nile spread muds of seven sorts, each of a different colour. In the house where Septima lived one could hear the dying sound of the Mediterranean's shore and, from below the house, sparkling lines of blue spread out fanlike to the skyline. The palms of Septima's hands were reddened with gold, and her fingertips were painted; her lips smelt of myrrh and her eyelids, glistening with oil, flickered pleasingly. Thus she would walk to the servants' house, carrying a basket of soft loaves.

Septima fell in love with Sextilius, a young freeman, the son of Dionysia. But to be loved is not permitted to those who know the subterranean mysteries; for they are under the sway of the adversary of love, who is called Anteros. And just as Eros directs the flashing of eyes and sharpens his arrow-points, Anteros turns glances aside and dulls the edge of his enemy's bolts. He is a beneficent god who sits among the dead. He is not cruel like the other. He possesses the nepenthes that bring forgetfulness. And knowing that love is the worst of earthly pains, he hates and cures love. However he is powerless to expel love from a heart where love is lodged. Then he takes possession of the other heart. Thus Anteros struggles against Eros. That is why Sextilius could not love Septima. No sooner had Eros brought his torch into the heart of the initiate than Anteros, incensed, possessed himself of him whom she would have loved.

In Sextilius' lowered eyes Septima recognised the power of Anteros. And when the purple uncertainty came upon the evening air, she set off by the road that leads from Hadrumetum to the sea. It is a quiet road where, leaning against the polished walls of the tombs, lovers drink date-wine. The breeze from the east breathes its perfume over the necropolis. The young moon, still veiled, diffident, comes and goes. Many of the dead, embalmed, sit enthroned about Hadrumetum in their sepulchres. And there Phoinissa slept, Septima's sister and, like her, a slave, who died at sixteen, before any man had breathed her scent. Phoinissa's tomb was narrow as her body. The stone constrained her breasts, that were supported by bandages. Close against her low forehead, a long flagstone cut short her sightless gaze. From her blackened lips the odour of the spices in which she had been steeped still exhaled. On her chaste hand shone a ring of green gold incrusted with two pale and hazy rubies. She brooded eternally in her sterile dream on things she had never known.

Under the virgin whiteness of the new moon, Septima stretched herself out on the kindly earth next to her sister's narrow tomb. She wept and she crushed her face against the sculptured garland. And she placed her mouth close to the conduit into which libations were poured and breathed out her passion:

'Oh my sister', she said, 'turn from your sleep and hear me. The little lamp that lights the dead in their first hours has gone out. You have dropped the coloured phial of glass we gave you. The thread of your necklace has parted and the golden beads are scattered about your throat. Nothing of ours is now yours, and now he who wears on his head a sparrowhawk possesses you. Hear me, for you have the power to convey my words. Go to the cell you know and supplicate Anteros. Supplicate the goddess Hathor. Supplicate the one whose dismembered corpse was carried by the sea in a coffer to Byblos. Have pity, my sister, on the sorrow you do not know. I conjure you, by the seven stars of the Chaldean magicians. By the infernal powers that are invoked in Carthage, Iao, Abriao, Salbaal, Bathbaal, receive my incantation. Cause Sextilius, son of Dionysia, to be consumed with love for me, Septima, daughter of our mother Amoena. Let him burn in the night; let him seek me out next to the tomb, oh Phoinissa! Or lead us both into the same dark and powerful dwelling-place. If he refuses to permit Eros to inflame our breaths, pray to Anteros that he freeze them. Scented corpse, accept the libation of my voice. *Achrammachalala!*'

The bandage-swathed virgin at once arose and, teeth bared, penetrated into the earth's depths.

And ashamed, Septima wandered among the sarcophagi. She remained in the company of the dead until the second watch. She kept watch upon the fugitive moon. She offered her breasts to the biting of the salt sea-wind. She was caressed by the dawn's first golden light.

Then she returned to Hadrumetum, and her long blue shift floated behind her.

Meanwhile Phoinissa was stiffly wandering the circles of hell. And he who wore on his head a sparrowhawk did not listen to her plaint. And the goddess Hathor remained stretched out in her painted wrapping. And Phoinissa could not find Anteros, because she did not know desire. But in her withered heart she felt the pity the dead have for the living. On the second night, at the hour when corpses come forth to accomplish incantations, she turned her bound feet towards the streets of Hadrumetum.

His face turned to the diamond-shaped decorations of the ceiling of his room, throbbing with the sighs of sleep, Sextilius was breathing regularly. And the dead Phoinissa, swathed in scented bandages, seated herself beside him. And she had neither brain nor inward organs; but in her breast they had replaced her dried heart: and, at that moment, Eros fought with Anteros, and he took hold of Phoinissa's embalmed heart. There and then she desired the body of Sextilius, that it might lie between herself and her sister Septima in the house of shadows.

Phoinissa laid her scented lips upon Sextilius' living mouth; and, like a bubble, his life escaped him. Then she came to Septima's slave's cell and took her by the hand. And, sleeping, Septima succumbed under her sister's hand. Almost at the same hour of the night, Phoinissa's kiss and Phoinissa's handclasp encompassed the deaths of Septima and Sextilius. Such was the funereal outcome of the struggle of Eros against Anteros; and the infernal powers received at the same time a slave and a freeman.

Sextilius lies in the necropolis of Hadrumetum, between the enchantress Septima and her virgin sister Phoinissa. The text of the incantation is inscribed on the tablet of lead, rolled and pierced with a nail, that the enchantress slipped into the libation-conduit of her sister's tomb.

Clodia, shameless matron

She was the daughter of Appius Claudius Pulcher, consul. When she was only a few years old she distinguished herself from her brother and sisters by the shameless lustre of her eyes. Tertia, her elder sister, was soon married; the younger yielded entirely to her caprices. Her brothers, Appius and Caius, were already unwilling to share the leather frogs and nutshell chariots that were made for them; later they were unwilling to share *sesterces*. But Clodius, handsome and effeminate, was his sister's companion. Clodia persuaded them, with burning glances, to dress him in a sleeved tunic, to cover his head with a little bonnet of golden threads and bind him under the breasts with a supple girdle; then they draped him in a flame-coloured veil and led him into the little rooms where he bedded with the three of them. Clodia was his favourite, but he also took the virginity of Tertia and the youngest.

When Clodia was eighteen her father died. She remained in the house on the Palatine Hill. Appius, her brother, governed the estate and Caius was preparing for public life. Clodius, still delicate and beardless, slept between his sisters, both of whom he called Clodia. They began to go secretly to the baths with him. They would give a quarter of an *as* to the great slaves who massaged them; then they would have it given back to them. Clodius was treated as his sisters were, in their presence. Such were their pleasures before marriage.

The youngest married Lucullus, who carried her off to Asia, where he was making war on Mithridates. Clodia took for husband her cousin Metellus, an honest, dull-witted man. In those troubled times he was conservative and narrow-minded. Clodia could not support his rustic coarseness. She already had dreams of new things for her dear Clodius. Caesar was beginning to win over men's minds; Clodia thought she should bring him down. She had Pomponius Atticus bring Cicero. Her circle was given to sniggering and gallantry. About her were found Licinius Calvus, the young Curio, known as the 'wench', Sextus Clodius who ran her errands, Egnatius and his cronies, Catullus of Verona and Caelius Rufus, who was in love with her. Metellus sat heavily in this company, not uttering a word. They would recount the scandals concerning Caesar and Mamurra. Then Metellus, appointed proconsul, left for Cisalpine Gaul. Clodia remained in

Rome with her sister-in-law Mucia. Cicero was completely captivated by her huge, blazing eyes. He thought he could repudiate his wife Terentia and supposed Clodia would drop Metellus. But Terentia discovered everything and reduced her husband to a state of terror. Cicero, fearful, renounced his desires. Terentia wanted more than that, and Cicero was obliged to break with Clodius.

Meanwhile Clodia's brother was busy. He was making love to Caesar's wife, Pompeia. On the night of the feast of Bona Dea there should have been women in the house of Caesar, who was Praetor. Pompeia alone offered the sacrifice. Clodius dressed himself, as his sister had been accustomed to disguise him, as a female cittern-player and entered Pompeia's quarters. A slave-girl recognised him. Pompeia's mother gave the alarm and the scandal became public. Clodius endeavoured to defend himself and swore that, at the time, he had been in the house of Cicero. Terentia prevailed upon her husband to disown him; Cicero witnessed against Clodius.

From then on Clodius was finished in the noble party. His sister had just turned thirty. She was more ardent than ever. She had the idea of having Clodius adopted by a plebeian, so that he might become a tribune of the people. Metellus, who had returned, guessed what she had in mind and laughed her to scorn. At that time when she no longer had Clodius in her arms, she let herself be loved by Catullus. Her husband Metellus was odious to them: his wife resolved to be rid of him. One day, when he returned, worn out, from the senate, she handed him a drink. Metellus dropped dead in the atrium. Henceforth Clodia was free. She quit her husband's house and quickly returned to the Palatine Hill, where she shut herself up with Clodius. Her sister absconded from Lucullus' household and joined them. They resumed their life *à trois* and gave vent to their hatred.

At first Clodius, become a plebeian, was designated tribune of the people. Despite his feminine grace, he had a powerful and trenchant voice. He brought about Cicero's exile; he had his house razed to the ground before his eyes and vowed the ruin and death of all his friends. Caesar was proconsul in Gaul and could do nothing. Nevertheless Cicero won influence through Pompey and contrived his recall the following year. The young tribune of the people was infuriated. He violently attacked Milo,Caesar's friend, who was beginning to man-oeuvre for the consulate. Lying in wait by night, he tried to kill him, knocking his torchbearing slaves off their feet. Clodius' favour with the people was on the wane. Obscene refrains were sung about Clodius and Clodia. Cicero denounced them in a violent speech: in it, Clodia was dubbed Medea and Clytemnestra. The brother's and sister's rage finally burst forth. Clodius tried to set fire to the house of Milo, and the slaves on guard struck him down in the darkness.

Then Clodia was desperate. She had taken and rejected Catullus, then Caelius Rufus, then Egnatius, whose friends had introduced her to low taverns: but she loved only her brother Clodius. It was for him she had poisoned her husband. It was for him she had enticed and seduced bands of incendiaries. When he died, she had nothing to live for. She was still beautiful and lustful. She had a country house on the road to Ostia, and gardens close to the Tiber and at Baiae. She took refuge there. She sought to distract herself, dancing lasciviously with women. That was not enough. In her mind she dwelt on the debaucheries of Clodius, whom she still saw as beardless and womanish. She remembered that he had once been taken by Cilician pirates, who had made use of his tender body. A certain tavern also came back to her memory, where he had gone with her. The pediment of the door was scrawled all over with charcoal, and the men who drank there gave off a strong smell and were hairy-chested.

And so Rome drew her back once more. In the first watches of the night she would prowl the streetcorners and the alleyways. The sparkling insolence of her eyes was still the same. Nothing could extinguish it, and she tried everything, even staying out in all weathers and bedding down in the mud. She progressed from the baths to the stone recesses the whores frequented; she was familiar with the cellars where slaves played at dice, the mean pothouses where crooks and carters got drunk. She waylaid passers-by in flagstoned byways. She died one stifling night as a result of a strange return to an old habit. A cloth-fuller had paid her a quarter of an *as* and he waited for her in the half-light of dawn to take it back and strangled her. Then he threw her corpse, the eyes staring, wide open, into the yellow waters of the Tiber.

Petronius, novelist

He was born in days when green-robed mountebanks used to make trained piglets jump through flaming hoops,when bearded porters in cerise tunics shelled peas into silver platters under the libidinous mosaics at the entrances of villas, when, in the provincial towns, upstart freedmen were intriguing to obtain municipal office, when at dessert reciters would chant epic poems in a language packed with words borrowed from the *ergastulum* and with turgid redundancies imported from Asia.

His childhood was spent among such elegancies. He never twice-running donned the same Tyrian garment. The silverware was swept into the atrium with the household filth. The meals were made up of the delicate and the unexpected, and the cooks ceaselessly varied their composition. There was no cause for astonishment, on opening an egg, to find therein a warbler, nor to hesitate to cut into a statuette imitated from Praxiteles and sculpted in *foie gras.* The gypsum seals of the amphorae were diligently gilded. Little Indian-ivory boxes contained sultry perfumes for the guests. The ewers were pierced in divers fashions and were filled with coloured waters that unexpectedly spurted out. All the glassware represented iridescent monstrosities. When one laid hold of certain urns, the handles came away in one's hands and the sides burst open to shower one with artfully painted flowers. Scarlet-cheeked African birds cackled in golden cages. Around the brilliant walls, behind inlaid lattices, howled numerous dog-faced Egyptian apes. In precious alcoves, crawled slender creatures with supple glowing-red scales and azure-flecked eyes.

Thus Petronius lived an effeminate life, thinking the very air he breathed was scented expressly for his use. When he became an adolescent, having shut up his first beard in an ornately-decorated casket, he began to look about him. A slave by the name of Syrus, who had served in the arena, showed him what he had not known. Petronius was small, swarthy, and had a cast in one eye. He was not of noble descent. He had the hands of an artisan and a cultivated mind. Thus it was that he took pleasure in shaping words and in writing them out. They in no way resembled the words the ancient poets had conceived; for they strove to portray everything that surrounded Petronius. And it was only later that he had the vexatious ambition to compose verses.

Consequently he knew barbarian gladiators and crossroads braggarts, shifty-eyed men who feigned to be watching the vegetables while they were pilfering the meat, the curly-headed boys that accompanied senators on their strolls, the old chatterboxes that discoursed on street corners of the city's affairs, lascivious menservants and newly-rich whores, costerwomen and innkeepers, seedy poets and thieving servant-girls, dubious priestesses and vagrant soldiers. He fixed them with his squinting eye and caught exactly their manners and their intrigues. Syrus was his guide in the slaves' bath-houses, the prostitutes' cubicles and the subterranean retreats where circus supernumeraries exercised with their wooden swords. At the city gates, among the tombs, he recounted to him the tales of men who change their skins, that the blacks, the Syrians, the tavernkeepers and the soldiers that stood guard on the crosses passed from mouth to mouth.

When he was about thirty, avid for that varied liberty, Petronius began to write the story of wandering and debauched slaves. He recognised their ways among the transformations wrought by luxury; he recognised their ideas and their language amid the polished conversation at banquets. Alone before his parchment, leaning over a sweet-smelling cedarwood table, he drew with the point of his pen the adventures of an unknown people. By the light from his high windows, under the paintings of the panelled ceiling, he conjured up the smoky torches of hostelries and absurd nocturnal combats, wooden candelabras whirling about, locks forced by the hatchet-blows of the slaves of justice, greasy truckle-beds traversed by bugs, and the curses of local procurators in the midst of poverty-stricken mobs dressed in torn curtains and dirty dishcloths.

It is said that when he had finished the sixteen books of his invention he had Syrus come so that he could read them to him, and that the slave laughed and shouted out loud, clapping his hands. At that moment they conceived the plan of putting into execution the adventures Petronius had composed. Tacitus falsely reports that Petronius was *elegantiae arbiter* at Nero's court and that, jealous, Tigellinus had the order conveyed to him that he should kill himself. Petronius did not expire delicately in a marble bath, murmuring wanton little verses. He slipped away with Syrus and ended his life wandering the roads.

His appearance made it a simple matter to disguise himself. Syrus and Petronius took turns at carrying the small leather bag that contained their duds and their *denarii.* They slept out, close to the crucifixion-hillocks. At night they saw the little lamps of the funeral monuments cheerlessly burning. They ate sour bread and overripe olives. It is not known whether they stole. They were wandering magicians, country charlatans, and the companions of vagabond soldiers. As soon as he was living the life he had imagined, Petronius completely forgot the art of writing. They had faithless young friends, whom they loved, and who abandoned them at the gates of the *municipium,* helping themselves to their last *as.* With escaped gladiators, they practised every sort of debauch. They were barbers and waiters in the stews. For many months they lived on funerary loaves that they pillaged from the tombs. Petronius terrified travellers with his lack-lustre eye and his malign-looking swarthiness. One evening he disappeared. Syrus thought to find him in a grimy den where they had had connection with a tanglehaired harlot. But a drunken footpad had thrust a broad-bladed knife into his neck as they lay together, in the open country, on the stone floor of an abandoned burial-vault.

Sufrah, geomancer

The story of Aladdin erroneously relates that the African magician was poisoned in his palace and that his corpse, blackened and criss-crossed with little cracks by the force of the drug, was thrown to the cats and dogs; it is true that his brother was deceived by this appearance and had himself stabbed to death, having put on the robe of the holy Fatima; but none the less it is certain that the Moghrabi Sufrah (for such was the magician's name) was merely lulled asleep by the almighty power of the narcotic and escaped by one of the twenty-four windows of the great hall while Aladdin was tenderly embracing the princess.

Hardly had he touched the ground, having without trouble descended by one of the golden pipes that carry off the water from the great terrace, than the palace vanished and Sufrah was alone in the midst of the sands of the desert. Nothing remained to him, not even one of the bottles of African wine which he had gone to seek in the cellar at the demand of the deceitful princess. In despair he sat down under the blazing sun and, knowing well that the extent of the torrid sands that surrounded him was infinite, he wrapped his head in his mantle and waited for death. He no longer had any talisman: he had no perfumes wherewith to perform suffumigations; not even a divining-rod that could indicate to him a deeply hidden spring by which he might assuage his thirst. The night came; it was blue and hot, but eased somewhat the inflammation of his eyes. The idea then came to him to trace in the sand a figure of geomancy and demand of it whether he was destined to perish in the desert. With his fingers he traced the four great lines, composed of points, that are placed under the invocation of Fire, of Water, of Earth and of Air on the left, and on the right, of the South, the East, the West and the North. And at the extremity of these lines he drew together the odd and even points so as to compose of them the first figure. To his joy he saw it was the figure of the Major Fortune, from which it followed he would escape the peril, the first figure having to be placed in the first house of astrology, which is the house of the questioner. And in the house called the Heart of the Heavens he again found the figure of the Major Fortune, which showed him he would succeed and be glorious. But in the eighth house, which is the house of Death, it came about that the figure of Red took up its position – which indicates fire or blood and is of sinister presage. When he had set up the figures of the twelve houses he drew out of them two 'witnesses' and from these a 'judge', so as to be assured that his operation had been rightly calculated. The figure of the judge was that of Prison, from which he knew that he would find glory, at great risk, in an enclosed secret place.

Certain of not dying there and then, Sufrah applied himself to reflection. He had no hope of recovering the lamp, which had been transported with the palace to the centre of China. However, he mused, he had never enquired as to which was the true master of the talisman and the ancient possessor of the great treasure and the garden of precious fruits. A second figure of geomancy, which he read according to the letters of the alphabet, revealed to him the characters S.L.M.N., which he traced in the sand, and the tenth house revealed to him that the master of these characters was a king. Sufrah knew at once that the wonderful lamp had been part of the treasure of King Solomon. Then he attentively studied all the signs, and the Dragon's Head showed him what he was seeking – for it was linked by the Conjunction to the figure of the Youth, which denotes riches buried in the earth, and that of the Prison, in which might be read the position of sealed-up vaults.

And Sufrah clapped his hands: for the figure of geomancy showed that the body of King Solomon was preserved in that very earth of Africa, and that he still wore on his finger his all-powerful seal which bestows earthly immortality: so that the king must have been sleeping for myriads of years. Filled with joy, Sufrah awaited the dawn. In the blue half-light he saw some thieving Badawi passing by; when he beseeched them they took pity on his distress and gave him a small bag of dates and a gourd filled with water.

Sufrah set out for the place designated. It was an arid and stony spot, set between four bare mountains that rose like fingers to the four corners of the sky. There he traced a circle and pronounced certain words; and the earth trembled and broke open and exposed a marble slab with a ring of bronze. Sufrah seized the ring and three times invoked the name of Solomon. Immediately the slab rose and Sufrah descended by a narrow staircase into the cavern.

Two fiery dogs emerged from two niches placed one opposite the other and spat forth intersecting gouts of flame. But Sufrah pronounced the magic word, and the growling dogs vanished. Next he came upon an iron door which turned silently on its hinges as soon as he touched it. He traversed a corridor cut out of the porphyry. Seven-branched candelabra burned with an eternal flame. At the end of the corridor was a square chamber whose walls were of jasper. In the centre a brazier of gold gave off a rich, gleaming light. And on a bed cut from a single diamond, which seemed like a block of cold fire, was extended an ancient form, white-bearded, its brow encircled with a crown. Close to the king lay a gracious dried corpse whose hands were still stretched out to grasp his; but the fire of kisses was burnt out. And, on the hand of King Solomon, where it hung down, Sufrah saw the great seal shining.

He approached on his knees and, crawling to the bed, he lifted the shrivelled hand, slipped off the ring and took possession of it.

Thereupon the obscure geomantic prediction was accomplished. Solomon's sleep of immortality was broken. In a second his body crumbled and was reduced to a little handful of white and polished bones which the delicate hands of the mummy seemed still to protect. But Sufrah, struck down by the power of the figure of Red in the house of Death, belched forth all his lifeblood in a bright red torrent and fell into the somnolence of earthly immortality. The seal of King Solomon on his finger, he lay down beside the diamond bed, preserved from corruption for myriads of years in the enclosed and secret place he had read by the figure of the Prison. The iron door fell too on the porphyry corridor and the fiery dogs began watching over the immortal geomancer.

Frate Dolcino, heretic

He learned to know of holy things in the Orto San Michele church where his mother would lift him up so he could touch with his little hands the beautiful wax figures that hung before the Holy Virgin. His parents' house adjoined the Baptistery. Three times daily, at dawn, at noon and in the evening, he saw two brothers of the order of Saint Francis going by, begging bread and carrying off the scraps in a basket. He often followed them to the door of the monastery. One of these monks was very old. Indeed, he said he had been ordained by Saint Francis himself. He promised the child that he would teach him to speak to the birds and to all the poor beasts of the field. Very soon Dolcino spent his days in the monastery. He sang with the brothers, and his voice was cool and clear. When the bell rang to clean the vegetables, he helped them wash their greens around the great tub. Robert the cook lent him an old knife and allowed him to dry the porringers with his big towel. In the refectory, Dolcino loved to look at the lamp-cover upon which he saw the twelve apostles painted, with wooden sandals on their feet and little cloaks covering their shoulders.

But his greatest pleasure was to go out with the monks when they went from door to door to beg bread, and to carry their basket, covered with a cloth. One day, when they were going about in this manner, at the hour when the sun was high in the sky, they were refused alms in many houses belonging to the common people on the river's bank. It was terribly hot: the brothers were very hungry and thirsty. They entered a courtyard with which they were not acquainted and, as he laid down his basket, Dolcino cried out in surprise. For this courtyard was clad about in leafy vines and was quite filled with clear and delectable verdure; leopards leapt about there along with many animals from beyond the seas and they saw there young men and women, dressed in bright garments, who played peaceably on hurdy-gurdies and citherns. The peace there was profound, the shade deep and sweet-scented. They all listened in silence to those who were singing, and the song was in a strange mode. The brothers said nothing: their hunger and thirst they deemed satisfied; they did not venture to ask for anything. With great reluctance they decided to go: but, on the river's bank, when they turned, they saw no opening in the wall. They believed it was a necromantic vision until Dolcino found the basket. It was filled with white loaves, as if Jesus had, with his own hands, multiplied the offerings.

Thus the miracle of mendicity was revealed to Dolcino. Nevertheless he did not enter the order, having received a higher and more singular notion of his vocation. The brothers brought him with them on the roads when they went from one monastery to another, from Bologna to Modena, from Parma to Cremona, from Pistoia to Lucca. It was at Pisa that he felt himself drawn by the true faith. He was sleeping on the crest of a wall of the bishop's palace when he was awakened by the sound of a trumpet. In the square a crowd of children, bearing branches and lighted candles were pressing about a wild man who was blowing upon a bronze trumpet. Dolcino believed he had seen John the Baptist. This man had a long black beard; he was dressed in a dark-coloured hair-shirt that covered him from his neck to his feet, marked with a large red cross. An animal-skin was tied about his body. In a terrible voice he cried: *Laudato et benedetto et glorificato sia lo Patre;* and the children repeated what he had said aloud; then he added: *sia lo Fijo,* and the children again took up his words; then he added: *sia lo Spiritu Sancto;* and the children said the same thing after him; then, with them, he chanted: *Alleluia, alleluia, alleluia!* Finally he blew on his trumpet and began to preach. His words were rough as mountain wine, but they attracted Dolcino. Wherever the monk in his hair-shirt blew on his trumpet, there Dolcino came to wonder at him, wishing to live like him. He was an ignorant man, moved by violence; he knew no Latin; to command penitence he would cry: *Penitenz agite!* But he ominously promulgated the predictions of Merlin, of the Sybil, and of the Abbé Joachim that are written in *Il libro delle figure;* he prophesied that the Antichrist had come under the guise of Frederick Barbarossa, that his ruin was consummated and that the Seven Orders would soon be raised up, after him, according to the interpretation of Scripture. Dolcino followed him as far as Parma, where he was inspired to comprehend all things.

The messenger came before Him who must come, the founder of the first of the Seven Orders. From the raised stone at Parma whence, for years past, the podestà had spoken to the people, Dolcino proclaimed the new faith. He said that men must dress themselves in mantlets of white cloth, like the apostles that were painted on the lamp-cover in the refectory of the Friars Minor. He affirmed that it was by no means sufficient to have oneself baptised; but, so as to return entirely to childish innocence, he made himself a cradle, had himself wrapped in swaddling clothes and demanded the breast of a simple woman who wept for pity. So as to put his chastity to the test, he beseeched a burgher's wife to persuade her daughter that she should sleep next to him in a bed, perfectly naked. He begged a bag filled with *deniers* and distributed them to the poor, to thieves and to public women, declaring that men must no longer work but live after the fashion of the animals in the fields. Robert, the monastery cook, fled to follow him and feed him from a porringer he stole from the poor brothers. Pious men believed that the times of the Knights of Jesus of the Holy Virgin had returned, and of those who had once, wandering and frenzied, followed Gerardo Secarelli. Blissful, they thronged about Dolcino and murmured 'Father, father, father!' But the Friars Minor saw to it they were chased out of Parma. A young girl of a noble line, Margherita, ran after him by the gate that opens onto the road to Piacenza. He dressed her in a sack marked with a cross and brought her with him. The swineherds and the cowherds gazed thoughtfully at them as they skirted the fields. Many quit their beasts and came to them. Some women prisoners whom the men of Cremona had cruelly mutilated, cropping off their noses, implored their protection and followed them. Their faces were wrapped in white cloths; Margherita taught them. Not far from Novarra they all established themselves on a wooded mountain and lived their lives in common. Dolcino established neither any rule nor any order, being certain that such was the doctrine of the apostles, and that all things must be in charity. Those who so wished nourished themselves on the berries from the trees; others begged in the villages; others rustled cattle. Dolcino and Margherita lived freely in the open air. But the men of Novarra were not minded to understand them. The peasants complained of thefts and of their scandalous ways. They had a band of armed men come to encircle the mountain. As for Dolcino and Margherita, they set them on an ass, their faces to its crupper; they led them to the great square of Novarra. By the law's command they were burned on the same pyre. Dolcino asked only one clemency: that in their torment, they be left clothed, among the flames, in their white mantlets, like the apostles on the lamp-cover.

Cecco Angiolieri, malevolent poet

Cecco Angiolieri was born malevolent in Siena, on the same day that Dante Alighieri was born in Florence. His father, grown rich in the wool trade, inclined towards the Empire. From childhood Cecco was jealous of the great, despised them, and mumbled prayers. Many nobles were no longer willing to submit themselves to the pope. Nevertheless the Ghibelines had yielded. But among the Guelphs even there were the Blacks and the Whites. The Whites were not especially averse to imperial intervention. The Blacks remained faithful to the Church, to Rome and to the Holy See. Cecco was by instinct a Black, perhaps because his father was a White.

Almost from his first breath, he hated him. At fifteen he claimed his share of the family fortune, as if old Angiolieri were dead. He grew angry on being refused and left the paternal home. Thenceforth he never ceased to complain, to chance acquaintances and to the heavens. He came to Florence by the great highway. The Whites were still predominant there, even after the Ghibelines had been expelled. Cecco begged for his bread, testified to his father's harshness, and lodged at length in the squalid quarters of a cobbler, who had a daughter. She was called Becchina, and Cecco believed he loved her.

The cobbler was a simple man, devoted to the Virgin, whose medals he wore, and was convinced that his devotion entitled him to cut his shoes from inferior leather. He would converse with Cecco concerning holy theology and the excellence of grace, by the light of a resin candle, before the time came to go to bed. Becchina would wash the dishes, and her hair was constantly in a tangle. She used to mock Cecco for his twisted mouth.

About this time the rumour began to spread about Florence of the excessive love of Dante Alighieri for Beatrice, the daughter of Folco Ricovero de Portinari. Those who were lettered knew by heart the *canzoniere* he had addressed to her. Cecco heard them being recited and found much fault in them.

'O Cecco', Becchina said, 'you mock at this Dante, but you cannot write such beautiful verses for me.'

'We shall see about that', Cecco said with a sneer.

And first he composed a sonnet in which he criticised the measure and the sense of Dante's *canzoniere.* Next he made verses for Becchina, who did not know how to read them and who burst out laughing when he declaimed them to her, because she could not bear the amorous grimacing of his mouth.

Cecco was as poor and as unadorned as a stone in a church wall. He fervently loved the Mother of God – and this rendered the cobbler indulgent towards him. Both had converse with some wretched ecclesiastics, in the pay of the Blacks. High hopes were entertained of Cecco, who appeared learned. But there was no money for him. Thus, despite his praiseworthy faith, the cobbler was obliged to marry Becchina to a coarse neighbour, Barberino, who sold oil. 'But oil can be holy!', the cobbler would say in self-extenuation. The marriage took place about the same time as Beatrice married Simone de Bardi. Cecco followed Dante's example in sorrow.

But Becchina did not die. On the ninth of June 1291 Dante was drawing on a tablet, and it was the first anniversary of the death of Beatrice. He found that he had portrayed an angel whose face was like the face of his beloved. Eleven days later, on the twentieth of June, Cecco Angiolieri (Barberino being busy in the oil-market) obtained from Becchina the favour of a kiss upon the lips, and he composed an ardent sonnet. Hate did not diminish in his heart. He wanted money with his love. He could not get any from usurers. He hoped to obtain it from his father and left for Siena. But old Angiolieri refused his son even a glass of acid wine and left him sitting in the street outside the house.

Cecco had seen a bag of newly-minted florins in the hall. It was the revenue of Arcidosso and Montegiovi. He was dying of hunger and thirst; his robe was torn, his shirt was stinking. He returned, dusty, to Florence and, on account of his rags, Barberino showed him the door.

In the evening Cecco went back to the hovel of the cobbler, whom he found singing a submissive hymn to Mary by the smoky light of his candle.

Weeping piously, the two embraced. After the hymn Cecco told the cobbler of the terrible and desperate hatred he bore his father, an old man who threatened to live as long as Botadeo, the Wandering Jew. A priest who came in to confer about the needs of the people persuaded him to await his deliverance in the monastic state. He took Cecco to an abbey where they assigned him a cell and an old robe. The prior decreed he should be called brother Henry. In the choir, at night, as they sang he would touch with his hand the flagstones, as cold and bare as himself. Rage contracted his throat when he thought of his father's riches; it seemed to him that the sea would run dry before the old man died. He felt himself so deprived that there were moments when he thought that he would like to be a scullion in the kitchen. 'That is a thing', he said, 'to which one might well aspire.'

At other moments he was caught up in the folly of pride: 'If I were fire', he thought, 'I would burn the world; if I were the wind, I would blow a hurricane; if I were water, I would drown the world in a deluge; if I were God, I would thrust it out into space; if I were pope, there would be no more peace under the sun; if I were emperor, I would cut off heads all about; if I were death, I would seek out my father... if I were Cecco... that is all my hope...' But he was *frate Arrigo*. He then returned to his hate. He procured a copy of the *canzoniere* for Beatrice and compared them patiently with those he had written for Becchina. A wandering monk told him that Dante spoke of him with disdain. He sought the means to avenge himself. The superiority of the sonnets to Becchina seemed to him evident. The *canzoniere* for Bice (he gave her her common name) were abstract and pallid; his were filled with force and colour. To begin with, he sent insulting verses to Dante; then he took it into his head to denounce him to the good King Charles, Count of Provence. Finally, none paying heed to his verses or to his letters, he remained powerless. In the end he grew weary of nourishing his hatred in inaction; he threw off his monkish robe, reverted to his open-necked shirt, his worn jacket, his rain-faded hood and returned to seek the assistance of the devout friars who worked for the Blacks.

A great joy awaited him. Dante had been exiled; in Florence only the shadows of the parties remained. The cobbler humbly murmured to the Virgin of the coming triumph of the Blacks. Cecco Angiolieri forgot Becchina in his delight. He dragged about in the gutters, ate hard crusts, ran on foot behind the envoys of the Church that plied between Rome and Florence. They saw he could be of use. Corso Donati, the violent chief of the Blacks, returned to Florence and, being powerful, employed him – among others. On the night of the tenth of June 1304 a rabble of cooks, dyers, smiths, priests and beggars invaded the noble quarter of Florence where the Whites' fine houses were situated. Cecco Angiolieri brandished the resinous torch of the cobbler – who followed at a distance, admiring the decrees of heaven. They burnt everything, and Cecco set fire to the woodwork on the balcony of the house of the Cavalcantis, who had been friends of

Dante. That night he staunched with fire the thirst of his hatred. The next day he sent the 'Lombard' Dante, at the court of Verona, some insulting verses; and the same day, as he had desired for so many years, he became Cecco Angiolieri: his father, as old as Elijah or Enoch, died.

Cecco hurried to Siena, smashed open the coffers and plunged his hands among the bags of new florins, repeating to himself, time and again, that he was no longer the poor friar Henry, but noble, lord of Arcidosso and Montegiovi, richer than Dante, and a better poet. Then he conceived that he was a sinner and that he had desired his father's death. He repented. There and then he hastily scribbled a sonnet demanding of the pope a crusade against all those who had insulted their parents. Avid to make his confession, he returned in haste to Florence, embraced the cobbler, and beseeched him to intercede on his behalf with Mary.

He burst in upon the church-candle merchant and bought a massive candle. Unctuously, the cobbler lit it. The pair wept and prayed to Our Lady. Until a late hour the cobbler's quiet voice could be heard as he sang songs of praise, rejoicing in his candle and wiping away his friend's tears.

Paolo Uccello, painter

His name, probably, was Paolo di Dono; but the Florentines called him Uccelli or Paul the Birds because of the great number of drawings of birds and painted beasts that filled his house: for he was too poor to keep animals or to procure for himself those he did not know. It is even said that, in Padua, he executed a fresco of the four elements and that, as an attribute, he gave the air the image of a chameleon. But he had never seen one, with the result that he portrayed it as a portly camel with a wide-open mouth. (Now the chameleon as Vasari explains, is like an agile little lizard, whilst the camel is a great clumsy beast.)

For Uccello did not bother himself with the reality of things, but rather with their multiplicity and the infinitude of lines, so that he painted blue fields, and red cities, and horsemen in black armour on ebony-coloured horses that breathed fire, and lances pointing like rays of light to every point in the heavens. And it was his habit to draw *mazocchi,* that is to say those wooden hoops which are covered with cloth and placed on the head so that the folds thereof, thrown backwards, entirely enclose the face. Of these Uccello drew pointed ones, square ones, and others with facets laid out in pyramids and cones so perfectly that in the folds of a *mazocchio* he laid bare a whole world of combinations. And Donatello the sculptor would say to him: 'Ah Paolo, you are forgetting the substance for the shadow!'

But the bird man went on with his patient work. He assembled circles, he divided angles, he examined creatures from every viewpoint, and he would go and question his friend the mathematician Giovanni Manetti about the interpretation of the problems of Euclid: then he would lock himself in and cover his sheets of parchment and blocks of wood with points and curves. He occupied himself continuously with the study of architecture, in which he was aided by Filippo Brunelleschi; but this was not with a view to erecting buildings. He limited himself to noting the way in which the lines rose from the foundation to the cornice and the convergence of right-angles at their intersections, and the way in which arches turned on their keystones, and the fanlike foreshortening of ceiling-joists that seemed to draw together at the ends of long halls. He also represented the beasts in all their movements and the gestures of men, in order to reduce them to simple lines.

Next, like the alchemist who bends over the mixtures of metals and reagents and watches over their fusion in his furnace to find gold, Uccello poured all these forms into the crucible of form. He united them, he combined them, he melted them together to bring about their transformation into the simple form upon which all others depended. That is why Paolo Uccello lived like an alchemist in the inner rooms of his little house. He believed he could transmute all lines into one ideal aspect. He sought to envisage the created universe as it was reflected in the eye of God, who sees all forms springing from a complex centre. About him lived Ghiberti, della Robbia, Brunelleschi, Donatello, each of them proud and the master of his art, making sport of the poor Uccello and his mania for perspective and pitying him his spider-infested house, bare of provisions. But Uccello was still prouder. With each combination of lines he hoped to have discovered the way in which to create. His aim did not lie in imitation, but in the power of developing all things like a master, and the strange series of pleated hoods seemed to him more revealing than the marble figures of the great Donatello.

Thus the bird man lived, and his pensive head was wrapped in his cloak; and he paid no heed to what he ate or to what he drank, but was wholly like a hermit. And so it was that one day, in a meadow, close to a circle of old stones embedded in the grass, he noticed a young girl, laughing, her head bound with a garland. She wore a long, light dress, caught about the hips by a pale ribbon, and her movements were as supple as the grass-stems she bent. Her name was Selvaggia, and she smiled at Uccello. He noticed the flexion of her smile. And when she looked at him, he saw the tiny lines of her lashes, and the circles of her pupils, and the curve of her eyelids, and the subtle plaiting of her hair, and in thought he drew the garland that bound her forehead in a multitude of positions. But Selvaggia knew nothing of that, because she was only thirteen. She took Uccello by the hand, and she loved him. She was the daughter of a dyer of Florence, and her mother was dead. Another woman had come into the house, and she had beaten Selvaggia. Uccello brought her home with him.

Selvaggia would stay all day squatting by the wall upon which Uccello traced his universal forms. She never understood why he preferred contemplating lines, curved and straight, to looking at the tender face that looked up at him. In the evening, when Brunelleschi or Manetti came to study with Uccello, she would fall asleep, after midnight, under the criss-crossing of right-angles, in the circle of shadow that spread beneath the lamp. In the morning she would waken before Uccello, and she would be happy because she was surrounded with painted birds and beasts in colour. Uccello drew her lips, and her eyes, and her hair and her hands, and he fixed all the attitudes of her body; but he never painted her portrait as other artists do who love a woman. For the bird man did not know the delight of limiting himself to the individual; he did not remain at one place; he wished to soar, in his flight, above all places. And the forms and attitudes of Selvaggia were tossed, with all the attitudes of beasts, and the lines of plants and stones, and the rays of light and the undulations of terrestrial vapours and of the waves of the sea, into the crucible of forms. And without a thought for Selvaggia, Uccello seemed forever bent over the crucible of forms.

Meanwhile there was nothing to eat in Uccello's house. Selvaggia dared not tell Donatello or the others. She held her tongue and she died. Uccello depicted the stiffening of her body, and the folding of her thin little hands, and the line of her poor closed eyes. He did not realise she was dead, any more than he had realised she was alive. But he tossed these new forms among those he had collected.

The bird man grew old, and no one any longer understood his paintings. They saw in them only a confusion of curves. They no longer recognised either the earth, or plants or the animals, or men. For long years he worked at his crowning achievement, which he concealed from all eyes. It was to encompass all his researches, and the subject bodied forth the thought behind it: it was Saint Thomas the doubter probing Christ's wound. When he was eighty, Uccello finished his painting. He sent for Donatello and reverently uncovered it in his presence. And Donatello exclaimed: 'Oh, Paolo, cover up your painting again!' The third man questioned the great sculptor; but more he was not minded to say. So Uccello knew that he had brought about the miracle. But all Donatello had seen was a tangle of lines.

And a few years later they found Paolo Uccello dead of overwork on his truckle-bed. His face was wreathed in wrinkles. His eyes were fixed upon mystery revealed. Tightly clasped in his hand was a small disc of parchment covered with interlacing lines that led from the centre to the circumference and returned from the circumference to the centre.

Nicolas Oyseleur, judge

He was born on the day of the Assumption and was a votary of the
Virgin. It was his custom to call upon her in all the vicissitudes of his
life, and he could not hear her name without his eyes filling with tears.
After he had studied in a little attic schoolroom in the rue Saint-
Jacques under the birch-rod of a skinny cleric, in company with three
children who mammered the Donatus and the penitential psalms, he
toiled over Occam's *Logic*. Thus he soon became bachelor and master
of arts. The venerable persons who instructed him observed in him a
great meekness and unctuousness of disposition. He had blubbery lips
from which poured words of adoration. From the day he obtained his
first degree in theology the Church had its eye on him. He served first
in the diocese of the Bishop of Beauvais who knew his qualities and
made use of them to warn the English besieging Chartres of various
movements of the French captains. When he was about thirty-five
years old he was made a canon of the Cathedral of Rouen. There he
was a good friend of Jean Bruillot, canon and succentor, with whom
he intoned beautiful litanies to Mary.

Sometimes he would remonstrate with Nicole Coppesquesne, who
was of his chapter, concerning his tiresome predilection for Saint
Anastasia. Nicole Coppesquesne never ceased wondering that so
sober-minded a girl had so enchanted a Roman prefect as, in a kitchen,
to render him enamoured of pots and cauldrons, which he fervently
embraced – to the extent that, face all blackened, he grew to look like a
demon. But Nicolas Oyseleur showed him how superior was Mary's
power when she restored life to a drowned monk. This monk was
lascivious, but he never omitted to do reverence to the Virgin. Rising
one night to go about his works of lewdness he troubled, as he passed
Our Lady's altar, to genuflect and pay her salutation. That same night
his lewdness led to his drowning in the river. But the fiends were not
able to carry him off and when, next day, the monks dragged his corpse
from the water, he opened his eyes, restored to life by the gracious
Mary. 'Ah!' the canon sighed, 'this devotion is a sovereign remedy,
and a venerable and discreet person such as yourself should sacrifice to
it the love of Anastasia.'

The Bishop of Beauvais did not forget the persuasive charm of
Nicolas Oyseleur when, in Rouen, he commenced the investigation for

the trial of Jeanne of Lorraine. Nicolas dressed himself in the short garments of a layman and his tonsure hidden under a hood, he was introduced into the little round cell, under a staircase, where the prisoner was confined.

'Jeannette', he said, standing in the shadows, 'it seems to me that Saint Katherine has sent me to you.'

'And who, then, in the name of God, are you?' said Jeanne.

'A poor shoemaker from Greu', said Nicolas – 'from our unhappy land, alas! And the Goddams have taken me, my daughter, as they have taken you – may your name be praised in heaven! Come now, I know you well; and many the time I have seen you when you used to come and pray to the most holy Mother of God in the Church of Sainte-Marie de Bermont. And along with you I have often heard the masses of our good curé Guillaume Front. Alas! Do you remember Jean Moreau and Jean Barre of Neufchâteau? They were my godfathers.'

Jeanne wept then.

'Have confidence in me, Jeannette', said Nicholas. 'When I was a child, I was ordained a cleric. Look: here is my tonsure. Confess, child; confess quite freely, for I am a friend of our gracious King Charles.'

'I shall make my confession to you most willingly my friend', the good Jeanne said.

Now a hole had been pierced in the wall; and outside, under a step of the staircase, Guillaume Machon and Bois-Guillaume took down notes of the confession. And Nicolas Oyseleur said:

'Jeannette, be firm and stick to your words – the English will never dare to harm you.'

The next day Jeanne came before the judges. Nicolas Oyseleur, together with a notary, was concealed in a window-recess, behind a curtain of serge, charged to place on record only the indictment and to leave blank the pleas in extenuation. But the two other clerks of the court raised an objection. When Nicolas reappeared in the room he made little signs to Jeanne that she should not seem surprised and, with a severe mien, he witnessed the investigation.

On 9 May, in the great tower of the castle, he urged that it was pressing that the question be applied.

On 12 May the judges assembled in the Bishop's house in Beauvais to deliberate whether it was of use to put Jeanne to the torture. Guillaume Erart thought it not worth while, there being matter enough without torture. Master Nicolas Oyseleur said that it seemed to him that, for the medicine of her soul, it would be a good thing were she put to the torture; but his counsel did not prevail.

On 24 May Jeanne was led to the cemetery of Saint-Ouen, where they had her mount a plaster scaffold. Next to her she found Nicolas Oyseleur who addressed her privily while Guillaume Erart preached. When she was threatened with the fire, she blenched; as he supported her, the canon winked at the judges and said: 'She will abjure.' He guided her hand to mark the parchment they gave her with a cross and a circle. Then he went with her under a little low door and stroked her fingers:

'You have done a good day's work, my Jeannette', he said. 'If it please God, you have saved your soul. Have trust in me Jeanne for, if you so wish, you will be delivered. Take back your womanly garments; do everything they command you; otherwise you will be in danger of death. And if you do what I tell you, you will be saved, you will meet with much that is good and nothing that is ill; but you will be at the disposal of the Church...'

The same day, having dined, he came to see her in her new prison. It was a commonplace room in the castle, reached by eight steps. Nicolas seated himself on the bed, by which there was a heavy block of wood bound with an iron chain.

'Jeannette', he said, 'you see how this day God and Our Lady have been most merciful towards you, for they have received you in the grace and mercy of our Holy Mother the Church; you must humbly obey the sentences and commands of judges and ecclesiastical persons; forsake your former imaginings and in no way return to them, otherwise the Church will forever abandon you. Here! Take these decent garments of a modest woman; be very prudent Jeannette; and make haste to have those locks shorn that I see are dressed like a boy's.'

Four days later Nicolas stole by night into Jeanne's room and took away the shift and petticoat he had given her.

'Alas', he said when they told him she had resumed men's dress, 'she has indeed relapsed and fallen deeply into evil ways.'

And in the chapel of the Archbishop's palace he repeated the words of Doctor Gilles de Duremort:

'We judges can but declare Jeanne a heretic and deliver her to the secular arm, praying them at the same time to treat her mildly.'

Before she was brought to the dreary cemetery he came in the company of Jean Toutmouillé to exhort her:

'Oh Jeannette', he said to her, 'do not conceal the truth: now you must think only of your soul's salvation. Believe me, my child: presently you must humble yourself among the assembly and, on your knees, make your public confession. For your soul's physic let it be public Jeanne, humble and public.'

And Jeanne beseeched him to recall it to her mind, fearing she would not dare before so many people.

He stayed to see her burn. It was then that his devotion to the Virgin became visibly manifest. No sooner did he hear Jeanne calling upon Saint Mary than he commenced to weep burning tears, so much did the name of Our Lady move him. Thinking him moved to pity, the English soldiers belaboured him and pursued him with swords raised. Had not the earl of Warwick taken him under his protection, they would have cut his throat. He contrived to mount one of the earl's horses and fled.

For days on end he wandered the roads of France, not daring to return to Normandy and in fear of the king's men. At length he came to Basle. Suddenly, on the wooden bridge, between the high, pointed houses with their ogival tiled roofs and blue and yellow pepperpot turrets, the light from the Rhine dizzied him: he felt as if he were drowning, like the lascivious monk, among the green water that swirled before his eyes; he died with a sigh; the word *Mary* choked on his lips.

Katherine la Dentellière, whore

She was born towards the middle of the fifteenth century in the rue de la Parcheminerie, close to the rue Saint-Jacques, during the winter when it was so cold that, in the snow, the wolves ran loose in Paris. An old woman, her nose red under her hood, took her in and raised her. At first she played with Perenette, Guillemette, Ysabeau and Jehanneton, who wore little shifts and dabbled their reddened fingers in the gutters to catch fragments of ice. And thus they watched the men who ensnared passers-by into the game that went by the name of Saint-Merry; and, under the awnings, they would greedily eye the buckets of tripe, and the long, bulging sausages and the heavy hooks on which the butchers hung quarters of meat. By Saint-Benoit-le-Bétourné, where the letter-writers have their booths, they would listen to the scratching of the pens and, under the noses of the clerks, they would blow out the candles in the evenings, through the tiny windows of the shops. At the Petit-Pont they would cheek the fishwives and quickly take flight in the direction of the Place Maubert, hiding in the nooks of the rue Trois-Portes; then, sitting on the brink of the fountain, they would chatter until the evening mists gathered.

Thus passed Katherine's first youth, before the old woman had taught her to sit before a cushion of lace and patiently intercross the threads of all the bobbins. Later she worked at her trade, Jehanneton having become a milliner, Perenette a lavender-girl, Ysabeau a glover, and Guillemette, the most fortunate, worked for a sausage-maker, her little face shining crimson, as if she had rubbed it with fresh pig's-blood. For those who had played at Saint-Merry things were taking a different turn; some were reduced to pawning penury on the Montagne Sainte-Geneviève, others shuffled the cards at Trou-Perrette and others clinked goblets of Aunis wine at the Pomme-de-Pin; others bickered at Grosse-Margot's; at midday they could be seen at the tavern door in the rue aux Fèves, and at midnight they left by the gate at the rue aux Juifs. As for Katherine, she intertwined the threads of her lace and, on summer evenings, she would take the air sitting on the bench at the church, where it was permissible to laugh and chatter.

Katherine wore a *chemisette* of Holland and a green surcoat; she was fond to distraction of clothes, and there was nothing she hated more than the sham-cuffs worn by girls of the commonality; she was every bit as fond of *testons,* of *blancs,* and especially of *écus d'or.* That is the reason she fell in with Casin Cholet, the tipstaff at Châtelet; under the cover of his office, he made a dishonest living. She often supped in his company at La Mule, opposite the church of the Mathurins; and after supper Casin Cholet would go and steal fowl beyond the fortifications. He brought them back under his great tabard and sold them advantageously to Machecroue, widow of Arnoul, the pretty poulterer at the Porte du Petit-Châtelet.

And very soon Katherine quit her trade of lacemaking; for now the red-nosed old woman was rotting in the cemetery of the Holy Innocents. Casin Cholet found his friend a mean little room, close to Trois Pucelles, and here he would come to visit her, late at night. He did not forbid her to show herself at the window, her eyes blackened with charcoal, her cheeks coated with white lead; and all the pots, glasses and fruit-plates in which Katherine offered food and drink to those who paid well were stolen from La Chaire, or Les Cygnes, or the Hôtel du Plat-d'Etain. Casin Cholet disappeared one day – the day he had pawned Katherine's dress and her girdle at the Trois-Lavandières. His friends told the lace-maker that, at the order of the provost, he had been whipped at the tail of a cart and expelled from the city of Paris by the Porte Baudoyer. She never saw him again. Alone, no longer having heart enough to earn her living, she turned whore, without a roof over her head.

At first she would wait at the doors of the hostelries; and those who knew her would take her behind the walls, in the shadow of the Châtelet, or against the Collège de Navarre; then, when it became too cold, an obliging old woman found her a place in the stews, where the mistress of the house gave her refuge. She lived there in a room whose stone floor was strewn with fresh reeds. Although she no longer made any lace, she was allowed to keep her name of Katherine la Dentellière. From time to time they let her out to walk in the streets, on condition that she returned at the hour when men customarily visited the stews. And Katherine would wander about outside the shops of the glover and the milliner, and time and again she would stop to look enviously on the sausage-maker's rosy face, laughing among her charcuterie. Then she would return to the stews where, at twilight, the mistress would light the candles that burnt red and guttered thickly behind the filthy window.

Katherine at length wearied of living enclosed in a flagstoned room;

she took to the roads. And thenceforth she was no longer a Parisienne, nor a lacemaker; but rather she was like one of those who haunt the outskirts of towns, seated on tombstones in cemeteries, to give pleasure to passers-by. These girls have no name apart from that which fits their appearance, and Katherine had the name of Museau. She would wander the fields and, in the evening, she would keep watch at the roadside, and her pale, sulky features could be seen among the hedgerow brambles. Museau learnt to tolerate the night's terrors when, brushing against the tombs, her feet would tremble. No more *testons,* no more *blancs,* no more *écus d'or;* she lived miserably on bread and cheese and water from her bowl. She had poor friends who called whisperingly to her from the distance, 'Museau! Museau!', and she loved them.

Her greatest sadness was to hear the bells of the churches and chapels; for Museau remembered the June nights when she would sit, wearing a green petticoat, on the bench under the holy porches. That was in the days when she envied the young ladies their finery; now she had neither sham-cuffs nor hood. Bare-headed, she stood waiting for her bread, leaning against a rough slab. And, in the cemetery night, her bare feet sinking in the sticky mud, she regretted the red candles of the stews, and the fresh reeds of her stone-floored room.

One night a bully who feigned to be a soldier cut Museau's throat for her girdle. But he found no purse in it.

160

Major Stede Bonnet, pirate by vagary

Major Stede Bonnet was a retired military gentleman who lived,
around 1715, on his plantations on the Island of Barbados. His fields
of sugar-cane and coffee-bushes gave him an income, and he took
pleasure in smoking the tobacco he had himself cultivated. Having
been married, he had not known domestic happiness, and men said it
was his wife that had turned his head. His mania, as a matter of fact,
scarcely took hold of him before his fortieth year, and at first his
neighbours and his domestics innocently humoured him therein.

This was Major Stede Bonnet's mania: that he commenced, at the
least occasion, to deprecate terrestrial procedures and to praise the
marine. The only names he uttered were those of Avery, of Charles
Vane, of Benjamin Hornigold and of Edward Teach. According to
him they were brave navigators and enterprising men. Those were the
days when they were roving the seas of the Antilles. If it happened that
they were called pirates in the Major's presence, he would cry:

'Then God be praised for having permitted these pirates, as you
would have it, to give an example of that open and common life our
forefathers lived. There were no possessors of riches in those days, no
custodians of women, no slaves to provide sugar, cotton or indigo: but
a generous God provided all things, and each and all received their
share. This is why I so much admire free men who share their goods
between themselves and live together the life of companions of
fortune.'

Wandering over his plantations, the Major would often clap a
worker on the shoulder:

'Well, imbecile, wouldn't you do better to stow in some store-ship or
brigantine bales of the wretched plant on whose leaves you pour out
your sweat?'

Almost every evening the Major assembled his servants in the
shelter of the lean-to where the grain was stored and there, by
candlelight, while the bright-coloured flies buzzed about them, he read
to them of the great acts of the pirates of Hispaniola and of Tortuga
Island. For the flysheets were warning the villagers and farms of their
depredations.

'Excellent Vane!' the major cried. 'Bold Hornigold, veritable horn
of plenty filled with gold! Sublime Avery, laden with the jewels of the

Great Mughal and the King of Madagascar! Admirable Teach who, on your fine Island of Overecok, have been able, successively, to master fourteen women and be rid of them, and who was inspired to deliver over the last of them (she was only sixteen) every evening, to your closest companions (out of pure generosity, great-heartedness and worldly wisdom)! Oh! How happy he would be who followed in your wake, who drank your rum with you, Blackbeard, master of the *Queen Anne's Revenge!'*

All these discourses were heard out by the Major's domestics in astonishment and in silence; and the Major's words were interrupted only by the slight, dull sound of little lizards as they fell from the roof, fear slackening the grip of the suckers on their feet. Then, screening the candle-flame with his hand, the Major would trace with his cane among the tobacco-leaves, all the naval manoeuvres of those great captains and would threaten all those who did not comprehend the niceties of these tactical evolutions proper to freebooting with *the law of Moses* (which is the way pirates designate a bastinado of forty blows).

Finally, Major Stede Bonnet could no longer hold back: and, having bought an old sloop with ten pieces of cannon, he equipped her with all that piracy calls for; to wit cutlasses, arquebusses, ladders, planks, grappling-irons, hatchets, Bibles (for swearing upon), pipes of rum, lanterns, soot for blackening the face, fuses to light between the fingers of rich merchants and a plentiful supply of black flags with white skull and crossbones and the name of the vessel: the *Revenge*. Then, abruptly, he ordered seventy of his men aboard and set sail at night, directly to the west, passing close to Saint Vincent to round Yucatan and scour the entire coast to Savannah (whither he never arrived).

Major Stede Bonnet knew nothing whatever concerning the sea. Thus, what with compass and astrolabe, he grew quite distracted, confusing mizzen with midden, foresail with forestay, prow with brow, gun-port with gunwale, hatch with match and giving the command 'Port arms!' when he meant 'Hard a-port!'; in short so much agitated was he by the tumult of unfamiliar words and the unaccustomed movement of the sea that, had the glorious desire to run up the black flag in sight of the first vessel he lit upon not maintained him in his resolve, he would have returned to Barbados. But on the first night they did not see even the fires of the meanest store-ship. Major Stede Bonnet decided they must attack a village.

Having drawn up his men in ranks on the bridge, he handed out new cutlasses and exhorted them to the greatest ferocity; then he called for a bucket of soot with which he blacked his own visage, ordering them to do likewise: this they did, not without merriment. Finally, judging in accordance with what he remembered that it would be meet to stimulate his band with some beverage fitting for pirates, he caused each of them to swallow a *pinte* of rum mixed with powder (not having the wine which is the ingredient customary to piracy). The Major's domestics obeyed; but, contrary to custom, their faces did not become inflamed with frenzy. More or less as a man they went to port and to starboard and, leaning their blackened faces on the rails, offered up the mixture to the villainous sea. After which, the *Revenge* being all but run aground on the shores of Saint Vincent, they unsteadily disembarked.

The hour was early and the astonished faces of the villagers did not arouse their ire. The major himself was not inwardly disposed to wrathful howling. Therefore he boldly purchased rice and dried vegetables, together with pickled pork for which he paid (in pirate fashion and, so it seemed to him, most ungrudgingly) with two casks of rum and an old cable. This done, the men succeeded, with some difficulty, in refloating the *Revenge;* and, puffed up with his first conquest, he put out again to sea.

He sailed all day and all night, not knowing what wind impelled him. Towards dawn on the second day, dozing against the wheelhouse, greatly inconvenienced by his cutlass and his blunderbuss, Major Stede Bonnet was awakened by a cry:

'Ahoy there, the sloop!'

And, at a cable's length, he saw the boom of a vessel riding at anchor. At the prow was a heavily-bearded man. A small black flag floated at the mast.

'Raise our deadly flag!' cried Major Stede Bonnet.

And remembering that his title appertained to the army of the land, following illustrious examples, he decided there and then to adopt another name. So, without hesitation he replied:

'The sloop *Revenge,* commanded by myself, Captain Thomas, with my companions of fortune.'

At which point the bearded man began to laugh.

'Well met, comrade', said he. 'We can sail in convoy. Come now and drink a little rum aboard the *Queen Anne's Revenge.*'

Major Stede Bonnet immediately realised that he had encountered Captain Teach, Blackbeard, the most famous among those he admired. But his joy was not so great as he might have imagined. He had the feeling that he was about to lose his pirate's liberty. Silent, he went aboard Teach's vessel; glass in hand, Teach received him most graciously.

'You please me mightily', said Blackbeard. 'But you are a reckless sailor. So take my word for it Captain Thomas, you will remain aboard our good ship and I shall have your sloop piloted by this fine fellow who goes by the name of Richards, and who is very experienced: and aboard Blackbeard's vessel you shall be at your leisure to profit by the free life of gentlemen of fortune.'

Major Stede Bonnet did not dare refuse. They relieved him of his cutlass and his blunderbuss. He swore an oath on the hatchet (for Blackbeard could not bear the sight of a Bible), and they assigned him his ration of rum and biscuit along with his share in future prizes. The Major had not imagined the life of pirates to be so regimented. He underwent Blackbeard's rages and the terrors of navigation. Thus, having left Barbados as a gentleman to be a pirate by vagary, he was obliged truly to become a pirate aboard *Queen Anne's Revenge.*

For three months he lived this life, during which time he was with his master in thirteen engagements; thereafter he found the means of returning to his own sloop, the *Revenge,* under Richards' command. In this he was prudent for, the following night, Blackbeard was attacked in the approaches of his Island of Overecok by Lieutenant Maynard, who arrived from Bathtown. Blackbeard was killed in the struggle and the Lieutenant ordered his head to be cut off and lashed to his yardarm: this was done.

Meanwhile poor Captain Thomas made off towards Carolina and, for several weeks, he continued to sail miserably about. Warned of his passage, the Governor of Charleston deputed Colonel Rhet to take him at Sullivan's Island. Captain Thomas allowed himself to be taken. He was brought to Charleston in great pomp under the name of Major Stede Bonnet which, as soon as he could, he had resumed. He was clapped in gaol until 10 November 1718, when he appeared before the Vice-Admiralty Court. The Chief Justice, Nicholas Trot condemned him to death in the following excellent discourse:

'Major Stede Bonnet, you are found guilty on two indictments of piracy: but you know that you have pillaged at least thirteen vessels.

As a result you could be indicted on a further eleven counts. But two will suffice us (said Nicholas Trot), for they are contrary to the Divine Law which ordains, *thou shalt not steal* (Exodus 20.15), and Saint Paul the Apostle expressly declares that thieves *shall not inherit the kingdom of God* (1 Corinthians. 10). But in addition you are guilty of homicide: and murderers (said Nicholas Trot) *shall have their part in the lake which burneth with fire and brimstone: which is the second death* (Revelation 21.8). And who, therefore, (said Nicholas Trot) *shall dwell with everlasting burnings* (Isaiah 33.14). Ah! Major Stede Bonnet! I have just cause to fear that the religion wherewith you were imbued in your youth (said Nicholas Trot) has been much corrupted by your evil life and by your undue application to literature and to the vain philosophy of these times; for if *your pleasure* had been *in the law of the Lord* (said Nicholas Trot) and if you had *meditated night and day* therein (Psalm 1.2), you would have found that the *word* of the Lord was *a lamp unto my feet, and a light unto my path* (Psalm 119.105). But this you have not done. Therefore it only remains for you to trust in the *Lamb of God* (said Nicholas Trot) *which taketh away the sin of the world* (John 1.29), who *is come to save that which is lost* (Matthew 18.11), and has promised that *him that cometh to me I will in no wise cast out* (John 6.37). So if you should determine to return to him, late though it be (said Nicholas Trot), like the workers of the eleventh hour in the parable of the vineyard (Matthew 20.6,9). He might still receive you. Meanwhile the court pronounces that you be taken hence to the place of execution where you will be hung by the neck until you are dead.'

Major Stede Bonnet, having listened with contrition to the discourse of the Chief Justice, Nicholas Trot, was hanged the same day at Charleston as a thief and a pirate.

Burke and Hare, murderers

Mr William Burke rose from the basest of beginnings to an eternal renown. He was born in Ireland, and began life as a shoemaker. For many years he plied this trade in Edinburgh; there he befriended Mr Hare, over whom he had a great influence. There is no doubt whatever that, in the collaboration between Messrs Burke and Hare, the inventive and simplifying faculty was Burke's. But their names remain as inseparable in the art as are those of Beaumont and Fletcher. They lived their lives together, worked together, and they were taken together. Hare never contested the popular favour that attached itself to the name of Burke. Such complete disinterest has never received its recompense. It is Burke who has bequeathed his name to the special procedure that honours both collaborators. The monosyllable *burke* will long survive on the lips of men to whom the person Hare will have vanished into the oblivion that unjustly swallows up obscure toilers.

Mr Burke would seem to have brought to his work the magical fantasy of the green isle of his birth. His mind must have been steeped in the tales of folklore. There is in what he did, as it were, a distant breath of the *Thousand-and-One-Nights*. Like a caliph wandering in the nocturnal gardens of Baghdad, he desired mysterious adventures, intrigued as he was by tales of the unknown and of men from foreign parts. Like a great black slave armed with a scimitar, for him there was no end more proper to his enjoyment than the death of others. But his Anglo-Saxon originality consisted in his being able to draw the greatest advantage from the play of his Celtic imagination. When his artistic pleasure was at an end, what, pray, did the black slave do with those whose head he had cut off? With a wholly Arabian barbarism, he carved them into quarters so as to preserve them, salted, in a cellar. What profit did he obtain of this? None. Mr Burke was infinitely superior.

In a sense, Mr Hare served as his Dinarzade. It would appear that Mr Burke's inventive power had been singularly excited by the presence of his friend. The illusion of their dreams permitted them to make do with a garret in which to lodge their grandiose visions. Mr Hare lived in a little room on the sixth floor of a teeming tenement in Edinburgh. A settee, a great chest and, doubtless, a few toilet-utensils, comprised all the furniture. On a small table a bottle of whisky and three glasses. As a rule, Mr Burke received only one person at a time; and never the same. His habit was to invite an unknown passer-by, at nightfall. He would roam the street to scan the faces that aroused his curiosity. Sometimes he chose at random. He would address the stranger with all the politeness of which Haroun-al-Rashid would have been capable. The stranger would climb the six stories to Mr Hare's garret. They would surrender the settee to him; they would offer him Scotch whisky to drink; and Mr Burke would question him regarding the most unusual incidents in his life. Mr Burke was a perfectly insatiable listener. The narrative was always interrupted before daybreak by Mr Hare. The form Mr Hare's interruption took was always the same, and was most imperative. To cut short the recital, it was Mr Hare's custom to slip behind the settee and apply both his hands to the mouth of the storyteller. At the very same moment Mr Burke would seat himself on the man's chest. The pair would remain in this position, motionless, dreaming of the end of the story which they never heard. In this way Messrs Burke and Hare finished a great number of tales the world will never know.

When the narrative was definitively brought to an end, along with the breath of the narrator, Messrs Burke and Hare would unravel the mystery. They would undress the stranger, admire his jewellery, count his money and read his letters. Some of this correspondence was not without interest. Then they placed the corpse in Mr Hare's great chest to cool. And here Mr Burke demonstrated the powerful practicality of his mind.

In order to drain the last drops of pleasure from the adventure, it was necessary that the corpse be fresh, but not warm.

In those early days of the century, medical men were fervent students of anatomy; but because of the principles of religion, they experienced great difficulties in obtaining subjects for dissection. As a man of intelligence, Mr Burke was aware of this scientific gap. It is not known how he became acquainted with a venerable and learned practitioner, Dr Knox, who held a chair in the Faculty of Edinburgh. Perhaps Mr Burke had attended courses of lectures, although his imagination must have inclined him rather towards artistic tastes. It is certain that he promised Dr Knox to aid him to the best of his abilities. Dr Knox, for his part, took it upon himself to pay him for his trouble. The tariff followed a descending scale, from the bodies of young persons to those of the aged. These were of small interest to Dr Knox.

This was also Mr Burke's opinion – for ordinarily they had less imagination. Dr Knox became famous among his colleagues for his anatomical knowledge. Messrs Burke and Hare profited from their life as dilettantes. It is no doubt fitting to place at this time the classic period of their existence.

For the all-powerful genius of Mr Burke soon led him beyond the norms and rules of a tragedy in which there was still a story and a confidant. Mr Burke developed, quite on his own (it would be puerile to invoke the influence of Mr Hare) towards a kind of romanticism. The setting of Mr Hare's garret did not meet his needs; he invented the nocturnal procedure, in the fog. Mr Burke's numerous imitators have somewhat dulled the originality of his manner. But this is the original tradition of the master.

Mr Burke's fecund imagination grew tired of the endlessly similar narratives of human experience. The outcome had never lived up to his expectation. He came to be interested only in the real aspect, for him always different, of death. He localised the entire drama in the *dénouement*. The quality of the actors no longer concerned him. It was a matter of chance. The one prop in Mr Burke's theatre was a linen mask, filled with pitch. On foggy nights Mr Burke would set out, carrying this mask in his hand. He was accompanied by Mr Hare. Mr Burke would wait for the first passer-by and walk before him; then, turning, he would apply the mask to his face, suddenly and firmly. Forthwith Messrs Burke and Hare would lay hold, each on his side, of the actor's arms. The linen mask, filled with pitch, introduced a simplification of genius in that it simultaneously stifled both cries and breath. What is more, it had an air of tragedy. The fog blurred the player's gestures. Some actors seemed to be miming drunkenness. At the end of this scene Messrs Burke and Hare took a cab, disrobed the player in their drama; Mr Hare took charge of the costumes, and Mr Burke provided Dr Knox with a corpse, fresh and in good order.

Here, at varience with the majority of biographers, I shall leave Messrs Burke and Hare, haloed in their glory. Why destroy so fine an artistic effect by leading them languishingly to the end of their career, by exposing their failures and their disappointments. There is no call to see them otherwise than on foggy nights, their mask at the ready. For the end of their life was commonplace, and like so many others. One of the two seems to have been hanged, and Dr Knox had to quit the Faculty of Edinburgh. Mr Burke has left behind him no other works.

Circa idem tempus pueri sine rectore sine duce de universis omnium regionum villis et civitatibus versus transmarinas partes avidis gressibus cucurrerunt, et dum quaereretur ab ipsis quo currerent, responderunt: Versus Jherusalem, quaerere terram sanctam ... Adhuc quo devenerint ignoratur. Sed plurimi redicrunt, a quibus dum quaereretur causa cursus, dixerunt se nescire. Nudae etiam mulieres circa idem tempus nichil loquentes per villas et civitates cucurrerunt ...

THE CHILDREN'S
CRUSADE
(1896)

The Goliard's Narrative

I, a poor goliard, a miserable clerk wandering the woods and the roads to beg, in the name of Our Lord, my daily bread, have myself seen a spectacle of piety and heard the words of little children. I know that my life is not especially holy, and that under the wayside lime trees I have yielded to temptation. The brothers who give me good wine see plainly that I am not accustomed to drinking it. But I do not belong to the mutilating sect. There are wicked people who put out children's eyes, and who saw off their legs and tie their arms, so as to expose them and implore pity. That is why, seeing all those children, I was afraid. Doubtless Our Lord will defend them. I speak haphazard because I am filled with joy. I laugh for the springtime, and because of what I have seen. My mind is not very strong. I received the clerical tonsure when I was twelve, and I have forgotten the Latin words. I am like the grasshopper: for I leap, hither, thither, and I buzz, and sometimes I spread coloured wings and my small head is transparent and empty. They say Saint John is fed on grasshoppers in the desert. He must have eaten a great many of them. But Saint John was not a man made like ourselves.

I am filled with adoration for Saint John, for he was a wanderer and uttered words without coherence. It seems to me they must have been very sweet. The spring too is very sweet this year. Never have there been so many pink and white flowers. The meadows look newly laundered. Everywhere the blood of Our Lord sparkles on the hedges. Our Lord Jesus is lily-coloured, but his blood is vermilion. Why? I do not know. It must be written in some parchment. If I had been skilled in letters, I would have parchment, and I would write thereon. In that way I would eat well every evening. I would go to the monasteries to pray for the dead friars and I would inscribe their names on my roll. I would carry my roll of the dead from one abbey to another. That is something our brothers find pleasing. But I do not know the names of my dead brothers. Perhaps Our Lord no longer troubles himself to know them. All those children did not seem to me to have names. And it is certain that Our Lord Jesus Christ favours them. They filled the road like a swarm of bees. I do not know from whence they came. They were very little pilgrims. They had pilgrim's staffs of hazel-wood and birch wood. They bore the cross on their shoulders; and all those crosses were of many colours. I saw green ones, that must have been made from leaves stitched together. They are untamed and ignorant children. They are going towards I know not what. They have faith in Jerusalem. Jerusalem, I think, is far away, and Our Lord must be nearer to us. They will not reach Jerusalem. But Jerusalem will come to them. As it will to me. The end of all holy things is joy. Our Lord is here, on this pink-flowered thornbush, and upon my lips and in my poor words. For I think of him and his sepulchre is in my thoughts. Amen. I shall lie down here in the sunlight. This is a holy place. The feet of Our Lord have sanctified all places. I will sleep. In the evening may Jesus cause all the little ones who bear the cross to sleep. In truth I tell him so. I feel very sleepy. I tell him so, truly, for perhaps he has not seen them, and he must watch over little children. Midday weighs heavy upon me. Everything is white. So be it. Amen.

The Leper's Narrative

If you wish to understand what I am to tell you, know that I cover my head with a white hood and that I wield a hardwood rattle. I no longer know how my face fares, but my hands frighten me. They go before me like scaly and livid animals. I should like to cut them off. I am ashamed for that which they touch. It seems to me they spoil the red fruits I gather, and the poor roots I grub up seem to wither at their touch. *Domine ceterorum libera me!* The Saviour has not expiated my pale sin. I am forgotten down to the resurrection. Like the toad sealed under the chill moonlight in a lightless stone, I shall remain locked in my hideous matrix when the rest arise in their cleansed flesh. *Domine ceterorum, fac me liberum: leprosus sum.* I am alone, and I am afraid. Only my teeth have kept their natural whiteness. The beasts are afraid, and my soul would flee. The daylight shuns me. Twelve hundred and twelve years since, their Saviour saved them, and he has not had pity on me. I have not been touched by the bloody lance that pierced him. Perhaps the blood of the Lord of others would have healed me. I often dream of blood: I could bite with my teeth; they are uncorrupted. Since he has not thought to give it me, I long to take that which is his. That is why I lay in wait for those children who came down from the Vendôme country to this forest of the Loire. They had crosses and they were in His service. Their bodies were His body, and He has not permitted me to share in His body. I am enclosed on earth in a pale damnation. I watched so as to suck innocent blood at the throat of one of His children. *Et caro nova fiet in dies irae.* In the day of wrath my flesh will be renewed. And behind the rest there marched a red-haired child. I marked him: I sprang suddenly; I stopped his mouth with my frightful hands. All he wore was a coarse shirt; his feet were naked, and his eyes remained placid. He looked at me without surprise. And then, realising that he would not cry out, the wish came upon me to hear again a human voice and I took away my hands from his mouth, and he did not wipe his mouth. And his eyes seemed elsewhere.

'Who are you?' I said.

'Johannes the Teuton', he replied. And his words were clear and salutary.

'Where are you going?' I went on.

'To Jerusalem, to conquer the Holy Land.'

I laughed then, and I asked him:

'Where is Jerusalem?'

And he replied:

'I do not know.'

And I asked him further:

'What is Jerusalem?'

And he replied:

'It is Our Lord.'

Then I fell to laughing again, and I enquired:

'What is this Lord of yours?'

And he told me:

'I don't know; he's white.'

And these words put me in a frenzy, and I opened my teeth under my hood, and I leant over towards his cool young throat and he did not shrink, and I said:

'Why are you not afraid of me?'

And he said:

'Why should I be afraid of you, white man?'

Then great tears troubled me, and I threw myself down upon the ground, and I kissed the earth with my terrible lips and I cried:

'Because I am a leper!'

And the Teuton child looked at me closely and said:

'I don't understand.'

He had not been afraid of me! He had not been afraid of me! My monstrous whiteness is like that of his Lord. And I took a fistful of grass and wiped his mouth and his hands. And I said to him:

'Go in peace to your white lord, and tell him he has forgotten me.'

The child looked at me without saying anything. I escorted him out of the blackness of that forest. He went on his way without trembling. In the sunlight, I watched his red hair vanishing into the distance. *Domine infantium libera me!* Let the sound of my wooden rattle reach you, as does the sound of the bells. Master of those who do not know, deliver me!

The Narrative of Pope Innocent III

Far from the incense and the chasubles, in this room of my palace with its faded gilt, I can very readily talk with God. I come here to think of my old age, without being supported under my arms. During mass my heart rises up, and my body grows stiff; the lambency of the sacred wine fills my eyes and my thought is smoothed with holy oils; but in this solitary place of my basilica, I may bend under the weight of my earthly tiredness. *Ecce homo!* For the Lord does not surely hear the voice of his priests by way of the pomp of pastoral letters and bulls; and no doubt neither paintings nor jewels please him; but in this little cell he has perhaps taken pity on my imperfect babbling. I am very old, Lord, and I stand here before thee dressed in white, and my name is Innocent, and thou knowest that I know nothing. Forgive me my papacy, for it has been commanded, and I have submitted to it. It is not I who ordained these honours. I like it better to see thy sky through this round window than in the magnificent reflections of my stained glass. Let me weep like any other old man and turn towards thee this pale and wrinkled face which I raise only with great effort above the flood of the eternal night. The rings slip along my withered fingers as my last days slip away from me.

My God! I am thy vicar here, and I hold out to thee my hollowed hand, filled with the pure wine of thy faith. There are great crimes. There are very great crimes. For these we can give absolution. There are great heresies. We must punish these pitilessly. Now, as I kneel, white in this white chamber that has lost its gilt, I am suffering a great anguish, Lord, not knowing whether the crimes and the heresies are those of the papacy or those of the small circle of daylight in which an old man merely joins his hands. And then I am troubled in regard to that which concerns thy sepulchre. It is still surrounded by the infidels. We have not been able to reclaim it. No one has taken thy cross to the Holy Land; but we are steeped in torpor. The knights have laid down their arms and the kings no longer know how to command. And I, O Lord, I blame myself and I beat my breast; I am too feeble and too old.

Hear now, Lord, the tremulous whispering that rises from this little cell of my basilica, and give me counsel. My servants have brought me strange news, coming from the regions of Flanders and Germany down to the towns of Marseilles and Genoa. Ignorant sects are coming into being. Naked women who do not speak are to be seen walking in the streets of the cities. These silent and shameless women point to the sky. Many madmen have preached ruin in the squares. The hermits and the wandering scholars proliferate rumours. And by I know not what sorcery, seven thousand children have been enticed out of their houses. There are seven thousand of them on the road, bearing the cross and the pilgrim's staff. They have nothing to eat; they are unarmed; they are helpless, and they put us to shame. They are ignorant of all true religion. My servants have questioned them. They reply that they are going to Jerusalem to conquer the Holy Land. My servants have told them that they cannot cross the sea. They have replied that the sea will separate and will dry up so that they may pass. Good parents, pious and sensible, do their utmost to hold them back. They force the bolts in the night and leap over the walls. Many are the sons of nobles and courtiers. It is most pitiful. Lord, all these innocents will be delivered over to shipwreck or to the adorers of Mahomet. I see that the Sultan of Baghdad lies in wait for them in his palace. I tremble lest the mariners seize their bodies and sell them.

Permit me, Lord, to address you according to the formulae of religion. This children's crusade is no work of piety. It cannot win back the Sepulchre for Christians. It adds to the number of vagabonds who wander on the edges of the authorised faith. Our priests cannot protect them. We are compelled to believe that the Evil One possesses these poor creatures. Like the swine on the mountain, they are going in a troop towards the precipice. As you know, Lord, the Evil One readily lays hold of children. He took on the appearance, once, of a ratcatcher, so as to lead away with the sounds of his musical pipe all the children of the city of Hamelin. Some say these unfortunates were drowned in the River Weser, others that he imprisoned them in the side of a mountain. Beware lest Satan bear away all our children to the torments of those not of our faith. Lord, you know that it is not good that faith be renewed. No sooner did it appear in the Burning Bush than you had it shut up in a tabernacle. And when it escaped from your lips on Golgotha, you ordained that it be enclosed in ciboria and monstrances. These little prophets will overturn the edifice of your Church. That must be forbidden them. Will you receive those who know not what they do, in despite of those consecrated to you, who wear in your service their albs and their stoles and who, to come unto you, resolutely resist temptations? We must let these little children come unto you, but by the way of your faith. Lord, I address you according to your institutions. These children will perish. Let there not be, under Innocent, a new massacre of the Innocents.

Forgive me now, my God, for having asked counsel of thee in my popely quality. The trembling of age overcomes me. See my poor hands. I am a very old man. My faith is not that of the little children. The gold of the walls of this cell is worn with time. They are white walls. The circle of thy sun is white. My robe too is white, and my dried-out heart is pure. I have spoken according to thy rule. There are crimes. There are very great crimes. There are heresies. There are very great heresies. My head nods with feebleness: perhaps there is no need to punish or absolve. Life gone by gives pause to our resolutions. I have seen no miracle. Enlighten me. Is this a miracle? What sign hast thou given them? Has the time come? Wouldst thou have it that a very old man such as myself be equal in whiteness to thy little shining-white children? Seven thousand! Though their faith be ignorant, wilt thou punish the ignorance of seven thousand innocents? I too, I am Innocent. Lord, I am as innocent as they. Do not punish me in my extreme old-age. Long years have taught me that this troop of children *cannot* succeed. Nevertheless, Lord, is this a miracle? My cell remains quiet, as in other meditations I know that there is no need to implore thee, for thee to manifest thyself; but I, from the height of my extreme old-age, from the height of thy papacy, supplicate thee. Instruct me, for I do not know. Lord, they are thy little innocents. And I, Innocent, I do not know, I do not know.

Narrative of Three Little Children

We three, Nicolas who does not know how to speak, Alain and Denis, have set out on the roads to go to Jerusalem. We have been walking a long time. White voices called us in the night. They called all the little children. They were like the voices of dead birds in the winter.And to begin with, we saw many poor birds stretched out on the frozen earth, many little birds with red breasts. Then we saw the first flowers and the first leaves, and we wove them into crosses. We sang outside the villages, as we had been accustomed to do for the new year. And all the children came running to us. And we went onwards like a troop. There were men who cursed us, not knowing the Lord. There were women who held us by the arm and questioned us, and covered our faces with kisses. And then there were good souls who brought us wooden porringers, warm milk and fruits. And everyone had pity on us. For they knew not where we were going and had not heard the voices.

On the earth there are thick forests, and rivers, and mountains, and paths filled with brambles. And at the end of the earth is the sea we are soon to cross. And at the end of the sea is Jerusalem. We have neither leaders nor guides. But to us all roads are good. Although he does not know how to speak, Nicolas marches as we do,Alain and Denis, and all regions are similar, and similarly dangerous for children. On all sides there are thick forests, and rivers, and mountains and thorns. But all around the voices are with us. There is a child called Eustace who was born with closed eyes. He keeps his arms stretched out before him, and he smiles. We see no better than he. A little girl leads him and carries his cross. Her name is Allys. She never speaks and never cries; she keeps her eyes fixed at Eustace's feet, so as to catch him when he stumbles. We love them both. Eustace will not be able to see the sacred lamps of the sepulchre. But Allys will take his hands to help him touch the stone slabs of the tomb.

Oh! The things of the earth are beautiful! We remember nothing because we have never learnt anything. All the same, we have seen ancient trees and red rocks. Sometimes it is dark for a long while. Sometimes we march until evening through empty meadows. We have cried the name of Jesus in Nicolas' ears, and he knows it well. For his lips can open for joy, and he strokes our shoulders. And thus they are not unhappy; for Allys watches over Eustace, and we, Alain and Denis, we watch over Allys.

They told us we would meet with ogres in the forest, and with werewolves. These are lies. No one has frightened us; no one has done us harm. The solitaries and the sick come and look at us, and the old women light lamps for us in the huts. They ring the church bells for us. The peasants stand up in the furrows to watch us. The animals look at us too, and they do not run away. And whilst we have been marching, the sun has grown hotter, and we no longer gather the same flowers. But all stalks can be woven into the same forms, and our crosses are always fresh. So we are very hopeful, and soon we shall see the blue sea. And at the end of the blue sea is Jerusalem. And the Lord will let all the little children come to his tomb. And the white voices will be joyful in the night.

Narrative of François Longuejoue, Clerk

This day, the fifteenth of the month of September, the year twelve hundred and twelve after the incarnation of Our Lord, have come into the dispensary of my master Hugues Ferré many children who demand to cross the sea to go to see the Holy Sepulchre. And seeing that the said Ferré has not sufficient merchant vessels in the port of Marseilles, he has commanded me to call upon master Guillaume Porc, to make up their number. Masters Hugues Ferré and Guillaume Porc will bring the ships to the Holy Land for the love of Our Lord J.-C. There are presently spread about the city of Marseilles more than seven thousand children, of whom some speak barbarian tongues. And the aldermen, rightly fearing a scarcity, have met in the city hall whence, after deliberation, they have commanded our said masters in order to exhort them to provide and dispatch the ships with great diligence. The sea is not at present especially favourable, by reason of the equinoxes, but it is to be considered that such an affluence might be dangerous to our good city, the more so because these children are all famished by reason of the length of the journey and know not what they do. I have had the sailors called out in the port, and ships equipped. At the hour of vespers they can put to sea. The throng of children is not in the city, but they are roaming the sands and collecting seashells for signs of a voyage and it is said that they are amazed at the starfish and think them fallen alive from the heavens to show them the way to the Lord. And concerning this extraordinary occurrence, this is what I have to say: first, that it is desirable that masters Hugues Ferré and Guillaume Porc promptly conduct this foreign turbulence outside our city; secondly, that the winter has been particularly hard, so that this year the earth is poor, as the merchants well know; thirdly, that the Church has not been apprised of the design of this horde coming from the North, and that it will not involve itself with the folly of an army of children (turba infantium). And it is proper that masters Hugues Ferré and Guillaume Porc be commended, as much for the love they bear our good city as for their submission to Our Lord, in sending their ships and convoying them in this time of equinox, and in great danger of being attacked by the infidels that scour our sea in their feluccas from Algiers to Bougie.

The Kalander's Narrative

Let God be glorified! Praised be the Prophet who has permitted that I be poor and wander through the towns, invoking the Lord! Thrice blessed be the holy companions of Muhammad who founded the order to which I belong! For I am comparable to him who was stoned out of the infamous city I do not deign to name and who took refuge in a vineyard where a Christian slave had pity on him and gave him grapes, and as the day declined was touched by the words of the faith. God is great! I have passed through the cities of Mosul, and of Baghdad and of Basrah, and I have known Salah-ed-Din (God has his soul) and his brother the sultan, Seif-ed-Din, and I have looked upon the Commander of the Faithful. I live very well on a little rice which I beg, and the water they pour into my calabash. I preserve the purity of my body. But the greatest purity resides in the soul. It is written that the Prophet fell on the ground in a deep sleep. And two white men came down to the right and to the left of his body and held him there. And the white man to his left slit open his chest with a golden knife and drew out the heart, from which he expressed the black blood. And the man on his right slit open his belly with a golden knife and drew out the viscera, which he purified. And they returned the entrails to their place, and thenceforth the Prophet was pure to proclaim the faith. There was a purity such as belongs properly to angelic beings. Nevertheless children too are pure. Such was the purity the seer-woman desired to engender when she saw the glory about the head of Muhammad's father when she sought to couple with him. But the father of the Prophet coupled with his wife Aminah, and the glory disappeared from his forehead, and thus the seer-woman knew that Aminah was to conceive a pure being. Glory be to God who purifies! Here, under the porch of this bazaar I can rest. I shall hail the passers-by. There are rich merchants squatting there, who deal in jewels and in cloth. There goes a kaftan worth fully a thousand dinars! For my part, I have no money and I am as free as a dog. Let God be glorified! Now that I am in the shade, I recall the beginning of my disclosure. First I speak of God, other than whom there is no God, and of our holy Prophet who revealed the faith, for that is the origin of all thoughts, whether they be uttered by mouth or traced with a pen. Secondly, I consider the purity wherewith God has gifted the saints and the angels.

Thirdly, I reflect upon the purity of children. I have, in fact, just seen a great number of Christian children who have been bought by the Commander of the Faithful. I saw them on the open road. They were going their way like a flock of sheep. It is said they came from Egypt, and that Frankish ships disembarked them there. Satan possessed them, and they sought to cross the sea and make their way to Jerusalem. Let God be glorified! It has not been permitted that so great a cruelty be accomplished. For those wretched children would have died on the way, having neither assistance nor victuals. They were wholly innocent. And, seeing them, I threw myself upon the ground, and I struck the earth with my forehead, praising the Lord in a loud voice. Now such was the condition of those children. They appeared not to know where they were, and they seemed not to be distressed. They kept their eyes set on the distance. One of them I saw was blind, and a little girl held him by the hand. Many of them had red hair and green eyes. They were Franks who belong to the emperor of Rome. They falsely adore the prophet Jesus. The error of these Franks is manifest. First, it is proven by books and by miracles that there is no word other than that of Muhammad. Next, God permits us daily to glorify him and beg our livelihood, and he ordains that the faithful protect our order. Lastly, he has refused insight to these children, who have set out from a far country, tempted by Iblis, and he has not manifested himself to prevent them. And had they not by good fortune fallen into the hands of the Faithful, they would have been seized by the Fire Worshippers and chained in deep caverns. And those accursed-ones would have offered them as a sacrifice to their ravening and detestable idol. Praised be our God, who does well all that He does, and who protects even those who do not confess him. God is great! I go now to the shop of that goldsmith to beg my share of rice and proclaim my contempt of riches. If it please God, all those children will be saved by the Faith.

Little Allys' Narrative

I can no longer go properly because we are in a burning-hot land where two wicked men from Marseilles have brought us. And at first we were tossed about on the sea in a lightless day, in the midst of the fires of heaven. But my little Eustace was not afraid of anything, because he saw nothing and I held both his hands. I love him very much and I came here because of him. For I do not know where we are going. It is so long since we left. The others speak to us of Jerusalem, which is at the end of the sea, and of Our Lord who will be there to receive us. And Eustace will know Our Lord Jesus, but he did not know what Jerusalem is, whether a city or the sea. He took flight to obey the voices he heard every night. He heard them at night because of the silence, for he does not know night from day. And he asked me about these voices, but I could tell him nothing. I know nothing, and all that troubles me is Eustace. We were marching next to Nicolas, and Alain and Denis; but they boarded another ship, and not all the ships were there when the sun came up again. Alas! What became of them? We shall see them again when we come to Our Lord. It is still a long way off. They speak of a great king who will summon us and who rules in the city of Jerusalem.Everything in this country is white, the houses and the clothing, and the women's faces are covered by a veil. Poor Eustace cannot see this whiteness, but I tell him of it and he is glad. For he says that it is a sign of the end. The Lord Jesus is white. Little Allys is very tired, but she holds Eustace by the hand so that he should not fall, and she has no time to think of her tiredness. We shall rest tonight, and Allys will sleep, as she is used to, next to Eustace and, if the voices have not abandoned us, she will hear them in the empty night. And she will take Eustace by the hand to the white end of our journey, for she must show to him the Lord. And the Lord will assuredly have pity on Eustace's patience and permit Eustace to see him. And then perhaps Eustace will see little Allys.

The Narrative of Pope Gregory IX

Here is the devouring sea that seems innocent and blue. Its ripples are soft and it is bordered in white like a divine robe. It is a liquid sky, and its stars are living. From this throne of rocks, where I have been brought in my litter, I meditate upon it. It is truly in the midst of the lands of Christianity. It received the sacred water in which John the Baptist washed away sin. All the saints have looked upon its waters, and it has rocked their transparent images. With my eyes I question you, great mysterious anointed-one that knows neither ebb nor flow, cradle of azure set in the terrestrial ring like a liquid jewel. Give me back my children, O Mediterranean Sea! Why have you taken them from me?

I never knew them. My old age was not caressed by their fresh breath. They did not come to supplicate me with their tender half-open mouths. Only, like little vagabonds, filled with a wild and blind faith, they launched themselves upon the promised land and were annihilated. From Germany and Flanders, from Savoy and from Lombardy they came to your perfidious waves, holy sea, murmuring indistinct words of adoration. They went to the city of Marseilles, they went to the city of Genoa. And you carried them in ships on your broad back, crested with foam; and you rolled over and you stretched out to them your glaucous arms, and you kept them. And the rest, by bringing them to the infidels, you betrayed, and now they weep in the palaces of the orient, captives of the worshippers of Mahomet.

Once a proud king of Asia had you beaten with rods and put in chains. O Mediterranean sea! Who will pardon you? You are wretchedly guilty. It is you I accuse, you alone, treacherously limpid and clear, imperfect image of the sky; I call you to justice before the throne of the Highest, to whom all created things are answerable. Consecrated sea, what have you done with our children? Raise towards Him your cerulean face; hold out to him your fingers shuddering with bubbles; bestir your innumerable empurpled laughter; let your murmuring speak, and account for yourself.

Dumb at all your white mouths that come and die at my feet in the sand, you say nothing. In my palace in Rome there is an ancient cell with faded gilt that age has made pale as a dawn. It was Pope Innocent's habit to retire there. They say he meditated long there on the children and their faith, and that he demanded of the Lord a sign. Here, from this throne of rocks, in the open air, I declare that this Pope Innocent himself had a childish faith and that he shook his weary head in vain.I am far older than Innocent: I am the oldest of the vicars the Lord has installed here below, and I am only beginning to understand. God does not manifest himself. Did he help his son in the Garden of Gethsemane? Did he not abandon him in his last agony? O childish faith that invokes thy aid! All evil and every trial reside only in ourselves. Faith has perfect confidence in the work fashioned by His hands. And you have betrayed its confidence. Do not be surprised, divine sea, at my words. All things are as one before the Lord. Man's superb reason, in comparison with the infinite, is worth no more than the little gleaming eye of one your creatures. God accords the same share to the grain of sand and to the emperor. The gold ripens in the mine as infallibly as the monk meditates in his monastery. The constituent parts of the world are as guilty, one as the other, when they do not follow the lines of goodness; for they proceed from Him. In his eyes there are neither stones, nor plants, nor animals nor men, but creations. I see all those whitening skulls that bounce about beneath your waves, and that dissolve in your waters; they glimmer for a moment only in the sunlight, and they may be damned or chosen. Extreme old age humbles pride and enlightens religion. I have as much pity for that little mother-of pearl seashell as I have for myself.

That is why I accuse you, devouring sea, that has swallowed up my little children. Remember that Asian king that punished you. But that king was not a centenarian. He had not suffered sufficient years. He could not comprehend the things of the universe. Therefore I shall not punish you. For my indictment and your murmuring would die at the same moment at the feet of the Most High, just as the soughing of your droplets dies from moment to moment at my feet. O Mediterranean Sea, I pardon and absolve you! I accord you most holy absolution. Go, and sin no more. Like you I am guilty of faults of which I am unaware. With your thousand moaning lips you incessantly confess on the sands, and I confess to you, great holy sea, with my withered lips. We each confess the other. Absolve me as I absolve you. Let us revert to ignorance and candour. So be it.

What shall I do here on earth? There will be an expiatory monument, a monument to unknowing faith. Ages to come must know our piety, and not despair. God drew to him the little crusader

children, by the holy sin of the sea; innocents were massacred; the
bodies of the innocents will have their place of refuge. Seven ships were
sunk on the shoals of Reclus; on that island I shall build a church for
the New Innocents, and there I shall install twelve prebendaries. And
you will restore to me the bodies of my children, innocent and
consecrated sea; you will fetch them to the sands of the island; and the
prebendaries will deposit them in the crypts of the chapel; and above
them they will light eternal lamps in which will burn holy oils, and they
will show to pious travellers all those little white bones laid out in the
night.